Praise for
On the Enemy's Side

On the Enemy's Side is a journey into a real historical drama of the Iranian Revolution in 1979, told through a prison cell. A breath-taking story about love and courage, it uncovers the world of Iran's ethnic and political diversity in the most intimate way. More crucially, the book is about finding an inner compass that leads through chaos, destruction and violence. With each sentence, one learns to be more historically aware, tolerant, courageous and loving. Heartbroken, a reader survives and thrives together with its protagonists, two outcasts who found themselves in the heart and hell of political turmoil and zeal, how to escape their own prejudices and hatred, starting a different kind of revolution.

Botakoz Kassymbekova,
historian and author of *Despite Cultures*

In his powerful debut, *On the Enemy's Side*, Hamour Baika tells a necessary love story: Set against the backdrop of the Iranian hostage crisis in 1980s Iran, he explores the complicated moral territory of a same-sex love between a political prisoner and interrogator. It's necessary because it's a story rarely told about gay men, especially in the Middle East during this time period. It's necessary because it's told with such urgency, beauty, and sensitivity. Baika layers in a hidden—and forbidden—history of gay men, giving those men a voice.

John Copenhaver,
award-winning author of *Dodging and Burning*

ON THE
ENEMY'S
SIDE

HAMOUR BAIKA

Washington, DC

Published by Unrolling Script in the United States of America

Publisher's note: This is a work of fiction. Names, characters, organizations, places, and events are the products of the author's imagination or are used fictitiously. Any resemblance to actual persons, living or dead, is purely coincidental.

Cover design by Jessica Bell
Interior design by Mirajul Kayal
Logo design by Spark4Hope

ISBNs: 978-1-7346337-0-2 (paperback)
978-1-7346337-2-6 (limited first edition hardback)
978-1-7346337-1-9 (ebook)
978-1-7346337-3-3 (audiobook)

Library of Congress Control Number: 2020903205

www.HamourBaika.com

For Anand, my love and joy

Karoun Prison, Ahwaz

A warm breeze brushed against Waleed, one of five men blindfolded and roped to five poles along the back wall of the prison yard. From beneath his hastily tied blindfold, Waleed could see the sandstorm's effects on the unpaved ground. He could make out the occasional pebbles that glistened under the first faint rays of the rising sun. Some twenty feet away, he estimated, he heard the footsteps of a guard, and the sound of a paper unfolding. Waleed imagined it had to be the hand-written court verdict, issued a few hours earlier, in the dark of the night.

"In the name of God, the Compassionate, the Merciful. Truly, any action against the Islamic Republic is an act of rebellion against God."

Waleed had heard that the judge wouldn't be present. Probably he couldn't be bothered to wake up before dawn. He heard the labored breathing of the four other men tied to the poles next to him. *I'm not alone*, he thought, but the notion did little to console him. His knees were shaking but he did his best to stand straight up against the injustice of the verdict being spat out. The verdict that made a mockery of justice.

He felt his existence crumbling, just like eggshells shattering between the teeth of a hungry jackal. Waleed's heart pounded faster and faster, making it harder to breathe. He wished he'd had a chance to see his family one last time. To see the pride in his mother's face as Waleed pulled faces that made his toddler nephew giggle. But that wouldn't happen. His last memory of them would be the last time they were together, with his mother wailing, "Why are you taking him? He's done nothing."

He had told her he would come back soon but neither of them believed it.

So instead of going back home, he was waiting to be shot in Karoun Prison. He could almost smell death, like dust so thick it blocked one's nostrils. Three days ago, when he'd been arrested, execution seemed inconceivable.

He regretted the troubles he'd caused his family as a child. The time when he climbed the *konar* tree and fell off as the branch broke. His dad had to leave work and rush him to the hospital. He had never seen his dad so worried. He went home with a lot of bruises, but fortunately without a concussion. He should have picked up the fresh *konar* from the ground, just like his mother had said. He hoped his parents would forgive him.

Waleed wondered what heaven felt like. He tried to cheer himself with the thought that when an innocent man is killed, he would go to paradise. Barely nineteen years old, he hadn't had the time to really sin. But in the eyes of the new regime, being Arab was sufficient evidence of guilt.

His thoughts were interrupted by a monotone voice. It felt like an eternity for the guard to finish reading the verdict. "The Islamic Revolutionary Court of Khuzestan

Province finds these individuals guilty of exploding oil pipelines, establishing a sabotage and assassination ring that received financial aid and explosives from the Baathist regime of Iraq, and having attempted assassinations and sabotage. The Court condemns them to execution."

Waleed heard shuffling sounds. He imagined they were caused by the boots of his executioners, standing in equal intervals in a single line. He knew the men were armed. Their heavy presence was already suffocating him. He squeezed his eyelids tightly together and awaited the inevitable. The next time he opened his eyes, Waleed would see how everything looked on the other side.

Then he finally heard it: the sound of guns being pulled off of the guards' shoulders, clacking against uniforms in their descent. Probably Kalashnikovs. The sounds of their movements were quickly muffled by the frantic beating of Waleed's heart.

An officer barked with forced bravado, "Ready!"

Waleed's heart felt as if it would explode.

"Aim!"

A burning feeling scorched his chest. Stomach cramps knotted his body. His brain felt like it had been set ablaze. The combined sensations made him feel like vomiting.

"Fire!"

The guns thundered. Waleed heard several shots, bullets flying forward and making their connection with flesh. He suddenly imagined his execution as if watching it from above, like a ghost. He pictured the bullet whistling through the air, piercing his gray shirt and entering his ribcage.

He scrunched up his face and awaited the final impact. The earthly life was over. He was ready for the departure. In just moments he would see heaven and be reunited with his grandma. She would feed him one of her legendary cookies made of raisins and date molasses. He tried to open his eyes to see her in the afterworld. But he couldn't. The blindfold was now soaked with sweat, making his forehead itch.

Waleed waited. He listened. He heard nothing but the scuffing sound of the guards' boots. He breathed in and smelled both gunpowder and fresh blood. Something was wrong. This was not heaven.

He breathed in again. His lungs had shrunk. His heart in his chest was still banging. He felt the rope, the pole. Waleed still was trapped in the prison. He heard voices in great agitation, even though he couldn't make out what was said. He heard the scrape of boots as an officer approached him.

The next thing he knew, his body was being pulled away. Though his hands were tied together, he clutched the pole with all of his power. He locked his fingers around it more strongly than he had the strength to. As he resisted, more hands began yanking him away, tearing him from the pole.

He heard a howling so frightening it paralyzed him. He had never heard such a thing in his life. Like the shriek of a wounded wolf. Suddenly Waleed felt a raw pain in his throat and realized the wolf howl was his own voice.

He stopped howling when he heard someone shout, "Take off his blindfold, you idiot!"

Waleed's head was roughly pulled back and, within a second, he could see. It wasn't dark anymore. It was much brighter as the sun rose.

What he saw frightened him more than death. He found himself in the yard, still confined in Karoun Prison.

His lips trembled as he slowly looked to either side. Four bodies were tied to the four poles, but slumped forward. Still blindfolded, but now bleeding from the chest.

They were dead. Quiet. Peaceful.

He felt the sour taste of his stomach acid. He forced it back down. Getting sick at the sight of the bodies would have defiled these men. He didn't know them but the deceased always must be treated with respect.

Was this a cosmic joke? Did someone press rewind on his death? Waleed wanted to be at peace like the others. He turned around to see the face that kept yelling at him. He saw the face of evil. He recognized the voice spitting words at him. It was the same voice that had read the verdict a few minutes earlier.

From behind a chipped tooth, his breath smelled densely sour. The goo in his eyes had been pulled but not washed away. The face held a hysterical expression.

Waleed found the wolf inside again and screamed as loudly as he could. He hoped to wake up from the nightmare. But as much as he cried, he stayed exactly in place. The guards angrily seized his body and told him to stop.

"Shut up. Why are you screaming like a beast?"

He was quickly distracted by a louder group of voices a few feet away. An officer was bawling out a member of the death squad. The man who had been assigned to execute Waleed.

"What the hell is wrong with you? Can't you aim?"

"Wasn't my fault. No one taught me how to shoot."

"What are we gonna do with him now?"

"Kill me. Please kill me," Waleed wanted to say. But his tongue would not obey. The sun was rising and the reality of still being in prison weighed heavily on him. He felt his body hit the ground. The guards pulled on his arms to bring him to his feet. He suddenly felt defiant and kicked back at them as hard as he could.

One of the guards yelled, "Be happy you're alive, you filthy dog!"

The guards were dragging him now. He resisted. He kicked, howled, and shook. *Please God, don't let me go back*, he pleaded, no longer sure whether he was saying it to himself or saying it out loud. But nothing was as real as the bitter truth that he was still alive. And still in custody. Still a prisoner of the Islamic Republic of Iran.

Within hours, Waleed had a reputation in Karoun Prison. Among the many prison guards and prisoners who had heard him screech, he was now known as the Beast.

Ahwaz

Hesam thought he was done being a foreigner after returning from Italy, yet it turned out his country also had unfamiliar lands. He wondered if he'd made the biggest mistake of his life when he decided to serve the masses. Every sight reminded him he didn't belong here.

Even in mid-spring, the air felt heavy with humidity and the heat punished the residents. The whole city smelled like the cellar of the childhood house where Hesam's mother used to make grape vinegar.

Hesam had arrived a few hours earlier that morning and was driving the patrol Jeep of the Revolutionary Guards. The yellow color made it less formidable, but it was still difficult for Hesam to drive the large vehicle, since he hardly had any experience driving even a small sedan. Next to him, Naser sat on the passenger side. While they had just met, Hesam looked up to him. The man was about twenty-four, he estimated, two years older than himself—yet he knew what he was doing. Naser was someone he had to impress.

"So you're coming from Tehran?" Naser inquired.

"Yeah." Hesam didn't want to explain that he was in fact coming from Rome. But his airplane did land in Tehran last week, so technically he wasn't lying. He'd convinced himself he wanted to serve the revolution. So he quit his medical studies and returned. But deep inside, he knew he was trying to escape from Umberto. The fact that the Cultural Revolution had led to armed clashes in universities throughout the country only provided an urgent cover story, so that Hesam didn't have to even think of his headaches in Rome.

The Cultural Revolution had been announced a few days before. The universities were to be purged of what the central government called un-Islamic elements. Oppositional student associations refused to close their offices inside universities, so they collided with the Revolutionary Guards and local Revolutionary Committees that came to throw them out of campuses. Confrontations broke out in several cities, including Ahwaz.

Hesam thought these parties should have moved their offices out of university campuses. But that meant they couldn't as easily use their subversive ideas to mislead young students. Still, he would have found a way of avoiding armed clashes.

The vehicle jerked as Hesam drove over a pothole. He noticed another one in the broken-up asphalt and maneuvered the Jeep to avoid another jolt. The streets were needled here and there by palm trees and occasional eucalypti. People dressed lightly due to the heat. But Hesam was shocked when he spied a man in a tank top. That struck him as somehow anti-revolutionary, looking like a European—or worse still, American. Two women walked toward the car from the opposite direction. They were dressed in sleeveless tunics that only extended down to their knees. How was this any different from Italy? The women hurriedly turned into a side street as soon as they noticed Hesam's Jeep. That was the difference. Of course, he personally supported the right to choose one's own clothing. But Hesam was now affiliated with the Corps that opposed it. He decided he'd never harass women for what they wore.

Against this background of Persians in modern clothing, Arabs stood out. Having never been to the south, Hesam had never seen Arabs before. They looked the way he had seen them in movies. Their men wore traditional white robes and red scarves over their heads. Hesam took a mental note that he should learn what to call those. Their women resembled dark ghosts as they were covered in black, head to toe. *They must be sweltering*, Hesam concluded.

"Well, we definitely need more help over here," Naser said, interrupting his reverie. "Happy you came."

Hesam tried to pay more attention to his passenger. But instead, his thoughts drifted back to the prisoner he'd seen earlier in the morning. Or was he just a detainee? He had long eyelashes, his eyes the color of violins. Intense, deep, warm. Hesam almost could hear the melody. It captured his soul. So he called him the Enthraller.

The teenager had immediately become his obsession. Why was he in prison? What had he done? Was it some petty crime or a political offense? Hesam wondered for a moment what the anti-revolutionaries were doing to the youth of his country. Several times during the morning, Hesam had felt the urge to go back to the prison and track him down—to find the Enthraller before he was lost or freed.

He noticed his new colleague was still talking. What was his name again? Naser. His name was Naser. Hesam tried to pull himself together.

"… all hands on deck. We don't really get that much help from Tehran, especially with all the riots everywhere."

When Naser paused, Hesam tried to fill the silence to show he was engaged. "Anti-revolutionaries are corrupting our youth," was all he managed to get out of his mouth.

"That's right." Naser grew more spirited. "This is exactly what they want. Turning our universities into battlefields."

"Terrible." Hesam hoped he sounded supportive enough. But he was still thinking of the prisoner. He had to collect his thoughts. A biker moving toward them suddenly changed direction to ride away from the Jeep.

"Killing our Brothers to further their own goals. And to serve the Americans."

Hesam was at a loss for words. He had a running list of to-do's in his mind: Find lodging, discover the stores in the neighborhood, learn about his new job, and try to make sense of this new city. He'd come back to Iran to serve his people. But what did that really mean? Hesam decided to let his superiors at the Revolutionary Guards Corps guide him.

Naser must have noticed his stress. "You're afraid, Brother?"

Hesam contemplated how to reply.

"Don't be," Naser continued. "As long as you have God, you have nothing to fear. You're in good hands. I'll help you. You'll be one of the best in the Corps."

Hesam nodded and tried his best to give a sincere smile. He had to rely on Naser's guidance. Even though Naser was not a socialist comrade. Not even a fellow nonbeliever. But at least Naser was familiar with the duties.

"Right now we have to take control. The anti-revolutionaries are doing their best to create disunity. That's their best weapon. If the people start to distrust us, they have already won. So we have to be very careful. And stern. We can't be soft on them or else the whole revolution is in jeopardy."

Hesam looked around. The streets were quiet. Some pedestrians stared at the yellow Jeep as he drove by while others averted their eyes.

Hesam had to explain his situation without looking incompetent or naïve. "Uhhh…I only joined the Corps a few days ago," he mumbled sheepishly.

"You're brand new. I get it," Naser reassured him. "Right now we want to make sure the city is safe. We question anyone suspicious. We make sure they don't start any trouble."

Naser acted as if the instructions made perfect sense. But how could he tell who was suspicious? That was what Hesam didn't know. The biker changing direction? The women turning away? He didn't know if any of these were suspicious. But he decided against voicing his uncertainty.

Hesam drove the vehicle onto the White Bridge. He observed the green grass and more palm trees as they advanced toward the river. The White Bridge was the only landmark of Ahwaz he had ever seen prior to arriving in the city—and that was on a postcard. The massive curved metal structure hovered over the two ends of the bridge. The Karoun River had brown water that seemed too lazy to flow. The palm trees did not seem as lively as on the postcards.

Hesam looked in the mirror. His drab camouflage uniform didn't add any cheer to his outlook. His boots were too warm for the weather. He hadn't had time to shave in the morning, but he knew that the new authorities had declared it more pious for men to not shave their beard. He didn't want to start on the wrong foot with the Guards over a clean shave. From inside of the Corps, he could be more effective. He could have a positive impact on his colleagues so they would focus on the enemies, instead of harassing members of the public for the length of their skirt or their facial hair.

Naser had a full beard and a buzz haircut. He looked like any member of the Revolutionary Guards. And right now, Hesam depended on Naser's support.

Hesam looked out at a small crowd of men wearing traditional Arabian white robes. "Why do they have to dress like this? This is not Saudi Arabia," Hesam suddenly spat.

Naser nodded. "Let's see what they are up to."

Hesam was cheered by Naser's agreement. Maybe his instincts were right. He cut over to the right lane and slammed on the brakes. The men stared at them as the dust under the tires rose in a cloud. Naser got out of the car, visibly touching his pistol on the side of his belt. Hesam followed.

"What's going on over here?"

Five Arab men stood on the corner. One was smoking a cigarette. Two others were fidgeting with their rosary beads. Both had dark skin and black eyes. One had a gray beard and a front tooth was missing. None replied to Naser's question.

"Are you deaf? I said, 'What's going on?'"

The oldest with the missing tooth answered, "Nothing. Just standing."

"Standing? Don't you have jobs?"

"We're just talking. Nothing illegal."

"You have no business gathering here like a nasty mob. Go home."

Hesam wondered if they had to be rude, but then he remembered Naser's words: *Stern, we can't be soft on them.* He creased his eyebrows, put his feet farther apart, and brought his hand closer to his belt.

The men just stared at them without taking a step. Naser moved his pistol. "Go home. Disperse."

The old man protested: "I am old enough to be your father."

"Didn't ask you how old you are. Just go home before I force you to."

The youngest man approached them and yelled, "Why are you harassing us? We did nothing wrong. Just standing on the street. Is that a crime?"

Hesam rubbed his palm on his pants to wipe off the sweat. He wanted to tell the young man to just appease Naser and do as told. But he stayed quiet and tried to look stern.

"If we weren't Arab, you would have no problem about leaving us alone. But you want no Arabs here. Is that what your revolution brings us?"

Hesam wanted to interject that the revolution meant Iran was a country for all Iranians, including Arab Iranians. But he had to follow Naser's lead.

"Shut your mouth and go home," Naser roared.

One of them took the hand of the young guy. He turned to Naser and said, "Forget it. We're going." He spoke to the young guy in Arabic. The other men started talking as well.

The young man wasn't about to walk off. He turned red as he barked at Naser, "You shut your mouth. If you're a man, put your gun down and then we talk."

"That's enough," Hesam found himself yelling. He had to de-escalate before anyone got hurt. "Everybody go home."

"You go home. You have no honor," the young man objected.

"What's your name?" Naser shouted.

"Najeeb."

What a coincidence it was that his name meant "honorable" in Persian.

"It should be naa-Najeeb." Naser called the guy dishonorable.

Hesam didn't like the way Naser was fueling the argument rather than calming it. If Naser weren't his boss, Hesam would have told him to back off.

Suddenly, Naser took out his pistol and pointed it at the sky. "You were always traitors. The first to sell the country to Iraqi Baathists. Sons of bitches."

"You're sons of bitches." Najeeb spat on the ground.

"You just signed your own arrest warrant," Naser said as he rushed closer. "Cuff him," he instructed Hesam.

Hesam took Najeeb's hands from behind and cuffed them. Naser slapped the man on the face with his pistol.

"Calm down," Hesam muttered.

The other men started yelling.

"Leave him alone."

"He's young. Forgive him."

"He doesn't know what he's saying. Let him go."

Hesam saw the blood coming out of Najeeb's nose.

The oldest man begged, "Officer, you slapped him. Now we are all even. OK? Be the bigger man. Let him go."

The commotion grew louder. Then a sudden thunder startled Hesam. It took him a second to realize Naser had just shot into the air. "Next time, I will shoot directly at you."

After a second of indecision, Hesam shoved Najeeb toward the car. He stumbled but didn't fall.

"You won't subjugate the Arab nation. We never bow our heads to you."

"Shut up before I shut you up," Naser intervened.

Hesam opened the door and pushed Najeeb into the back seat. The quarrel on the street continued.

Naser turned to the crowd and shouted, "If anybody else wants to go with him, let's go."

As the men approached the car to plead for Najeeb's release, Hesam hurried to the driver's seat. He felt his heart rate go up and his hands get shaky. He started the car and they took off in another cloud of dust.

Minutes ago, Hesam hadn't been sure how to do his job. Now he'd just made his first arrest.

Najeeb kept speaking in Arabic, mumbling expletives. His volume was reduced from fear. Periodically he would lick the blood from his nose as it trickled down to his lips.

Hesam pushed down on the gas pedal. They were heading back to Karoun Prison. He was going to have another chance at finding the Enthraller.

Karoun Prison, Ahwaz

Bahram felt like the stench of prison was suffocating him. A mix of stale sweat, piss, and mold. He tried to breathe shallowly in a vain effort to reduce his intake of the odor. He was locked in a ward of numerous cells. He didn't know how many because he was assigned to the first cell by the front door of the ward. About twenty-five other men of different ages occupied the same cell. They were sitting on the floor, standing around or occupying both levels of the five bunk beds. While the room was built for ten men, hundreds of arrests in the aftermath of the Cultural Revolution had led quickly to prison overcrowding. Even the hallways were full. Additional detainees were sent to other prisons and even packed into the conference room at city hall.

Sitting on top of a bunk bed, Bahram attempted to not look directly at anyone. Out of the corner of his eye, he noticed a middle-aged man searching for a place to sit. The cell was already hot and Bahram didn't want yet another warm body next to his. In his peripheral vision, he thought the man gave up and looked away. Bahram glanced at him but then their eyes met. Bahram felt irritated that he was caught. He had no choice now. He reluctantly signaled for the man to sit next to him. Bahram lifted his foot off of the ladder and scooted over. His thighs touched the guy on his other side, who didn't move.

The man climbed up and sat next to him. "Hello, my name is Vargha," he said as he extended his hand.

"Bahram," he replied, offering his chosen name.

They squeezed each other's hands, a gesture of solidarity for being political detainees.

Bahram looked away, fearing the man would start a conversation. The Revolutionary Guards were on edge. They'd proved yesterday that they had no hesitation to use their weapons. They just wanted to scare the people so no more confrontations would break out on the campus of Jondi Shapour University. He just hoped to be lost among other detainees and released after a short time. He wasn't from Ahwaz, so the Guards would have to dig deep to find real evidence against him.

Bahram jerked his foot, keeping tempo to a silent melody in his head. As he settled in his thoughts, he dropped his shoe.

"Excuse you," someone yelled from the bottom level of the bunk bed.

"Oh, shut up," Bahram grumbled.

If not for the sound of keys jiggling, indicating the guards were coming, a fight might have broken out over the fallen shoe. Just then, a guard entered the cell and looked around. "Where are we gonna put them?" he called to someone outside.

"Just shove them in there," another guard replied from the hallway.

"I don't think that'll work. They already stink." He looked at Bahram. "Just like pigs."

Bahram lifted the corner of his lip to show his disgust. He noticed several new detainees in the hallway.

"Pigs are harmless animals," murmured Vargha.

Bahram knew well that Muslims considered pigs to be unclean. By contradicting that belief, Vargha was implying he wasn't a Muslim. He was either a socialist or a member of a religious minority. Either one would be enough reason for his detention. Bahram didn't feel like chatting. So he didn't take the bait and looked away.

"Let me give you a piece of advice," Vargha persisted. "You don't wanna stand out in prison."

Bahram found himself responding, despite his preference for silence. "How the heck do I stand out?"

Vargha hesitated, perhaps searching for the right words to say. "I saw the way that guard stared at you."

"And?"

"Try to not catch their attention. If you talk back to the guards, they will go out of their way to make your life miserable." He exhaled loudly. "To make an example of you."

Bahram smirked. "There are hundreds of detainees. I doubt he'll remember me."

"You're like my son. You're a...good-looking young man. And your eyes...anybody will remember those eyes."

Bahram squinted. He wondered if the man was an informer, placed in the cell to gain detainees' trust and gather information. Or maybe they had met somewhere before. Or maybe he was threatening to disclose Bahram's activities to the Revolutionary Guards.

Defensively, Bahram insisted, "I've done nothing wrong. I was just in the wrong place at the wrong time."

"And where was that?"

Bahram realized he was now caught in a conversation. "Outside the city hall," he said, even as he regretted his answer.

"I heard people got shot there yesterday."

In fact, they had. The Revolutionary Guards had opened fire on parents of student detainees kept in the conference hall. Whatever Vargha knew, Bahram did not want to volunteer any additional information. "That's what I heard too."

"So you went there hoping to find a detained sibling? Or a friend?"

Vargha didn't seem threatening. But Bahram had no reason to trust him. He thought of the day before. Maybe he did stand out. Maybe that was why, out of everyone waiting outside the city hall, he was one of the few to get arrested. But he kept silent and stared into space.

The same guard entered the cell again. "You, you, you." The guard pointed at the men sitting on the floor. "And you four on top of the bunk bed—get out." He looked at Bahram.

Bahram shrugged, pretending it didn't matter to him. But he wondered if they were going to be released—or taken somewhere even worse. Was Vargha right that his looks got him into trouble?

Vargha climbed down the ladder. Bahram followed. They walked out of the cell.

Several guards watched the new batch of detainees who stood in the hallway. The eight men just selected were lined up along the barred walls of the cells on the opposite side. The guard stood too close to Bahram and yelled, "Hold your hands behind your back."

Bahram obeyed. He felt a coarse rope surround his wrists and press them together. Then a piece of black cloth appeared. Bahram convinced himself that these were only scare tactics. He should just stick to his story. Or maybe he was about to be freed. He closed his eyes as the guard fastened the blindfold around his head. The guard made sure to squeeze it tightly over his eyes.

Bahram thought of Vargha's warning: "Anybody will remember those eyes."

"Are you deaf?" From behind his blindfold, Bahram heard the same guard bark at someone nearby. "Move."

All of a sudden, he heard a commotion break out in the cell on his right.

"Get him out of the cell. He's crazy."

"He keeps screaming and kicking like a rabid dog."

"Get him to a madhouse."

Bahram heard a high-pitched howl.

"Freaking Beast."

"Shut up!" The guard yelled so loudly he startled Bahram. "You're lucky I'm in a hurry. Otherwise, I'd beat you so bad you'd forget your own name."

Someone shoved Bahram on the shoulder to push him forward. "What are you waiting for? Move!"

Bahram was unable to walk straight, since he couldn't see or use his hands to guide him through the halls. He heard the Beast howl again, so he sped up, but his shoulder slammed into a brick wall.

He heard laughter from the guards. "Watch where you're going, blind man!"

"He's creeping like a mole!"

Amid the ridicule and the howls from the Beast, Bahram kept moving his feet. But he knew he was not going to be freed. Not with this prelude. He guessed he was being taken to yet another stinky, overcrowded cell. Possibly one worse than this.

Hesam followed Naser's directions, trying to memorize the roads to the prison so he could find his way back the next time. He knew that many streets had been renamed after the revolution.

"So where are we? This is not Pahlavi Street." Hesam guessed it couldn't still bear the former monarch's name.

"Who calls it that? Emam Street is the correct name. But we already drove past that. This is Prison Road."

Not very creative with street names, Hesam noted. He drove toward the gates. A crowd blocked the road to the prison. Men and women in regular clothes and *dishdashas* were arguing with the prison guards. As the guards saw the yellow Jeep approaching, they started yelling at the crowd to clear the way.

"Slow down, but don't stop," instructed Naser.

Hesam did as told. As the car moved closer to the people, they slowly cleared a path for the vehicle—everyone except one young woman who was engaged in a heated discussion with a guard.

Hesam honked. She ignored the sound and continued to argue.

A middle-aged woman in black *chador* approached the young woman and pulled at her hand. "Step aside or they'll shoot." She repeated her warning, trying to convince the young woman to get out of the way. "Weren't you at the city hall yesterday? Step aside." She finally wrenched the young woman out of the road.

Hesam slowly drove past. He listened carefully to the story about city hall. He guessed one of the Revolutionary Committees, which had appeared out of nowhere, had begun acting as if they were legitimate security forces.

Hesam pushed the accelerator and entered the prison.

"Go over there," Naser said.

He parked the car as indicated, eager to make a good impression on his mentor.

A guard walked toward the car. "Welcome, Mr. Bridegroom! How are you?"

"Brother Mansoor," Naser greeted him.

Hesam looked at Naser. "I didn't know you just got married."

"I didn't, thanks to all the clashes at the university. Even today, we're here babysitting criminals instead of attending the Friday sermon."

Hesam wasn't a Muslim, so he preferred babysitting criminals. Although he doubted that the way they'd arrested Najeeb really made him a criminal.

Naser got out and opened the door for Najeeb.

"What are you doing?" Mansoor protested.

"What do you mean? We just arrested this idiot," Naser replied.

"We can't have more detainees here."

"Hah?"

"What do you think, Mr. Bridegroom? The prison is packed three times its capacity. We just moved about a dozen detainees out of here."

"Put them in the hallways."

"The hallways have more detainees than they can handle."

"Come on. He's just one guy. Throw him anywhere," Naser insisted.

"Sorry, Brother. The orders are from Haj Agha himself."

Hesam imagined Haj Agha was probably the warden.

Naser was irritated. He turned to Hesam. "You watch him. I'll be right back."

Hesam looked at the building. Somewhere inside the prison, the Enthraller was held captive. If it weren't for this unwanted detainee, there would be a chance to look for the guy.

Hesam noticed Najeeb couldn't get out of the car with his hands tied.

"Close the door. Let him toast a little," Mansoor instructed.

Hesam didn't want to upset his colleague. Plus, Najeeb kept him from searching for the Enthraller. He closed the door on Najeeb and walked a few steps into the shade.

A meaty black fly attacked his mouth as if wanting to drill into his jaw. Hesam smacked his own face. The fly relocated to his ear. Then to his cheek. Then he scratched his cheek. "What the hell?"

Najeeb noticed his irritation and sneered.

Hesam remembered a verse of a poem he had heard years ago. If he remembered correctly, it was from the epic Book of Kings and probably referred to the Arab conquest of the Persian Empire many centuries ago. It went something like, "Despite drinking camel milk and eating crocodiles, Arabs have gained the audacity to dream of the Persian crown. Spit in the face of such fate."

He had witnessed contempt toward Arabs from Persians. He distinctly remembered his math teacher in northeastern Khorasan province. Every time a student was not listening to lessons, the teacher would say, "What are you, an Arab? Shut up and listen, silly boy. Maybe you'll learn something."

Hesam looked over at Najeeb in *dishdasha*. For some reason, he remembered how Umberto used to wrap some sheets around his body and call it a toga. Umberto with his toned body and curly hair looked like a grown-up cupid.

Why did he keep thinking about Umberto? He'd come to Iran to avoid the whole situation.

Mansoor signaled to Hesam to come over. He shook his hand. "Welcome, Brother."

"I'm Hesam."

"You're new."

"Started today."

Mansoor took a Winston pack out of his pocket and offered one. Hesam took a cigarette but struggled with the lighter. Mansoor helped. Hesam carefully took a puff and broke into a string of coughs.

"You don't smoke, do you?" Mansoor laughed.

"First time."

"Well, you don't have to smoke to fit in. And you already proved you know how to make an arrest. Now give me that." Mansoor took the cigarette from Hesam, softly pressed it against the brick wall, and then put the remainder back into the pack.

Hesam changed the subject to cover up the ineptitude he felt. "Is it going to get any worse than this?"

Mansoor drew his eyebrows together.

"I mean, does it get any hotter?"

"Hot? Man, this is nothing. This is just a bit on the warm side."

"Geez, I don't know if I can survive the summer." He immediately regretted showing weakness to this stranger.

"You'll get used to it."

Naser came out of the front door, looking even more irritated. "Hey Hesam, we have to take him out of here. They won't budge."

"And don't bother taking him to the city hall," Mansoor mocked.

Naser shook his head. "Have to take him to Kian Pars."

"Kian Pars?" Hesam asked. "Where's that?"

"Not too far. Have to take him to the house of a former SAVAK officer."

Hesam recognized the name of the disbanded intelligence agency of the Shah's regime. But why send detainees there?

Naser volunteered the answer before Hesam could ask. "The house was confiscated months ago. The bastard had a mansion in Kian Pars."

Mansoor added, "The nicest area in the city. While we live in Kampolo."

Naser continued, "You don't live in Kampolo anymore. Anyway, we're using the house as a detention center now. There's no more space here. So, let's go."

Hesam nodded. The prospect of driving under the sun didn't appeal to him. He would rather be trying to find the Enthraller.

As he opened the car door, he looked at Najeeb. The blood on his face had dried but sweat was rolling down his forehead.

Hesam looked into the mirror as he sat behind the wheel. Najeeb stared right into his eyes through the mirror. Hesam felt goose bumps on his arms and was pleased that the military fatigues hid them. He switched on the engine and waited for Naser to get in.

Former SAVAK House, Ahwaz

Judging from the outside, Hesam thought the house probably used to be really nice. But the plants had grown over and into each other. An untrimmed branch of a honey locust tree, armed with thorns, posed a threat to unsuspecting passersby. Probably no one took care of the garden since the confiscation of the house. Once inside, he could see damaged plasterwork and holes in the ceiling of the living room. Hesam imagined a crystal chandelier once hanging there. The carpet was dirty and faded from the sun. Hesam could see the outline of where the rugs used to lay.

The air felt fresh. Hesam saw an AC unit blowing cold wind into the room. The unit was smaller than the built-in frame. Someone had stuffed soiled rags into the gaps. A table stood in the corner of the living room next to a couple of chairs.

Hesam watched Naser lead Najeeb into the house.

"So…is there a basement where we keep them?"

"Basement?" An older guard dragged his feet as he entered

the living room. His red eyes caught Hesam's attention. "Where is this one from?"

"He's new."

"You don't say." The older guard turned to Hesam and asked, "Have you heard of the Karoun River? It passes through the city."

Hesam still didn't get the point. "I know. I crossed the bridge several times."

"What a brilliant recruit! River equals no basements. Not unless you wanna welcome the river into your lovely basement, you—"

"Like I said, he's new," Naser interrupted.

"Why can't they send us people who can actually be useful? I haven't slept for two days. Can't keep up with all these freaking arrests. Now this madness at the city hall. All these dead bodies we have to get rid of."

Hesam tried not to react to this revelation.

"I need guards who can help investigate the detainees," the guard continued. "Who should be charged? Who should be freed? What to tell the families that gather at the gates? Not a Tehrani boy looking for basements."

Hesam wasn't from Tehran, but he decided to keep quiet.

"I know, Brother," Naser sympathized. "We'll get through it. You go have lunch. We'll take care of things here."

The man with red eyes looked at Naser and nodded. "God bless you." He then turned to Hesam. "Sorry. Didn't mean to go off on you. I'm Ahmad," he extended his hand.

"Hesam."

"Yeah." Ahmad crept out of the room. "Two days I haven't slept," he repeated aloud. "We need help. This can't work. How many days can I…" His voice faded out as he exited.

"Turn on your radio on the way home," Naser advised.

Hesam remembered the short news story they'd heard on the way about an American military operation to rescue the hostages in Tehran. The helicopters had crashed near Tabas. But he really wanted to ask about all the dead bodies in Ahwaz, whom Ahmad just mentioned.

"Hey, can you stay here for a bit?" Naser asked. "I have some personal stuff to take care of. Was supposed to get married last week."

"Yeah, of course. No worries."

"You can start by booking this idiot." Naser pointed to Najeeb and left.

"Will do," Hesam replied.

Now situated in the air-conditioned room, Najeeb looked better. The blood on his face had turned brown. Hesam resisted the urge to wipe his face clean.

"Let me go," said Najeeb. "The Revolutionary Guards are ready to kill. I don't deserve to die."

"You're not gonna die."

"Yeah? They shot innocent people at the city hall yesterday."

Hesam revisited the events leading to his arrest: His only true crime was looking like an Arab, a foreigner. Hesam lowered his head and saw his boots. Too warm for this weather. Najeeb was wearing sandals. Judging by the footwear, Hesam was the foreigner, not Najeeb.

"Let me go," Najeeb pleaded.

Hesam looked at his face. For the first time he saw the young man's dark brown eyes. They immediately reminded him of the seductive look of the Enthraller.

Hesam looked around: No one else was in sight. Only three men had seen Najeeb in custody. Mansoor, who wanted no more detainees. Agitated Ahmad, who was too tired to care. And Naser, who was busy re-arranging his own wedding. No one was likely to remember Najeeb.

Hesam had returned to Iran to serve the country. Not to add to the number of the dead. He took a breath, shook his head clear, then took the key out of his pocket and un-cuffed Najeeb.

"Run, and don't tell anyone," Hesam instructed.

Najeeb's jaw slightly dropped. He looked at Hesam in disbelief, and rubbed his wrists as if to ensure the handcuffs were in fact gone. Then he looked around and then back at Hesam. "*Ay wallah*. Thanks." He peeked outside and then slowly slipped through the door without turning around.

"No more dead bodies on my watch," Hesam whispered to himself.

Abadan

Bibi closed the tap on the wall and dropped the T-shirt back into the washing bowl. She could imagine Bahram's shiny brown eyes staring at her as he insisted he wash his own clothes. Now that he'd gone missing for a few days, Bibi found things to do around the house to distract herself. She wiped her hands with her *chador* and wrapped it around her waist.

She couldn't concentrate on the laundry. Bahram had never disappeared like this before. She walked to the front gate. Just a few years ago, Bahram had first appeared at the same front gate, unexpectedly offering to work for Bibi if she let him stay in her house. So much had changed since then. Bibi went out, walked down the alley, and knocked on a green metal gate.

"Parvin *Khanum*? Open the door. It's Bibi." She paused a bit and then knocked again on the gate with an open palm. "Parvin *Khanum*."

The gate opened and Majid emerged. He was wearing a

striped blue polo shirt. The fine hair on his cheeks reminded her that he was quickly growing up into a young man. His dark skin glowed under the sun. "*Salam,* Bibi *Khanum.* How are you today?"

"Thank God, I'm not bad. How are you, son?"

"Fine, thanks. My mom is not home. She's gone to the market. You need help with something?"

"Majid *jan*, have you heard from Bahram?"

"Not since he went to Ahwaz. Why?"

"I haven't heard from him since then, either. Are you sure he hasn't called?" She noticed Majid scratching his thumb.

"No, Bibi *Khanum.* If he'd called, I would've let you know."

"This is not how it's done, no. There are the youth and there are the elderly. What happened to respect? He wasn't like this before. He hasn't been himself for a few months. He wouldn't have been so inconsiderate before, leaving me worried like this."

"I'm sorry. I don't know what to say." Majid ran his fingers through his short curly hair.

"You've been friends for years. Hasn't he told you anything? He's been acting strange."

"No. He said he was going to see a friend in Ahwaz."

"I know what he said. Doesn't he think I'm worried? With all these clashes?"

"It's all right. Nothing's gonna happen to him. I'm sure he'll call soon."

Bibi wished she had a telephone in her own house so she wouldn't have to depend on anybody else. "God is my witness, I don't want to be a bother."

"No, what are you talking about? You're like my grandma."

"Thank you, son. Let me know if he calls."

"Definitely, I will."

"God be with you." Bibi turned away.

"Bye, Bibi *Khanum*."

Bibi paused and turned back. "Majid, dear?"

Majid peeked out of the gate. "Yes?"

"You see what's happening. Clashes and imprisonment. Unrest everywhere. Isn't it better if you suspend your activities? Think of your studies."

"Bibi *Khanum*, I'm not endangering Bahram. I promise you."

"Not for Bahram. For yourself! You're young. You have a thousand dreams. Leave the politics for the politicians."

"I really don't do much."

"What do I know? I'm just an old woman. You are the brave young men. But I do know a few things. I've raised men like you."

"I promise there's nothing to worry about. I'm doing nothing illegal."

"OK, son. You decide. But be careful."

"Definitely."

"May God protect you. And Majid *jan?*"

"Yes?"

"Your cuticles are going to bleed. Stop digging at them."

Bibi headed home. She was so unsettled that she neglected to close the gate.

Former SAVAK House, Ahwaz

Hesam stepped onto the porch. He'd had a long day. He wanted to rest but had no desire to return to the inn, with its gray walls and fluorescent lights, and even worse, its dusty tile floors. They were so dirty, he couldn't even walk barefoot. He had to wear the boots as if they were slippers.

He looked at the sky. The sun was starting to disappear in the west. He placed his hands on the metal railing of the porch, only to quickly pull them away. He had underestimated how hot the railing would be. He shook his hands until the pain receded. He didn't even have the time to go to Karoun Prison and look for the Enthraller. He thought again of those beaming eyes.

He looked at the garden. Everywhere he looked, there were signs of neglect. The bougainvillea bushes had grown into a giant green ghost. The fig tree didn't have enough leaves to cover up the branches. The oleanders had much foliage, but only a few flowers. The leaves on lower plants resembled those of nasturtiums, but the yellow flowers were so tiny he couldn't be sure. With a little work, the garden could be beautiful. Full of flowers. But as long as the house was being used as a detention center, Hesam doubted anyone would water the plants or trim them.

Hesam heard the door open behind him.

"Is Ahmad being testy with you too?" the guy asked as he adjusted his glasses and pulled his soft black hair away from his forehead. Unlike many in the Revolutionary Guards Corps, he didn't have a buzz haircut.

"He's had really long shifts." Hesam was careful to not complain.

"Who hasn't?"

"You're right."

"I'm Saeed." He extended his hand. Saeed stood taller than Hesam. His glasses didn't hide the sadness in his eyes. A few strands of hair fell back onto his forehead. He was younger than Hesam, maybe nineteen or twenty.

"Don't worry too much about Ahmad's complaints. He's a bit older. He doesn't have the energy we do." Saeed took off his glasses and examined them in the light. "We're the young men of the revolution!" Saeed sat on the steps, took a pack of cigarettes out of his shirt pocket, and offered one to Hesam.

"No, thank you. I don't smoke."

Saeed shrugged and lit his cigarette. "So where do you live, Brother?"

Hesam hesitated but couldn't find a reason to lie. "In an inn, not too far from the Clock Circle."

"You live in an inn?"

"I arrived just a couple of days ago," Hesam explained.

"I see. And you're coming from…?"

Hesam took a deep breath and weighed his options. He wasn't sure if he could trust this stranger, even though he looked harmless enough. He decided to tell the truth. "I was studying in Italy."

"Rome?"

Hesam nodded.

"So you came back to serve our country."

Hesam stared at the sky and didn't respond.

"Beautiful, isn't it? The sky will take new colors as the sun goes down. Like a magic canvas. But after the sun is gone, it's a bit sad. You have to wait a whole night to see sunlight again. Even though the light here means a heat that'll drive you crazy." Saeed took another puff of his cigarette. "And you've been working with Mr. Bridegroom, right? Poor thing. He had to reschedule his wedding because of all this."

"Yeah." Hesam opted for brief answers, still unsure how much to trust his colleague. It sounded like Saeed had enough words for both of them.

"So are you going to the wedding?"

"Well…um…I haven't really been invited."

"Naser has good manners. He probably just forgot. Come with me. It's no problem."

"Well…" Hesam hadn't been to a wedding in a long time. He'd gone to Umberto's sister's ceremony, but that was held in a Catholic church. He didn't even know what a wedding in Ahwaz would entail.

"You should come. It's impolite not to."

Hesam thought it would be rude to show up uninvited, but he decided to yield to Saeed's judgment. "Sure."

Saeed inhaled one last time and then threw his cigarette butt off the railing. It landed among many cigarette butts on the ground. Saeed moved to the side and patted his hand on the step. Hesam sat down next to him.

"Lucky man, Naser." Saeed leaned closer to Hesam and spoke softly. "I heard his bride is really pretty." Saeed playfully nudged Hesam with his shoulder. "I've seen her picture."

Hesam forced a smile.

"I can't wait to get married. Have someone who expects me at home every evening. Maybe a couple of kids. You know?"

"Yeah."

"God is my protector, but my companion is just loneliness."

Hesam realized that Saeed made a habit of sharing elaborate and poetic responses. He looked away, unwilling to show he wasn't impressed with the impromptu verse.

"I'm a poet in a soldier's body," Saeed declared. "But I'm doing this for now. I'm hoping to save some money and get a house, put some money aside for a wedding and whatnot."

"So what should I wear to this wedding?"

"A jacket and a button-down shirt. Don't wear a tie!"

"I know. I know."

"Naser is a conservative guy."

"Yeah. I guess that's obvious. So, when is this wedding?"

"Thursday. I know the address. I can take you."

"Thanks, man." Hesam began to relax a little with his new coworker.

Saeed looked at Hesam's boots and snorted. "Do you have any other shoes? Literally, any other shoes?"

"I like these. They complete the uniform."

"You can wear something less heavy, or even shoes like these." Saeed straightened his leg to show off his tan Oxfords. "You can find fancy Italian shoes in Abadan. That will help with your homesickness."

Hesam forced a smile in response to the mention of Italy. But Italy meant Umberto and that memory still hurt. "I actually do wanna go to Abadan at some point. Maybe after I settle down a bit."

"Well, don't settle down in your inn, genius." Saeed slapped his hand on his lap. "I know what you're going through. It takes a while, but you'll get used to this. Trust me."

"Yeah? Where are *you* from?"

"Tabriz."

"Wow. You're a long way from home."

"You too."

"Yeah. My family is from Ferdows, but they live in Mashhad. That's where I was before going to university in Rome. How come you ended up here?"

The grin on Saeed's face vanished. "It's a long story. Maybe one day…" He paused. "You know what? You seem like a good guy. Why don't you come and live with us?"

Hesam frowned.

"It's nothing fancy. It's a bachelors' house. There are two of us now: me and Mansoor."

Hesam had already met Mansoor, who had offered a cigarette when Hesam had Najeeb baking in the car. Hesam wished he had apologized to Najeeb before letting him go free.

"There's a third bedroom we can empty for you," Saeed said, interrupting Hesam's thoughts.

"I don't want to bother."

"It's no bother. You will contribute to the rent and what-not. Besides, you won't find a place so easily. No one wants to rent to a single man."

"Why not?"

"Single men could be trouble. Anything from anti-revolutionary activities to drugs…this is Ahwaz, not Italy."

Hesam looked around to see if anyone was watching. "Do me a favor and keep that between us. I don't want people to think I'm westernized. They'll lose respect for me."

"Of course not, genius. It's our little secret. But seriously, it's a good deal. I won't cheat you."

"I'm sure it beats my little room in the inn."

"It's a done deal then." Saeed extended his hand and shook Hesam's. "If we get lucky, we can even find someone to clean and cook for us. We're not good at tidying up. And even worse at cooking. Just last week, Mansoor cooked a meal. It tasted like mud and rice."

Hesam chuckled with relief. It had turned out to be a good day after all. Hesam had found himself a new place to live, and a new friend he felt he could trust. At least, a little.

MAY 1, 1980

Karoun Prison, Ahwaz

Hesam sat in his parked Jeep in front of the prison building, the engine running. Hands on the steering wheel, he wondered what his socialist comrades would think about seeing him driving an American vehicle. But he liked the power, the speed. Hesam loved the look of it.

The yellow color brightened his rides, making his life less grave. It complemented his camouflage uniform. The Jeep had previously belonged to some wealthy monarchist and had been confiscated by the Revolutionary Guards a few weeks before.

Hesam had moved in with Saeed and Mansoor the same day Saeed made the offer. The move was easy and involved carrying two duffel bags from the inn to his new room. His housemates were both Muslim. To prevent any invitation to attend the Friday sermon the following day, he shaved his beard in the morning. That would signal that he didn't follow every edict of the government. His face no longer itched. He adjusted the rear mirror and smiled at his reflection. The uniform looked good on him. If he found the Enthraller today, he'd make a good impression.

He turned off the engine and walked into the prison building, straight to the office. His first investigative case belonged to a Vargha Mobasheri. This back and forth between Karoun Prison and the makeshift detention center in Kian Pars meant he spent a lot of time in his favorite Jeep. But it also meant he couldn't spend much time in prison to look for his Enthraller.

As Hesam sat down to review Vargha's file, he heard noises from the prison yard. He stood up and looked out the window. The noise became clearer. Prisoners were screaming and moaning. Hesam walked out of the office toward the yard.

A guard by the door addressed Hesam. "You wanna have some fun?"

Hesam didn't understand, so he just ignored the question and stepped into the yard.

The image he saw made his chest shrink. He immediately pulled at his collar to breathe better. Tens of prisoners were sitting on the ground in lines. They were only wearing boxers and had their hands tied behind their backs. The guards punched, kicked, and lashed them with cable wires. The prisoners' bodies, dirty and sweaty, were becoming bloodstained under the assaults. The men's bare bodies contorted to protect their heads from the blows. Some fell on the ground as they got kicked on the side, shoulder, or stomach. The unpaved ground gave rise to a cloud of dust. Hesam stared at the men's bodies.

I love the male form. It's strong, yet intricate and beautiful, Hesam remembered Umberto saying. Hesam looked into the sky so the current ugliness wouldn't blur the mental image of that cherished memory. He closed his eyes briefly and he and Umberto were standing by the Trevi Fountain in Rome. The statue of a long-bearded man stood on top of waves. Flanking the bearded man were two young and muscular male figures who led two winged horses out of the fountain water. Umberto pulled Hesam's hand and continued, "I like this one, beardless." Hesam followed Umberto. "There's something sacrosanct about the human body," Umberto said as he tugged Hesam closer and wrapped his arm around his waist.

Hesam loved it when Umberto adored him.

Hesam's thoughts were interrupted by the prisoners' screams. Some begged the guards to stop. Others spoke in Arabic. A guard grabbed one of the prisoners by his hair to lift his head and then slapped him. The prisoner fell on the guard's boots. But the guard kicked him away.

"Stop, please. Please stop. Don't hit." The prisoner was bent, broken, and begging for mercy. He was young with untrimmed facial hair. Unlike the Pegasus riders' strong muscles, this man's bones accented stretches of limp filaments, getting dirty as dust mixed with his sweat. There wasn't any sanctity there.

Hesam walked away, back into the building. He looked hard at the guard by the door. "What is this all about?"

"Group punishment. It was the idea of one of the backup guards from Tehran."

"Punishment for what?"

"You haven't heard the news?"

Hesam walked back to his office and found a newspaper. The front page read, "Gunmen raid Iranian Embassy in London." The subtitle read, "Demand release of Arab prisoners in Iran." Hesam skimmed through the article, but it did not provide much detail.

Mansoor walked in and sat down. "You see what's happening?"

Hesam nodded as his eyebrows creased together. "They're being beaten for *this*? How do we know if our prisoners were somehow involved in this attack?"

"Well, I guess they have to be high-profile prisoners to instigate such an attack. Probably dangerous even."

"You *guess?*"

"Don't get snappy at *me*. Only members of a violent armed group could trigger an attack on the embassy."

Hesam grunted. He suspected there were innocent Arabs among the prisoners. After all, he had arrested Najeeb just for standing on the street.

"You're upset," Mansoor explained. "It's no party. This is a revolution. Bad things happen."

"Bad things happen because our colleagues are intentionally inflicting them."

Mansoor stared at Hesam. "You're kind. That's a good quality. But you need to put things into perspective. You're from a fancy European university. You're out of your element. They raided our embassy. Why can't you have compassion for the staff there?"

Hesam couldn't win this battle. If he was unable to change his roommate's mind, he definitely wouldn't be able to convince Naser that this was unjust. He flashed back on the prisoner being hit. Umberto's voice echoed in his head: *There's something sacrosanct about the human body.*

MAY 2, 1980

Former SAVAK House, Ahwaz

Hesam began to feel he was wasting his time driving back and forth between Karoun Prison and this house. Every day, his chances of finding the Enthraller diminished. Detainees were being assigned to other interrogators, freed, or even executed. Just this morning, a young guy from Jondi Shapour University was put to death. Hesam was mostly bringing messages from and to Karoun Prison and keeping watch in the Kian Pars house. To this date, they had assigned him only one case: Vargha Mobasheri, a middle-aged man in prison because the Corps disapproved of his Bahá'í faith. Hesam entered the living room.

"Oh, good! You're back," Naser greeted him.

"I thought today we'd go to the prison."

"*I'm* going to the prison." Naser brushed off the suggestion. "But I'm gonna have you open files for the ones here."

"I can help you there," Hesam pleaded. "Whatever you need."

"You will help me *here*. Why do you wanna go to the prison so badly? Trust me, it's a lot cleaner here. And the AC is better. Open files for as many as you can," Naser ordered. "Fill out the forms and find out why they were arrested."

Hesam crossed his arms with obvious defiance. "Whoever made the arrest should already know why."

"Brother Hesam, do you have an objection?" Naser responded sharply.

Hesam noted the tone and backed off quickly. "No, sir."

"Good." Naser walked toward the door, but then paused and turned around. "What did you put down as the reason for arrest of the guy you detained last Friday?"

Hesam thought of Najeeb, whom he had secretly freed, and stammered.

"Or you never filled out the forms because you never processed him?" Naser fixed him with a hard glance.

Hesam felt his pulse go up.

"I'm not mad you let him go. But you need to have a strategy. You can't just arrest people and then free them with no explanation."

"I'm sorry."

"It's OK. You'll learn. That's why I'm teaching you. Fill out the forms."

"Yeah. Of course. How many do we have here?"

"Ten, twelve." Naser clearly did not know. "Let me know when you find out."

"I was the watch guard all day yesterday. I haven't even seen inside of the bedrooms."

"The cells!" Ahmad corrected as he entered the living room.

"Good morning," Hesam greeted him.

Ahmad shook Hesam's hand. "They are all ready to be questioned."

"Hesam will open their files," Naser informed Ahmad. "But he's new. Help him out if you can."

"You know, I was up all night. My shift was supposed to end an hour ago," Ahmad replied to Naser.

"I'm going back to the prison."

"Well, if you want me back for another double shift, I need to go home and take a nap."

Naser exhaled noisily. He looked at Hesam and then back at Ahmad. "OK, I'll stay. You go rest. But bring me a detainee first."

As Ahmad walked out, Naser showed Hesam into a rectangular room. Shelves covered the small wall to the right of the door. Hesam guessed it used to be a library, but now the books were gone, replaced by loose papers scattered around. "I'll supervise as you process the first detainee. But you're on your own for the rest of them." Naser took a pile of papers from the shelf and put it on the table. Two chairs sat on opposite sides of the table: a regular chair and a school chair with a table arm.

"You sit the detainee on this chair, blindfolded, hands tied in the front. That's important because they need to write. Ahmad or someone else will take care of that. Plus, if you tie their hands from behind, it's harder to sit them down. Ask them who they are and why they were arrested."

"What if they don't talk?"

Naser patted Hesam condescendingly on the head. "Then you reprimand them a little. They'll talk. Or you can wait for me to come back. They wouldn't want that, though. I don't have much patience these days."

Hesam nodded.

"Do *not* free anybody else without my permission."

The hierarchical lines had been drawn. Hesam couldn't overstep them again.

He heard footsteps. Ahmad brought in a detainee, blindfolded and tied. "Sit your ass down," barked Ahmad. But the guy couldn't see anything to locate the chair. Ahmad put the chair close to the back wall and pushed the guy onto it. "He's all yours."

Naser looked at Hesam and mimed that he should watch how the process went. Naser approached the detainee.

He was quite young, probably seventeen. The hair on his face seemed soft. He was wearing a white tank top. Hesam guessed he probably had taken off his shirt due to the heat. In the south, men didn't mind showing their bare arms and shoulders. Back in the north where Hesam had grown up, this was not considered proper attire.

Naser suddenly raised his hand high and slapped the young detainee on the face. The gesture made Hesam wince. The detainee's face turned to the side from the impact of the blow.

"Why are you beating—"

Before he could finish his sentence, Naser slapped him again.

"What—" the detainee protested before he was slapped a third time. "Why—" And then a fourth. "If you're man enough, untie my hands and then beat," he finally managed to yell out.

Naser hit him again. "I ask the questions. Don't you forget that!" Naser held the prisoner's chin to focus his attention. Then, without warning, he punched him in the stomach. The young man let out a shriek and folded his body to protect his gut.

Naser waited a few seconds as the detainee gasped for air. Then Naser lifted his head by the hair and punched him again. The detainee's mouth let out a stream of drool.

"What's your name?"

"Bahram," he moaned.

Naser slapped him hard. The sound was almost like hitting someone with a whip. "Bahram what?"

The detainee struggled to breathe. "Bahram Karimi."

"Why were you arrested?"

"I don't know." Bahram moved his head reflexively as if to dodge the next blow.

Naser grabbed his neck and choked him. "I'm not in the mood for playing games. So don't waste my time. I will beat you so bad, you'll choke on your teeth. So answer my questions."

Bahram's face started to turn red as Naser pressed into his throat. Bahram couldn't protect himself with his hands tied together.

"You got it, or should I choke you to death?"

Bahram struggled to nod.

Naser freed his neck. "I repeat: Why were you arrested?"

"I was taken in front of the city hall. I haven't done anything."

"Why were you there?"

"I was passing by. I saw a crowd there. I wanted to see what was going on."

Naser sat on the table in front of Bahram. He pressed his foot on Bahram's chest. Hesam noticed that today Naser was wearing boots. He couldn't imagine kicking anyone during interrogation. Bahram's chest turned white under the pressure of Naser's foot.

"Did you know someone detained in the city hall?"

"No."

"I swear I'll beat you so bad, you'll be sorry to be alive." Naser nodded at Hesam, signaling him to get closer. "Lucky for you, I have to go. Brother Hesam will question you. If he complains to me that you didn't cooperate, I'll crush your balls." Naser lifted his foot and pressed Bahram's hands against his crotch. "His hand is even heavier than mine." Naser turned to Hesam. "Show him, Brother!"

Hesam hesitated. Naser signaled his head again. Hesam approached the detainee and slapped him. Bahram groaned.

Naser stood up, nodded, and walked into the hallway. He signaled to Hesam to follow him and then closed the door.

"Just be stern with them. I have to go now. You'll be alright, Brother Hesam."

Hesam exhaled and went back to the library-turned-interrogation room. He sat on the table and looked at the questions on the form.

Bahram remained silent, but still cowered perceptibly.

"Where do you live?"

"I don't live here."

Hesam paused for a second, then continued with an edge in his voice, "You're only making your own life more difficult." He waited for his words to sink in and then stood up.

The sound made Bahram jerk in his chair and fall off.

Hesam had underestimated the fear caused in the young prisoner. "Sit down."

Bahram tried to use his hands to get up, but he couldn't. Hesam put his hands around Bahram's waist to pull him off the ground. He softly placed him back on the chair, then noticed that the blindfold had become loose. He removed the prisoner's blindfold to tie it back on again and noticed the long eyelashes and eyes the color of violins.

Hesam gazed at him.

Bahram looked back, giving Hesam a look that pierced through his soul.

This was the Enthraller.

Hesam had just hit the same guy he was so eager to meet. Hesam choked on his own saliva as he dropped the blindfold.

He wanted to apologize. But that would weaken his authority. He cleared his throat to reestablish control and resumed. "How old are you?" he managed to say.

"Seventeen."

Five years younger than Hesam. He looked again at Bahram's face. His eyebrows were almost a straight line. Beneath the thin facial hair he could see cheeks that were still red from Naser's repeated slaps. His hair was in disarray, having been brutally pulled by Naser. His tank top showed the trace of the grooves of the bottom of Naser's boot. As Hesam considered the boot dirt that stained Bahram's chest, he also saw a fine covering of blond hair.

As he admired Bahram's chest, Hesam suddenly realized he had been staring at him.

Bahram filled the awkward silence. "You like to hit."

Hesam looked down with a sense of shame. "No. Just have to," he pushed back. "Sometimes."

Bahram looked at Hesam for a second. Then he smiled, showing small dimples on his cheeks.

Hesam felt his resolve slipping away.

"Nonsense. You didn't have to hit me," Bahram spat out. "You just like to do it."

"I don't," Hesam insisted. "Why don't you answer my questions so we don't have to…"

"What questions?"

"Where do you live?"

"In Abadan."

"Why are you in Ahwaz?"

"I came to find a job."

Hesam thought Abadan had a much better economy than Ahwaz. Why would anyone come from there to find a job?

"The whole place got crazy after the university shootings," Bahram continued.

"At seventeen, why aren't you at school?"

"I don't like school."

"Why? Don't you wanna be somebody some day?"

"I am somebody *now*," Bahram said with defiance, then looked Hesam up and down. "You're not from here."

"What do you mean?"

"Your questions. You're not filling out your form. Why do you care about my studies? You almost sound like a foreigner."

"Do you know many foreigners?"

"Of course. Everyone who lives in Abadan and works for the oil company knows foreigners. Used to, anyway."

"Tell me about that."

Bahram looked at Hesam coolly, as if considering how far he could go. "Do you have a cigarette?"

"Sorry, I don't smoke."

"You *are* a foreigner."

"You need to stop saying that."

"In Abadan, everyone smokes. People love their cigarettes so much they take pictures with them."

Hesam just stared. He had seen portraits of Abadanis with lit cigarettes, some sort of expensive watch, and Ray-Ban sunglasses.

"Can you get me some food then?" Bahram said, further testing the limits of Hesam's kindness. "I haven't eaten since yesterday morning."

"Yesterday morning?"

"They didn't even let us use the bathrooms yesterday."

Hesam was to blame for that. He was the only watch guard the whole day and he was afraid of dealing with all the detainees on his own. The help Naser had promised had never showed up.

"Or better yet, let me go," Bahram said audaciously. "It will save you from filling out your forms." Bahram pointed to the stack of papers on the table.

Hesam was momentarily charmed by the young man's nerve. But he could not betray his emotions. He feigned a scowl and shot back, "I can't just let you go."

Bahram exhaled.

Hesam felt his fascination with the prisoner grow. He worried it showed on his face. To hide his feelings, he pretended to look at his form. "Maybe it's enough for now," Hesam told the teenager. "I'll see what I can get you for lunch."

"It's only morning," Bahram pointed out with a small laugh.

Hesam wondered if he was laughing at him. "I'm gonna have to blindfold you now."

"Great," Bahram said sarcastically.

Hesam stood up and put the blindfold on without tightening it. He wondered if the prisoner would notice the difference. He wondered what Bahram was thinking. He opened the door and called out into the hall, "Ahmad *Agha*!"

Mansoor showed up at the door. "Ahmad's gone."

"OK. Could you take this one back to the cell?"

Bahram stood up unsteadily, the blindfold affecting his balance. "Thank you, officer. Your slaps reminded me of my school days."

Hesam wanted to ask why Bahram had been slapped at school, but Mansoor was already leading him back to the makeshift cell. Hesam felt every nerve in his body vibrate. The sensation lasted for some time.

MAY 4, 1980

Former SAVAK House, Ahwaz

Two days before, Ahmad had refused to bring Bahram back for a second questioning.

"My orders are to bring them to you so that you admit them first. No time for interrogation right now," he explained.

Yesterday, Hesam had spent most of the day in Karoun Prison. Today, he finally got a chance to be the one in charge, once Ahmad went home in the midafternoon. So Hesam went to a sandwich joint and bought a burger for Bahram. Upon returning, he placed the brown bag on the table in the library. The appetizing smell of grilled meat and ketchup filled the room. Then he stepped outside the library and called out, "Mansoor?"

When he approached, Mansoor looked slightly dazed, his eyes a bit pink as if waking up from an afternoon nap.

Hesam decided to ignore it. "Is Ahmad here?"

"Ahmad is gone for the day." Mansoor lowered his voice. "Honestly, it's much better without him. He's so whiny."

"Could you bring me a detainee from cell one? Bahram Karimi."

"Cell one? I thought we were going to cell four. Ahmad said—"

"I need to see this one first. Then, we can finish the admissions from cell four," Hesam insisted.

Mansoor paused for a moment. Then, his face opened into an ear-to-ear smile. "Smart," he said and pointed to his head. "I know what you're doing. You're interrogating one on the side, so you can take credit for whatever you might discover."

Hesam forced a grin to convince the man he was correct.

"I don't blame you," Mansoor continued, getting excited. "Everyone thinks we're idiots because we're young. But look at that wrinkled potato, Ahmad. It's not like he's doing anything extraordinary. Just whines the whole damn time."

Mansoor walked away. A few moments later he returned with Bahram, still blindfolded and with tied hands. Mansoor sat Bahram on the chair. "If he's an anti-revolutionary, I can help extract some intel," he boasted, pumping his fist up and down, making his biceps bulge.

Hesam wondered silently whether Mansoor was more interested in showing off his muscles than extracting information. "Great," he said to humor the guy.

Mansoor smiled and stomped his feet before marching out of the room.

Hesam paused for a moment, closed the door, and approached Bahram. He couldn't wait to see his eyes again. "I brought you lunch." He took off the blindfold so he could again see Bahram's deep brown eyes. For a second, Hesam wanted to kiss them.

Bahram looked at the bag on the table. "And it only took you two days," he said with a sting.

Hesam took a deep breath. "It took me two days to build up the courage to face you and say I'm sorry…for hitting you." Hesam reached for the bag on the table and took out a sandwich. It was still hot.

Bahram hesitated for a second, clearly confused by the apology. But his hunger took over and he grabbed the sandwich, took a big bite, and gulped with overt satisfaction.

Hesam tried not to smile at his enjoyment. He reached for the other sandwich. Furtively glancing at the detainee, he slowly reached for a napkin so the ketchup wouldn't spill over his uniform. When he looked back at Bahram, he had already devoured the burger and crumpled the empty wrapper.

"Is that for me too?" Bahram asked, looking warily at Hesam.

"Yeah, of course."

"Thanks. Can you untie my hands for a minute?"

After Hesam undid the knot, Bahram massaged his wrists where the ropes had left marks on his skin.

Hesam thought that the knot didn't have to be that tight. He picked up a glass bottle of Coca-Cola, wet with condensed moisture. "You want some soda?"

Bahram nodded with a full mouth. He took the bottle from Hesam and grunted his thanks between bites. Then he tipped back the bottle and gulped several sips.

Bahram looked sheepishly at his captor. "I was hungry."

"Yeah, I see."

Bahram wiped his mouth with the back of his hand and looked intensely at Hesam, causing the guard to avert his eyes. Fortified by the meal, he said with a sneer, "So what's your deal? You beat me up—then you bring me food?"

Hesam looked down to avoid those penetrating eyes.

Bahram continued his offensive, but with a dose of light sarcasm. "I thought 'good cop, bad cop' was played by two *different* cops!"

"I'm not playing," Hesam said a little too loudly. He tapped the pack of cigarettes in his side pocket but decided

Bahram was too young to smoke. He saw Bahram cock his ear, as if listening for something.

"Don't do anything stupid," Hesam said as he read Bahram's mind. "There are guards here who are happy to use their guns."

Bahram looked at Hesam with feigned innocence and leaned back in his chair. "Can I have a cigarette?" Bahram noted the shape of the packet in Hesam's pocket.

Hesam shook his head.

"Why not?"

"Because it's bad for you," he replied, at the risk of sounding nerdy.

"What are you, a doctor?" Bahram mocked.

"No. Not yet," Hesam shrugged.

Bahram looked at Hesam and furrowed his eyebrows. "So you were studying to be a doctor? And you're *here now*. Good choice! You got your priorities right."

Hesam ignored the provocation.

"And you're coming from abroad. From where, though? France?"

Hesam again felt vulnerable that the prisoner could easily detect his unfamiliarity with this environment.

"Or maybe you are a prim and proper English lad," Bahram imitated a bad English accent.

"Stop it."

"I've seen many foreigners at the National Oil Company. You have been abroad for a few years."

"Don't piss off your guard," snapped Hesam. "It's not in your interest."

"So you hit me and then bring me food. And then threaten to hit me some more? Are you sure you're OK? Like mentally?"

Hesam ignored the insult and resumed his interrogation. "Why are you here?" He waited for a response. Secretly, he liked that despite detention, Bahram's sarcasm and defiance remained intact. He was not a scared child.

"The food isn't enough to forgive you for beating me." Bahram ignored the question. "But you know what is? Letting me go."

"I can't let you go. Not until you go through the process."

"And what is this process? That *I* tell you why *you* arrested me?"

Hesam didn't reply.

"Go ask your Brothers," Bahram scolded. "They took me from the street. I was just standing around. That's not a crime."

"I'm not here to argue with you. And I'm sorry for hitting you."

Bahram shook his head in frustration.

"I'll get into trouble big-time if I free a detainee." He decided not to say that he had already angered his superior by freeing Najeeb.

"Fine," Bahram conceded. "To be honest, I'd rather talk to you than get hit by your Brother friend." He leaned back and crossed his arms, still rubbing his wrists occasionally to stimulate circulation. "So tell me. Why did you come to Iran? You could be a doctor for God's sake."

"I am serving the people."

"I'm sorry you think so. You don't know what you're doing. This is not what you think, this Revolutionary Guards Corps. Here's how to serve the people: Let me go. And if they fire you, so be it. I can see you have a good heart."

For a second, Hesam felt like Bahram was looking inside of him. The moment felt intimate, like talking philosophy with a lover. But he had to maintain his official façade. "I came back to serve my country. And I'm not turning back." He didn't want to admit he was lying.

"So you were living abroad but came back to Iran to serve the revolution. You must be a sympathizer of one of the socialist organizations. Smart enough to study medicine, but dumb enough to join the Corps."

An image of Umberto—and how he'd left him to return here—flashed in Hesam's mind. "Taunting me is not gonna work. You want me to hit you again so I feel guilty. Forget it. I'm not buying you another burger." Hesam laughed a little but Bahram didn't respond. Still, he felt he had gained the upper hand. "What do you know about socialist organizations anyway?"

"My guess is…since the Socialist Party of Iran is the largest one, you're probably associated with them. Right, comrade Hesam?"

Hesam felt like his opponent was dissecting his past with surgical precision. How could Bahram read him like that? Was his cover so thin that anyone could see through it? Did Naser see it too? He had to play his role better.

"Most of the supporters of the Party are from the upper middle class. The type who would go to university abroad," Bahram continued.

Bahram was clearly politically active to make such an observation. "I ask the questions, not you," Hesam barked.

"So is this how you serve your nation? You imprison random people?"

"If you've done nothing wrong, you'll be freed. You just have to go through the process. That's all."

Bahram was quiet for a moment.

Hesam felt he needed this teenager to believe him. "If you tell me the truth…if you're innocent, you'll walk. I promise you that."

"Yeah, yeah," Bahram grumbled.

Hesam felt he had allowed Bahram too many liberties and it would backfire on him. He threw the remains of the sandwich into a metal paint bucket that served as a garbage can. "I should be interrogating you." He picked up a sheet of paper from the table and slapped it down before Bahram. "We can continue to chat. I think I'll be in charge of your file."

"How lucky."

Hesam grabbed a pen from the bookshelf. "What, you prefer Naser?"

"Is that your Brother from the other day? He likes to hit."

"Yeah, I know. I'll keep you away from him." He placed the pen in front of Bahram.

Ahmad suddenly showed up at the door. "Hey! If I hear you're not cooperating with Brother Hesam, I'll make you regret it." He had noticed the blank sheet of paper in front of Bahram. "You understand? I will tie your feet to a *falak* and whip you until you cry like a girl."

Hesam froze at the intrusion. He hadn't expected Ahmad to come back today. This would prevent him from talking to Bahram more.

"I'll take him back and bring you someone from cell four," Ahmad offered.

Bahram held out his hands together, allowing Hesam to retie them.

Hesam wished he could kick Ahmad out of the room. But he had to act normal. He started looking for the blindfold.

"On the table," Bahram informed.

Hesam thanked him and knotted the blindfold behind Bahram's head. He briefly felt the softness of the youth's beard, wishing he could caress his cheek.

In a different setting, Hesam and Bahram would be together. Even their names rhymed in agreement. They could be friends with Mansoor, more so with Saeed. They could go to the movie theater and walk around the city.

Ahmad took Bahram back to the cell. Hesam was alone in the interrogation room. He noticed he was breathing heavily, his heart beating wildly.

Ahmad untied Bahram's hands, took off the blindfold, and pushed him back into the bedroom-turned-prison cell. Bahram stumbled.

Vargha jumped up to help. "Hope they didn't harass you too much."

"It's all good."

"What do they want from you? They didn't take anyone else a second time."

"They probably think I know something."

"Remember what I told you. Try not to stand out."

"They threatened to hit me with a *falak*."

"Well, there are too many prisoners to whip them one by one."

Bahram sat on his metal bed and closed his eyes. That would discourage Vargha from asking him any more questions. He thought of the day he first discovered the pain of a *falak*.

It was soon after he went to Abadan. He was fourteen and new in town. One day the literature teacher, Mr. Motamedi, was lecturing about the greatness of Persian literature. Bahram saw two of the Arab students exchanging glances. Bahram knew how it felt to belong to an ethnic minority.

"If the Persian literature is so great, why is it that they borrowed so many words from other languages? Arabic, for example. The entire Persian script is Arabic."

"Persians were forced to adapt after the Arab conquest. It's amazing how our students know nothing about history. What grade did you get in your history class?"

"The Arab conquest was more than thirteen centuries ago. Surely our literary experts had sufficient time to invent new words." From the corner of his eyes, Bahram saw the two Arab students staring at him.

Mr. Motamedi's smile tightened and he tried to continue. "There are hundreds of new words that came into existence over centuries. It's quite simple. Like two and two makes four."

"Or two and two makes five," Bahram chuckled. "The Persian way!"

Laughter broke out in the classroom. Mr. Motamedi demanded order. "You think my classroom is a circus? Come over here."

Bahram walked toward the chalkboard with a smirk. It wasn't his first time disrupting a lesson.

"This is a classroom," declared Mr. Motamedi. "It's not the street when yahoos like you can do whatever they please. You can keep your smart-ass comments to yourself. So you're a roughneck, ha? I'll teach you how to respect your elders. You've heard of the *falak*, right?"

"I'm not afraid," Bahram snapped back.

"Fantastic." Mr. Motamedi clapped his fist against his other open palm. "And stand properly when I'm talking to you. Look at you. Feet wide open like you're about to wet yourself."

Bahram reluctantly brought his feet together.

Mr. Motamedi turned to the class and lectured, "This is what happens to you when you don't study. And don't respect authority." Mr. Motamedi then ordered Bahram to take off his shoes and socks.

Bahram thought that the *falak* was just an empty threat. After all, it was usually for younger boys. This class was in their mid-teens. They were almost men.

Bahram didn't move. He imagined Mr. Motamedi not getting lucky at home so he was here to take out his anger on his students. With that ugly mug, no wonder he couldn't get any. The thought made Bahram smirk.

"And why are you smiling? Didn't I tell you to take off your shoes and socks? Are you deaf?"

"No. Are you?" Bahram blurted.

Mr. Motamedi turned red like chili *sambusa* sauce and lunged at him, slapping him hard on the face. "You won't take off your shoes, ha? Well, I'm sure half of this class would be delighted to watch you in pain."

Bahram was new in town and didn't really have any friends yet.

Mr. Motamedi faced the class. "I need two strong boys."

Asadi jumped up, the pathetic boy Bahram only knew by his last name. Another boy was also eager to volunteer. His face resembled a cat's.

"You, get on the ground," Mr. Motamedi instructed him angrily.

Bahram let out a grunt and obeyed.

"Go get the *falak* from the principal's office," Mr. Motamedi directed Cat-Face.

Asadi gleefully grabbed Bahram's calf and started pulling off his shoe and sock. "You stink," he lied.

Soon, Cat-Face showed up with a ruler and a *falak*: a wooden stick and a piece of rope that was tied to each end. Judging by how dusty the rope was, the *falak* hadn't been used in quite a while. Asadi tied Bahram's feet to the *falak*. He and Cat-Face held it up in the air.

Mr. Motamedi took the ruler and approached Bahram. "This is what happens when you can't control your tongue." He struck the ruler against the soles of Bahram's feet.

The pain shot through his body like a lightning bolt. He jolted and groaned. He pressed his teeth together to prevent any further moaning. The class was so quiet that Bahram could hear his own heavy breathing. The point of this humiliation was to scare all the students, so no one would challenge the teacher again.

Droplets of sweat glittered on Mr. Motamedi's forehead. He struck with the ruler again. And again. No sound could be heard other than the collision of thick ruler against Bahram's flesh. Asadi stared at Bahram with joy on his face, reveling in his classmate's pain.

The next blow hit the arch of his foot. The pain felt like he was being electrocuted. But Bahram was determined to not scream. That was the last bit of his pride, and he was going to hold onto it. He lost count of how many blows followed. A dozen? More? He squeezed his fists as if to catch the pain in them. He didn't moan.

Finally Mr. Motamedi barked to Asadi and Cat-Face to untie Bahram's feet.

Bahram bent his knees and looked at the soles. They were as red as a ripe tomato and the ruler seemed to have tattooed marks on his feet. One of the lines was starting to bleed at the edges. Bahram needed to get up, but the pain was excruciating. Cat-Face offered his hand to help him stand up.

Bahram stood on his clenched toes like a bad ballet dancer, then bent to pick up his sock. His soles shot pulsating shocks of hurt when he put them on the ground. He jerked and almost jumped up. The class laughed. He winced each time he attempted to retrieve a shoe and sock.

An Afro-Iranian student named Majid got up from his chair and approached Bahram. He lived on the same block. He signaled to Bahram to sit down.

"What the hell are you doing?" Mr. Motamedi shouted at Majid.

Unfazed, Majid went to the other side of the chalkboard by the door and collected Bahram's shoe and socks and brought them to him. Bahram was grateful for the help.

Mr. Motamedi accosted Bahram and declared to all assembled, "Learn courage from your classmate, Majid. Despite the risk of getting hit, he went ahead and gave this one a helping hand. That's real courage, not like the foolishness of talking back when you clearly don't have a clue."

Bahram tuned out Mr. Motamedi.

At dismissal, a student offered Bahram the carrier rack of his bicycle.

"Or you can sit on my crotch," Asadi hazed.

A crowd started to gather around them, sensing a brawl.

"Shut up or I'll shut you up," Bahram barked as he put his socks in his pocket. His feet hurt too much to wear them.

"Yeah? Let me see you try."

"Leave him alone," Majid intervened.

Bahram turned to Asadi and warned, "When I kick your teeth in, you'll have nothing to smile about."

"Kick my teeth? With your bloody feet? Let me get you a tampon to stop the bleeding."

"You *would* have tampons."

"That I'm gonna stick in your—"

"Stop it, you two," Majid yelled. "Come, I'll help you get home," he told Bahram.

"Thanks. I can walk though."

Bahram folded in the back of his shoes and pushed his feet in as far as he could. As he started limping home, a crowd of boys, led by Asadi, gathered behind him, throwing insults. They followed Bahram most of the way home.

Each step was a struggle. But he refused Majid's help in walking. The scorching sun made his feet sweat. The salt of the sweat burnt the open wounds. He undid the first two buttons of his shirt, hoping to cool off.

Bahram did not look back, but he knew most of the boys were gone. Only Asadi still followed them, imitating how Bahram limped.

As Bahram and Majid made their way home, Bahram noticed an Arab guy sitting on the steps in front of a house. He watched them calmly but steadily. He had olive skin and thin facial hair. He was wearing a red and white *keffiyeh*. His dark brown eyes glistened like stars. His body was covered by his white *dishdasha*, so clean that it shined, making him look otherworldly. Bahram estimated the guy was about sixteen.

Bahram continued to limp forward and felt humiliated that the stranger saw him like that.

"Hey, can you help this girl walk home?" Asadi asked the guy sitting on the steps of the house. "Or would your own skirt get in the way?"

Bahram looked at the guy to see how he'd react. He didn't.

"Don't be ignorant. Go home already," Majid told Asadi.

Bahram hoped the guy would beat up the annoying troublemaker.

Asadi continued taunting the stranger. "What is it? The cat got your tongue? Don't you speak Persian?"

The guy remained entirely calm, as if Asadi were invisible. Bahram envied his composure.

Asadi stepped in front of the stranger to block his view of Bahram. The guy slowly stood up. He was taller and bigger than Asadi.

Bahram used the distraction to pounce on him. He clutched at Asadi's throat from the back and the tormentor gave out a muffled scream. Then Bahram punched him in the lower back with all the force he could muster. Asadi groaned. Encouraged by his own power, Bahram tightened his arms around Asadi's neck.

Unable to withstand Bahram's weight, Asadi lost his balance and fell onto the ground in front of the stranger's feet.

"Bahram, stop it," Majid insisted. He helped Asadi stand up and ordered him to go home.

Asadi started to walk away. "This is not the end of it."

"Apologize." Bahram wanted to show off his power to the stranger.

"Go to hell." Asadi disappeared into an alley.

"He's an idiot," Majid offered as an apology to the stranger. "Let's go, Bahram."

Fascinated by the stranger, Bahram told Majid, "You go. I'm fine."

Majid shook his head and walked away.

"What's up with you?" the stranger asked Bahram in a smoky baritone voice.

For a moment, Bahram forgot his ache, lost in the tone of his voice. "Why did you let him insult you like that?" Bahram asked.

"Boys like him are just like flies."

"Flies?"

"If you keep swatting them away, they keep coming back. But if you ignore them, they will go away soon enough."

"What if they sting?"

The stranger grinned and extended his hand. "I'm Talib."

"Taleb," Bahram said in a Persian accent.

"No. Talib!"

He noticed the difference but wasn't sure how to pronounce it. He introduced himself and shook Talib's hand. "Nice to meet you."

"The pleasure is all mine." Talib smiled at Bahram. "So you think you're a thug?"

Bahram was happy he'd impressed Talib. "Hell, yeah!"

"You fold the back of your shoes, unbutton your shirt and think you're a thug?"

"I guess I'm not doing it right. I'm new here. Don't wanna be bullied."

Talib just stared into Bahram's eyes and didn't respond.

"Teach me how to be a real thug!"

"You think all Arabs are thugs?"

"No," Bahram protested. "You just sounded like you know what you're talking about. I want everyone to be afraid of me. To do what I want."

"So you think you're a king."

Bahram was tempted to say he used to be treated like one. But instead, he replied, "Just teach me to be a thug. I'll do whatever you want."

"Whatever I want?"

Bahram nodded.

Talib smiled and teased, "I want your ass."

"Deal!" Bahram said abruptly, going along with what he thought was a joke, but not wholly sure it was.

Talib laughed. "What kind of a thug-wannabe says that?"

Bahram lifted his foot and moaned softly.

"What happened to your feet?"

"Got the *falak* in class."

"Damn. A thug wouldn't put himself in that situation. No public embarrassment."

"Then show me how to be one."

Talib turned around and walked into the house, gesturing that Bahram do the same. Talib had Bahram sit in the living room at a coffee table. He grabbed Bahram's foot and inspected it. "Damn, it's all bloody and bruised. I guess you should be off your feet for a bit." He studied Bahram for a second and added, "You're a good-looking guy."

Bahram felt a wave of heat rush to his cheeks.

"Makes me wanna attack you." Talib placed Bahram's feet on his shoulders, positioning him to lie down on the table. "But in a good way." He bent over.

Bahram could feel Talib's breath on his face. It had been a while since Bahram had allowed someone to get so close.

Talib kissed him.

One kiss led to another, leading the pair to take off their clothes. Bahram felt vulnerable yet confident. Talib wasn't taking advantage of him. He imagined he was rewarding him for silencing Asadi before he could spit out any further insults. Talib dominated not only his body, but his soul. His desire.

Bahram held him tight and closed his eyes.

He had no idea how long it lasted. The next time he opened his eyes, they were panting at the same pace.

"I'm sorry," Talib announced as he broke their embrace.

Bahram took a breath. "You can attack me any time you want."

"Yeah? Well, I think we should take care of those bloody feet."

Talib left for the kitchen, returning with a large plastic bowl filled with ice and water.

As Bahram's feet soaked, Talib sat next to him. "You said you're new here. Where are you coming from?"

"Up north."

"Like Gilaki-speaking kind of north?"

Bahram didn't reply.

"Tell me whenever you're ready."

Relieved he didn't have to avoid a barrage of unwanted questions, Bahram said, "Most people are nice here. I didn't know what to expect when I came."

"That Afro-Iranian guy is nice. Majid, right?"

"You know him?"

"My family's lived in this neighborhood my whole life. I know everyone."

"That rude-ass idiot you saw is one of the few who's evil. I used to have the respect of my peers. So I don't know how to build it up from scratch."

"We'll think of something," Talib said as he took Bahram's hand. His skin warm. His touch reassuring.

Reminiscing about Talib made the time go by faster in prison. Bahram smiled. He pushed himself to remember all the sweet details of their relationship. He wasn't sure how long he'd be kept in custody and he had to retrieve every one of the good memories with Talib so they would last the whole detention period.

Bahram looked around the cell. Vargha was apparently praying, sitting with his arms crossed and eyes closed. Another detainee was sitting on the floor. The fourth was standing by the window and watching the backyard. They were both Jondi Shapour students who shared the same admiration for their physics professor. The one on the floor thought they may be expelled from school. The other had some hope.

Bahram closed his eyes again and wished he was walking with Talib in South Bowardeh, past Taj Movie Theater all the way toward the river to Arvand Gymnasium, where men worked out in their short shorts, but no one had sexy legs like Talib. Soon Bahram didn't even bother looking. The breeze would bring a hint of Talib's oil-based cologne that smelled like jasmine. Even this stuffy cell would feel like a walk in the gardens if Talib were around.

And this guard, Hesam. He seemed odd. His kindness unexpected. What was his goal? Bahram had to play along until he could convince Hesam to let him go. Before Hesam found out the real reason he had been arrested.

Sanandaj

Atefeh knew she had been cursed. She looked outside the window from the darkened room. No trace of Daniar. She drew the curtains together and walked back to the sofa. She turned the regulator on the kerosene lamp so the wick went back into the oil, dimming the light even more. Was Daniar coming back tonight? Or was today the day his luck ran out—the day he got killed?

Today was her twenty-first birthday. She used to think this was a blessed date. She married Daniar exactly three years ago. That year she had two celebrations, her birthday and her wedding. This year in contrast, she had nothing to celebrate. She heard on the radio that the first female member of the Shah's cabinet had been executed in the morning. The war tore her city apart. And instead of celebrating the day, she was crunched up in the dark, wondering if her husband would come back.

She used to be lucky. She happened to find out a secret about the son of the tribe's matriarch, Banoo. She blackmailed her to exile him and replace him with Daniar. She'd never expected the consequences to be so grave. Banoo's teenage son went missing on the way to Tehran. Atefeh thought maybe some relatives somehow got word of the scandal and killed him on the road. Or maybe he died in an accident in the mountains. Whatever the case, Daniar did replace him and Atefeh gained the same status as Banoo's daughter-in-law. But that had brought Atefeh nothing but misery. She was sure Banoo's son had cursed her for causing him so much shame.

She got pregnant soon after the wedding. Daniar used to say it didn't matter if they had a son or daughter. Atefeh gave him neither. Their baby girl was stillborn. He never said anything, but Atefeh felt in her heart that she'd let him down, her beloved husband. Then, the revolution removed the Shah and soon the war began. Kurds wanted autonomy but the new government wouldn't tolerate it. Kurdish groups boycotted the referendum. Seeing no other solution, an armed resistance soon took shape against the new government.

The army and the Revolutionary Guards Corps quashed the resistance. In a single month last year, tens of Kurds were summarily executed. An unknown number died in confrontations that ensued. But almost a year after the beginning of the war, acts of resistance kept flaring up, and so did the fatalities. Daniar joined a group. Because of his status in the tribe, he immediately became the leader. A young man living in a destroyed city with a wife who couldn't give him children, Daniar had no reason to live. At least that was what Atefeh thought. She wondered if he even cared that he could be killed any day.

Atefeh put her hands on her stomach. If only her body would cooperate and give her a child, that would be a reason for Daniar to stay home—to stay out of harm's way. She felt a twist in her belly as if someone was wringing out her insides.

Another explosion happened outside, followed by a series of single shots. She wrapped her arms around her legs.

"Please!" she prayed to Banoo's son. "Please forgive me. Lift this curse. I promise you I suffered enough. I'm so sorry for what I did to you."

More shots fired in the distance. Atefeh put her forehead on her knees. She was careful not to make a sound as she cried.

Karoun Prison, Ahwaz

Two rectangular metal sheets made up the gates of Karoun Prison. Above each, a fat isosceles triangle gave them the illusionary look of two large pencils. The sun had caused their green paint to fade. A large arch stretched over both pencil-triangles. An inverted arch, half the size, connected the highest points of each triangle, resembling an eye. It was a reminder of surveillance and control over prisoners' lives. On the left, the tall watchtower loomed over everything.

Today Mansoor served as one of the guards at the gate. Although it was an essential task, he found it the most boring of all posts. He preferred to be an investigator, like Hesam. But with so many prisoners, all members of the Revolutionary Guards Corps had to do what was required. They had some backup help from other cities, but not enough.

Family members of prisoners formed a crowd in front of the gates, waiting to see when their loved ones would be freed. The first wave of releases had come a few days prior, but that was only a small portion of the hundreds of arrests made during and after the clashes at Jondi Shapour University. Families hoped for many more to be set free. The newcomers would arrive and ask which prisoners had already been freed. Each new arrival would ask the same questions, hoping for better answers. No matter their personal agony, they had to act calm. They didn't want to give the guards, like Mansoor, excuses to delay any possible release. And he knew it.

A young woman approached the other guard at the gates and asked him for a prisoner. The guard was a backup from Tehran but Mansoor had forgotten his name.

"What's your relationship with him?" the guard asked her.

"He's my son."

"How old is he?"

"Sixteen."

The guard looked at Mansoor and smiled. "She says he's sixteen." He turned back to the woman and mocked, "How come he's sixteen and you're so young? How old were you when you had him?"

The woman pulled her headscarf to cover some of her face.

Mansoor looked away. He wished he was inside, or off duty. Or literally anywhere else.

"Where is his father anyway?"

"At work. Why do you need his father?"

"You look too young to have a sixteen-year-old. If he's a legitimate son, I need to see his father."

"God have mercy. Have some shame!"

The guard taunted, "Or maybe he doesn't have a father." He winked at Mansoor.

The woman raised her voice. "May God forgive you. You're here to safeguard the people. Not question their honor."

"Just tell me the truth: Are you his mother or his concubine?"

Her face turned red and she raised her hand and slapped the guard.

Mansoor thought maybe he should intervene, but the guard deserved it.

"Feisty! I like it. You're not my mother. But you can be my concubine, ha?" The guard leered as he licked his lips.

"You're shameless," yelled another young woman.

Mansoor looked to see who'd spoken up.

She accosted the guard, pulling the side of her *chador*. "Do you have no honor?"

"Get away from here. Who are you, little girl?"

"OK, that's enough." Mansoor interfered when he recognized who the second young woman was: Esmat, Naser's new bride. He walked toward her. "Forgive him, Mrs. Atri. He's a backup support from Tehran. He doesn't know."

The guard stepped backward, realizing that Mansoor knew Esmat. "I'm from Arak," he objected.

Mansoor wanted to tell him to shut up, but he didn't want to look bad in front of his boss's wife.

Esmat approached the guard. "That's no reason to insult the people. Don't people from Arak have honor?"

"Forgive him, please." Mansoor opened the gate for her to enter and glared severely at the guard. "Apologize. Now," he demanded.

"I'm sorry," he stuttered.

"Don't apologize to me. Apologize to her. You were rude to *her*." Esmat wasn't appeased.

The guard looked at the woman. "I'm sorry."

The woman looked down.

Esmat stood at the prison gate and looked at Mansoor. "Brother Mansoor, please find her son. Tell her what's happening with him. People have the right to know."

"Yes, Mrs. Atri. I will."

Mansoor was about to close the gate as Esmat entered but someone in the crowd shouted out: "Don't go away, daughter. Come back, please. Help me."

Esmat looked back and stepped out of the gate again.

Mansoor looked at the crowd, afraid he would get yet another task.

An older woman wrapped up in Arabic headscarf paced toward the gate. "Don't go, please." She had tattoos that elongated her eyebrows.

"What is wrong?" Esmat inquired.

"My son was arrested a few weeks ago. They want to execute him. But he's innocent. He's only nineteen. He's done nothing."

Esmat looked at Mansoor.

"His name is Saleh Moghadam," the old woman continued. "But he goes by Waleed. Everyone knows him as Waleed."

Mansoor knew exactly which prisoner that was. What a mess! The guards now had to deal with this situation and they blamed him for it. He opened his mouth but immediately shut it. Naser had to approve whatever they were going to tell his family.

"Do you know who that is?" Esmat faced Mansoor.

"I don't."

"OK." Esmat looked at the old woman. "*Khanum*, please wait for me. I'll be back."

"May God reward you, daughter. I will stay here."

"What is your name?"

"Rafat Moghadam."

"I'll see what I can do," Esmat said as she walked inside.

When she walked away out of earshot, the guard approached Mansoor. "Who's that?"

"You better pray to God she doesn't complain to Naser. That's his wife."

"What? What is she doing here?"

"She brings him lunch, you idiot. You really have to learn to shut your mouth."

Mansoor saw the old woman getting closer. He suspected she might be listening to their conversation.

"Please step aside. You can wait for her on the sidewalk."

The old woman looked down. Mansoor followed her glance to check if she saw something that he hadn't noticed before. The unpaved ground made it impossible to tell the difference between the street and the sidewalk. But she didn't complain. She stepped away.

Mansoor hoped she hadn't heard Naser's name.

MAY 12, 1980

Former SAVAK House, Ahwaz

Hesam crossed his arms as he paced around the room, waiting for Ahmad to bring in his first detainee. As more detainees were freed from Karoun Prison, detainees held in other locations were gradually transferred back to the prison. He was told to clarify the charges based on the information that the *detainees* gave him. This seemed the opposite of what should happen. When he'd taken part in anti-Shah protests in front of the Iranian Embassy in Rome, the police did not arrest and interrogate him to then come up with charges. But in Ahwaz, that was his duty. He couldn't make sense of the logic. Not to mention the variety of duties he had to perform: guard the prison gate, patrol the street, and interrogate detainees. He just wanted to spend time with his Enthraller: Bahram.

The door opened and Ahmad brought in Bahram and pushed him roughly into the chair. He tilted his head at Hesam, signaling to meet him outside. Hesam followed him into the hallway.

"How are you doing?"

Hesam was surprised at the question. "I'm doing well, thanks."

"Brother Naser told me to mentor you. We have many detainees and few guards. The backup support from Tehran is not going to stay here forever. We need to take advantage of this time and complete all the detainee files as well as we can."

"Yeah, I know."

"Well, do me a favor and help out with the charges for these guys."

"I know. I will." Hesam was tired of being infantilized by this man.

"Well, do it already before he forces me to attend your interrogation sessions."

"Excuse me?"

"Prove to Naser that you can do your job. Otherwise, I'll have to babysit you too, and I really don't…" Ahmad scratched his head.

"I'm not a child. I can do my job."

"Saying it is one thing. Doing it is something else."

Hesam gave Ahmad an angry look and went into the interrogation room. No one trusted him. They saw him as an inept foreigner. They probably resented that he didn't join them for the prayers. Worse, Hesam was afraid others would catch on and notice he was easy on Bahram. This had to be avoided at all cost. So he had to convince everyone of the opposite: He was an Iranian, dedicated to the revolution, and harsh on detainees. He had to prove that he belonged.

He untied Bahram's hands and removed the blindfold, being slightly rough, if only to keep up his charade. "Hello."

"Comrade Hesam."

"Don't call me that." Hesam loved the honorific, but he was afraid to be discovered. He quietly placed a piece of paper and pen on the table arm of Bahram's chair. He then sat on the desk and put his left foot on the table arm. "How are you?"

Bahram gazed into Hesam's eyes. "OK."

"I want you to write down the circumstances of your arrest."

"I already told you, I was arrested near the city hall, I didn't—"

"Write it down."

"But I already said everything. I was—"

"Write. It. Down."

Bahram stared at Hesam for a moment and then shrugged his shoulders. He took the pen and tried to place it on top of the piece of paper but it was stuck under Hesam's boot. Bahram unclenched his fist.

Hesam lifted the tip of his boot so Bahram could adjust the position of the paper. Bahram lowered his head and started writing. Hesam watched, quietly admiring his beauty.

But Hesam was on notice. He had to do his job. He couldn't let his interest in Bahram distract him from fulfilling his duties. His future was at stake.

After Bahram wrote about half a page, Hesam bent forward and said firmly, "Give it to me." He imagined Bahram was about to protest that he needed more time, but he said nothing and complied.

Hesam needed Bahram to know that he was in control, to understand that it was in his own interest to cooperate. That would benefit both of them. Bahram would be released, and Hesam would prove that he could do his job. Meanwhile, Hesam had to fight his own desires to walk over to Bahram and…

He shouldn't even think about that. He followed Naser's directions and, without looking at the writing, tore up the piece of paper.

"What was that?" Bahram protested.

Hesam felt he'd let him down. But he had to do his job. "This really doesn't help you. I've already wasted a lot of time on you. I've been patient with you but your time is running out. You either tell me what I wanna know, or I'll let you be in your cell for as long as it takes. You could be here for months. I can keep you here until you rot." Hesam surprised himself with the strength of his threats.

Hesam reached for another piece of paper. He attempted to hand it to Bahram, but it fell on the ground.

"Pick it up."

Bahram didn't budge.

Hesam wondered why Bahram was defying him. Was it because he knew Hesam had a crush on him?

Bahram stared into Hesam's eyes.

"You heard me. Pick it up."

Bahram remained resistant, his eyes burning into Hesam.

"You're a smart guy. I give you that. But be smart enough to know I can do to you as I please. You don't wanna end up in the infirmary with a black eye and broken limbs."

Something in Hesam shook. The threats were coming to him too easily. He wouldn't have to hurt Bahram, would he? Would Ahmad? He hoped that threats alone would suffice to scare Bahram. He had to put Bahram back in his place. Guards ordered, detainees obeyed.

Bahram only gazed longer into Hesam's eyes. This was the same look Umberto gave him when he said he wanted to return to Iran. Hesam knew the look of shock and quiet disappointment.

"I am smart enough to know this is not you," Bahram said quietly as if they were lovers reaching a moment of truth.

A chill ran through Hesam's body, raising goosebumps on his arms and legs. He was happy his uniform covered it up.

Bahram stood up, forcing Hesam to take his foot off the table arm. "You brought me food. You apologized for hitting me. This is not you."

Hesam looked into Bahram's eyes. He'd stood up to him, something Umberto never did, not even when Hesam abandoned everything and left without a genuine explanation. But in Bahram's resistance, Hesam felt tenderness.

"You are a noble man. You showed that to me. Don't let them take away your essence. You're above that."

Hesam struggled to ignore the flattery, even though it appeared sincere. Bahram could have simply asked again to be freed, but instead he chose to show concern for his interrogator. Hesam saw his own image in Bahram's eyes. He wondered if Bahram saw a better man in him than he saw in himself.

"I know you have power over me," Bahram said, almost in a sensual whisper. "But don't let it make you cruel."

Hesam felt conquered by the simplicity of Bahram's words. Or was it his sun-kissed skin, the stubble on his face, or his toned arms? Hesam extended his hand and took Bahram's. He squeezed it as he stood in front of him. Bahram didn't pull away.

Hesam drew Bahram closer. His heart pounded in his chest. He wondered if Bahram could hear it. His breathing intensified. He leaned forward and, as if in a daze, put his lips on Bahram's cheek. He puckered his lips and pressed slightly. Suddenly realizing the implications of his gesture, Hesam retreated backward a few steps.

Bahram didn't move for a second. "If you let me go, we can spend time together without having to worry about Ahmad."

Hesam wasn't sure if this was a sincere offer. Of course Bahram's main objective would be to be freed, not romance with Hesam. But the thought still tempted him. Hesam approached Bahram and put his palm on his hand, interlocking fingers. Bahram squeezed his fingers. Hesam put his other arm around Bahram's waist, enjoying how Bahram's breath felt, warm and insistent against his neck. His body odor smelled sweet.

Hesam moved his weight from one foot to the other. He put his hand behind Bahram's neck and held him steady as he studied every inch of Bahram's face. "You are beautiful."

Bahram looked away and bit his lower lip. "Stop."

"I'm the guard here. I can do as I please."

Bahram's face froze with no trace of a smile.

Hesam realized this could easily refer to rape. "I'm sorry. I didn't mean…many detainees are being freed. Even those who threw stones at the Revolutionary Guards that day were sentenced to only a few months imprisonment. Of course, they were dismissed from the university. But what I'm trying to say is: if your only crime…since your only crime was to be in the wrong place at the wrong time, you'll be freed once they go through your file."

"So why don't you do that? Release me."

"I don't have the authority. I let go of a detainee a few weeks ago and got into trouble," Hesam embellished a bit. "You will be transferred to Karoun Prison soon. But I will watch over you. I need to be with you."

"Said the jailer to the caged bird," Bahram observed. His words were harsh, but his face had a new kindness to it.

Hesam lifted Bahram's slender hands with fine hair emerging at the wrist. His nails were slightly overgrown but shapely and clean. Hesam kissed his fingers but heard footsteps in the hallway. He retracted quickly and stepped away from Bahram.

"Brother Hesam?" Ahmad opened the door and walked in. "Should I bring the next detainee? We have a lot of them to go through."

Hesam had no choice. But he would create a fresh reason to interrogate Bahram further. He needed to see him again soon.

"Did you get much out of him?"

Hesam didn't want Ahmed to beat Bahram to "help" the interrogation process. "I am making progress. He has become cooperative. I just need more time."

"Glad he finally cracked. Guess he realized the longer they stay stubborn, the longer they're stuck here. I'll go get the next idiot."

Ahmad took Bahram and returned a few moments later with Vargha. Hesam waited for Ahmad to leave and then lifted Vargha's blindfold. Hesam noticed gray hair in Vargha's stubble and dark circles under his eyes.

"Hello. Your name?"

"Vargha Mobasheri."

"From?"

"Dezful."

Hesam picked up the file from the desk. "It says that your crime is being a sympathizer of the wayward sect of Bahaism."

"I'm a believer of the Bahá'í faith."

Hesam remembered someone in his school when he was about twelve. The boy was younger than Hesam, probably in fourth grade or something. Hesam knew that other boys of his class picked on him and called him "the Bahá'í dog." But Hesam was from a family of nonbelievers, so he didn't get involved.

One day after school, he saw a group of boys around the Bahá'í kid. One of them was twisting the kid's hand behind his back. Another spat on his face and said, "We don't want you here." The boy started to cry. The first guy said, "Go away from our town." He pushed the boy on the ground. "Filthy dog."

They walked away and Hesam noticed that the boy's belongings were scattered on the ground. Hesam looked at the boy, wiping off the spit with his sleeve and crying. Hesam contemplated if he should help him gather his things. The boy collected his books and pencils from the ground and dusted off his pants and shirt. One of his books fell on the ground again. But the boy suddenly turned around and looked at Hesam, realizing he'd been watching the whole episode. The kid looked disappointed that Hesam hadn't come to his rescue. Hesam felt so embarrassed, he panicked and just walked away.

Hesam looked at the file to come up with the next question. "Why are you here?"

"You should tell me that, son. I haven't done anything illegal."

"Your file says you are charged with espionage."

"And how would I have done that? For whom?"

"The Americans. The Israelis."

"I don't know many Americans. I know a few. But anyone who works at the National Oil Company knows a few Americans. They were our technical experts."

"And what did you do at the oil company?"

"I was a construction manager. You see, I didn't have access to any sensitive information to give to Americans."

"And Israel?"

"I don't even know anyone from Israel. I get it: The Bahá'í World Centre is in Israel. So everyone says we spy for Israel. What spy? What information did I have to give anyone?"

"Why is your center in Israel? That raises so many questions."

"Our prophet was exiled and driven from city to city. He was in Baghdad and Istanbul too. He died in the eastern Mediterranean area in the Ottoman Empire. There was no Israel back then."

"You are also accused of collaborating with SAVAK."

"Again, what information did I have to share with SAVAK? I'm a simple construction manager. I have a family. I mind my own business."

"You could tell SAVAK who participated in anti-Shah demonstrations. Who distributed leaflets. Who wrote slogans on the walls."

"And how would I know these things? I don't interfere in politics. I obey the laws. I work and go home."

"So you didn't give information to SAVAK for them to harass the revolutionary folks?"

"SAVAK harassed me, too. Just like you're harassing me."

Hesam took a deep breath and slowly posed the next question. "Tell me about your organization."

"What organization? A few of us worked voluntarily to hold gatherings where we pray and socialize. We have moral classes for our kids to become honest members of society."

Hesam was running out of questions. "I heard your prophet says people shouldn't love their country."

"My son, don't rush to believe everything you hear. You're an interrogator and I'm sure you will find the truth when you finish your investigation. But that's a misquote. The prophet said that man shouldn't pride himself in loving his country, rather the entire world."

Hesam paused to think about the quote. The idea of transcending national borders sounded a bit like socialism. "That's a noble idea," Hesam affirmed.

Hesam heard Umberto's voice in his head as if it were real. *You're a noble man*, Umberto had told Hesam when he heard that Hesam was going to leave Rome to return home and serve the revolutionary cause. Hesam didn't dare to tell Umberto that his true intention was to escape his conflicting emotions for Umberto.

Hesam closed his eyes and rubbed his forehead. "You know what, Mr. Mobasheri? I'll investigate your claims. I just hope you told me the truth."

"I don't tell lies, my son. That's against my beliefs."

Hesam remembered the face of the Bahá'í kid, bruised and disappointed in his inaction. He decided this time would be different. He wouldn't allow other people's misconceptions to determine his own judgment.

MAY 14, 1980
Abadan

Bibi wore her sandals and walked to the front gate. She had not heard from Bahram in three weeks. She had called hospitals, police stations, and detention centers. Nothing. But she suspected Bahram might have been arrested. Now the detainees were slowly being freed. She asked her nephew in Ahwaz, Nosrat, to look for Bahram. She did not have a phone in her house, so she would go to Parvin *Khanum*'s to ask if they had received a call from him. The knock on the door lit a candle of hope in her. "Bahram, is that you? Bahram?" Bibi opened the gate.

"It's me, Bibi *Khanum*." It wasn't Bahram's voice. "Hello."

"Hello, Majid *jan*. Are you doing well?"

"I'm fine. Thank you. How are you?"

"Have you heard from Bahram?"

"I thought he was back."

Bibi squinted, her mouth partially open.

"Hundreds of detainees are being released. I thought he'd be among them."

"And why do you think he's been detained?"

Majid looked down. "I told you, Bibi *Khanum*. He was at the university when the clashes started. No one has seen him since."

"He told me he was going to Ahwaz to see a friend. He didn't say anything about political activities, no." She raised her index finger. "I warned you both not to get involved in these things. They have no use for anyone. And what are these papers in your hand?"

"It's a magazine I brought for Bahram."

"A political something? Don't bring it in here."

"Bahram would want to read it. He is—"

"No, Majid *jan*. And if there are these…magazines in this house, go ahead and take them out. We have enough trouble already. Bahram has disappeared for three weeks, and you're all about these dangerous magazines. Aren't you worried, no?"

"He'll be all right. Don't worry."

"I'm worried, son. Bahram was my support. He came to me as a boy. He was only fourteen, you know. I raised him to become a man. But I didn't raise him to give him up to one of these prisons for some godforsaken politics, no. Come and fetch any magazines he has in this house."

"Bibi *jan*, he may be back in a couple of days. He'd be upset if I go through his stuff."

"What upset? You are best friends. Have been for years. You are neighbors. What, you keep secrets from each other? I don't get it, no. All these mysteries and lies. All of sudden I hear of political activities. I say, no more. Go get whatever magazines he has."

"Bibi *jan*, please. He will be very upset if I search his room."

Bibi looked Majid up and down. "Are you afraid of my Bahram?"

Majid was taken aback. "I'm not afraid. Why should I be afraid of him?"

"He can be rough and rebellious. But he has to. He was the man of the house. He didn't have a father to give him structure. But he never once hit anyone without reason, no. With all these hooligans around here, someone needed to put them back in their place, you know." Bibi wondered if Bahram had made himself a few enemies.

"I have to go now. Please let me know when he shows up. I think it'll be soon."

"From your mouth to God's ears, Majid *jan*." Bibi gave up the idea of Majid cleaning out any political publications. She'd do it later on her own. "Go. May God watch over you."

Majid was about to leave but then turned around. "Bibi *Khanum*." Majid seemed to remember something. "Forgive me, but have you tried to learn which prison he may be in?"

"I've gone everywhere I could think of in Abadan. Nosrat *Agha* has checked with the prisons in Ahwaz. He's even gone to the hospitals. No one knows anything about his whereabouts. As if he became a drop of water and disappeared into the earth."

"Well…I've heard if you send money to prisons, they'll have to give it to the prisoner and get a signed receipt. If they give you such a receipt, you know which prison he's in."

"And if he's not there…" Bibi pondered.

"I'd love to say they'll give you the money back, but you know—"

"I'm not so naïve to think anyone would return free cash."

"They might. But if they give you a receipt with Bahram's signature…"

Bibi gazed into thin air for a moment. "It's worth a try. At least I won't have to worry about visiting the morgue. May God take my life. What am I saying?"

"He won't be in a morgue. All he did was read a few magazines. That's not a crime to get killed for."

Bibi gave Majid a reprimanding look.

"He will come back." Majid nodded.

"OK. I'll come with you to call Nosrat *Agha* from your house."

"Of course. You can come any time."

"Is your mother home?"

"Yeah."

"I won't stay long. Just to make a phone call." Bibi came out. She left the gate ajar so she wouldn't need a key to come back.

Ahwaz

As more prisoners were freed, Bahram and other detainees from the SAVAK house were transferred back to Karoun. Once in prison, the detainees were separated: common criminals in one group, and political prisoners in another. The latter mostly consisted of socialists, and therefore nonbelievers. The few supporters of the monarchy also were kept with the socialists, both because they were political prisoners and because they weren't thought of as true Muslims. Vargha was placed with the socialists as Naser stated that Muslims would not want to be in the company of an unclean pagan.

Today, Hesam got a chance to interrogate Bahram again. In a dingy, dark room that smelled like vinegar and sweat. Unlike the setting, the interrogation wasn't authentic. In fact, they sat together, held hands, and talked until Hesam could no longer justify being alone with Bahram. He stopped by an oleander bush and picked a flower. He wished he could take it back for Bahram. But instead, he just took the flower home to remind him of Bahram. He found Saeed in the living room, watching television with a half-full cup of tea in his hand. Hesam sat on the floor next to him and put the flower in the tea tray. "The oleanders smell so good."

Saeed looked at Hesam and then turned back to face the TV. "You in love, Brother?"

Hesam's cheeks felt hot. He had to deny that quickly. "No. But the flowers outside remind me of home. My grandma grew these amazing hyacinths for Noruz that gave the whole house such a lovely aroma." Hesam wondered if that was a good enough excuse. "We would sit on the balcony and talk, drink tea," he continued. "In the summer, we'd sleep on the rooftop. Watching the stars until we fell asleep."

"So you're homesick," Saeed concluded.

Hesam had avoided discovery. "I guess. You're from Tabriz, right?"

Saeed nodded.

"What brought you here to this hot…" Hesam didn't want to use the word *hell*. He chose to say, "desert?"

"It's a long story. You want some tea?"

"Sure."

"That cup is clean. Mansoor didn't want it."

Hesam poured some tea from the pot.

Mansoor entered the living room, brushing his teeth and wearing only a pair of boxers. "I'm going to bed now. Have a night shift." He managed to say everything with the toothbrush in his mouth. "So don't make too much noise. What you watching?" A drop of toothpaste foam fell on the carpet. He rubbed it with his foot.

"Nothing."

"Just talking," added Hesam, hoping Mansoor would leave without anything else falling from his mouth.

"OK," he said as he walked back to the bathroom.

Hesam looked at Saeed and smiled. Then he turned his attention to the TV. The volume was low so they couldn't really hear the news anchor.

"Good night," said Mansoor as he walked by to go to his room.

"Sweet dreams," answered Hesam.

"I guess it's because of the heat that the southern guys are so comfortable with their bodies," Saeed remarked. "I had to get used to that. In Tabriz, it's quite rude to be walking around topless like that. Southerners feel much more comfortable in their own skin—literally."

"When we visited my grandma and it was hot like this, I'd sit by the fish pool in the garden and cool my feet in the water. Felt good. But I felt shy to roll up my pants too high. They'd get wet all the way up to my knees."

"That would be refreshing to perform ablution like that."

Hesam didn't know how to respond.

"You don't pray, do you?" inquired Saeed. "So…are you a socialist? Something led you to leave Rome and come here to serve your country. Is it the Socialist Party of Iran?"

Hesam swallowed his saliva and looked away.

"It's wise to keep it quiet. We all have secrets."

Hesam looked at him oddly, considering his words. "What secret do you have?"

"One day, I'll tell you, Brother. One day."

"I never wanted to come here, you know. I wanted to go to Kurdistan and fight anti-revolutionaries there. Not only do we have to fight the random Iraqis, we also have to fight our own countrymen. What the heck is that? Why do some of them wanna secede? Iran shouldn't be chopped up for each ethnicity. You know what it is? I think it's some foreign agents trying to stir up trouble." Hesam realized he should have been more cautious with his words. "I'm sorry. You're from Tabriz, so you should be Azeri."

"You don't have to be apologetic. I'm with you on that. One Iran for all Iranians, be it Azeris, Kurds, or Arabs."

"Yeah. I was about to be deployed to Kurdistan, but then the clashes broke out in the universities and they sent me here. I'm watching detainees and investigating what they have done."

"Well, at least you're less likely to get killed."

"I'm not afraid of death."

"Yes, you are. I'm afraid of it too. That's why when things got serious in Tabriz, I came here. I just want a quiet life. Get married. Have children. And serve the country meanwhile."

Hesam wondered what serious events in Tabriz forced Saeed to leave. A grand ayatollah was against the draft constitution, and clashes arose from the disagreement between his followers and government forces. "What exactly happened in Tabriz?"

"You should be happy you're here," Saeed said, not answering directly as he cleaned his glasses. "Southerners are nice people. Kind and sincere."

Hesam gave up on his question. "But…for example, this Bahá'í detainee…I talked to his co-workers, friends, family members…There's no evidence he collaborated with SAVAK or has spied for anyone."

"So you support a Bahá'í detainee?"

"I don't know what else to do. No one likes them because of their religion but…"

"Well, I don't like Bahá'ís either. So you're talking to the wrong person, genius."

"But isn't it the anti-revolutionaries we're after? They're the ones who want to cause disunity."

Saeed remained silent.

"What should I do?"

Saeed reached out for a pack of cigarettes and took one out. "I don't know, Brother. When I have a moral dilemma and no way of solving it, I smoke." Saeed lit his cigarette.

"Does it help?"

"You wanna try?"

Hesam glanced at the pack and shrugged. "What the heck."

Saeed gave Hesam the pack and brought his lighter to his cigarette. Hesam sucked on the cigarette and it ignited.

"Inhale the smoke, keep it in your lungs for a moment, then—"

Hesam coughed, took the cigarette out of his mouth and inspected it as if surprised by the damage it caused.

Saeed burst into laughter.

"Keep it quiet before I get insomnia," yelled Mansoor, emerging from his bedroom.

Saeed and Hesam laughed at the man's blustery overreaction.

"No, don't get insomnia, my love," exclaimed Saeed.

Hesam banged on the floor with his hands as he chuckled.

"Hehe, laugh till you die. And get your smoking outside before you stink up the whole house."

"Not as stinky as your feet," Saeed joked.

Mansoor walked over to Saeed and held his foot next to Saeed's face. "Sniff it! Sniff it!"

"Put down your foot. I can see up your shorts."

Hesam put his cigarette on the tea tray as he laughed uncontrollably.

"You like what you see?" Mansoor mocked Saeed. "That's

what *men* have. Are you jealous?"

"Fine, fine!" Saeed held up his hands. "Your feet smell better than Hesam's oleander. Just get your balls out of my sight." Saeed took off his glasses.

Mansoor walked away grumbling. "I live with two children."

"My balls are bigger," Saeed called after him, then burst into laughter again.

MAY 17, 1980

Karoun Prison, Ahwaz

In the political prisoners' ward, Bahram sat on his bed at the corner of the cell. He wondered if the Revolutionary Guards had any idea that he supported the Socialist Organization to Alleviate Laborers' Struggles, SOALS. He didn't agree with all of their politics, but they were one of the few organizations that were active in Kurdistan. Bahram hoped he wouldn't be discovered.

He thought about the guard. Hesam had been investing an extraordinary amount of time in him. Bahram couldn't understand what was going on—until that day his interrogator kissed him. He hadn't seen it coming. Now they met regularly to share discreet affection. But the interrogations had ceased. Bahram doubted that Hesam had conducted any real investigation. He wondered if Hesam was going to release him as promised. He had to play on Hesam's emotions. Promise that if he were freed, there could be more to their relationship.

Bahram hoped that Majid had by now removed any evidence of political activity, even though it consisted solely of reading the magazines. Did Majid know about the stack of SOALS magazines in his bedroom? Hopefully, Hesam wasn't competent enough to investigate and find his house in Abadan. Meanwhile, Bahram had to distract him with tender moments.

Judging by the regime's strict social policies, Bahram's personal life posed a more serious threat to his freedom than his political beliefs. People were killed for…sodomy, as they called it. Now he had an ally in Hesam, who wouldn't use his personal life against him, since he shared the same inclinations. Back in Abadan, very few people knew of Bahram's personal life, and those who did would not dare speak a word. The way he'd publicly humiliated Asadi had taught everyone in the neighborhood to not mess with him.

Worse than his political ideals and personal propensity was his previous life, before he arrived in Abadan at the age of fourteen. But he didn't feel any real danger there. No one could connect the dots. Only Talib knew the story but he was out of the country, not that he would talk anyway. No. With a bit of luck, Hesam's infatuation would divert a thorough inspection into any of these problematic sides of his life.

He hoped Hesam was right, that they would free him soon. But how to speed the process? Perhaps he should come up with a coherent plan to charm him. Bahram wasn't sure how to do that. He'd never had to charm anyone on purpose. Back home, his sexual encounter occurred spontaneously. And with Talib, everything transpired without effort.

Talib. Bahram leaned against the wall and folded his leg on the bed. With few distractions in the cell, he spent a lot of time thinking about Talib.

He thought back to that blissful time. He was in Talib's

room one day after lovemaking, still naked, still glowing. He found Talib's *keffiyeh* on the chair by the side of the bed. He lifted it with both hands so to prevent the *agal* from moving. He stood in front of the mirror and placed the *keffiyeh* on his head.

Talib came back to the room wearing white pajamas. "You could wear your boxers first, babe. Not that I'm complaining." Talib came closer to Bahram, unwrapped the right side of the *keffiyeh* and then wrapped it again. "Pretty Arab boy," Talib approved.

Bahram held Talib's hands and pulled him closer. He stared at the two of them in the mirror.

"I like the way you are. You stay in my room, naked, wearing my *keffiyeh* and staring in the mirror with no shame."

"Why should I be ashamed?"

"Well…after what we just did, most boys would be ashamed."

"I like being with you."

"Yeah. Me too. But you know, guys in your position, they can be called names, harassed, bullied."

"I won't be bullied," Bahram defied. "I'm a thug, remember?"

"A thug you say?!" Talib snickered. "A thug who…" Talib instead tapped Bahram on the back.

"Are you calling me a butt-boy?"

"Shut up. I'm happy you're not ashamed."

"Good. Cause if you think I should be ashamed for being a faggot, I have news for you: You're a fag too."

Talib burst into laughter. As he moved, the *keffiyeh* on Bahram's head tilted to the side.

Bahram fixed it. "What are you laughing at? It's true. That's why you're with me. That's why you call me 'babe.'"

"Oh yeah? That's how it is? Who're you kidding? I'm a man."

"So you think I'm less than a man because I'm…passive?"

Talib shrugged his shoulders, pouting his lips. "Well, it's not so manly to…"

"So in your eyes, I'm less than a man." Bahram looked down, bruised. "And what about love? Don't you love me?"

"Hey, hey, hey…you know I love you. You wouldn't be here in my bedroom wearing my *keffiyeh* if I didn't. You beautiful thief of hearts."

Bahram stared into the mirror and flashed a wide smile at his own reflection.

"You're a sweet-talker, aren't you?"

Talib hugged Bahram from behind, Bahram basking in being enveloped by his firm warm body. They gazed into the image in the mirror. Talib lifted his hand and grabbed Bahram's chin. "*Kellesh helo.*"

Bahram absorbed the compliment with joy. "I love when you speak Arabic. But I have to say it's good that we both speak Persian. Otherwise, we wouldn't even be able to communicate."

"We don't need to talk. Our bodies already speak the same language." Talib squeezed Bahram's body in a combination of love and lust.

"I mean…if you spoke only Arabic and I spoke only Kurdish," Bahram insisted.

"I'd teach you Arabic, babe. But I see your point. It's good *and* bad. Like when they throw Arabs into Persian schools. If the kids can only speak Arabic, they're mocked for not knowing Persian. Don't Kurdish kids have the same problem?"

Bahram agreed that they should be able to speak their own language at school. And be able to benefit from the oil in Khuzestan. The entire country received its riches from the resources of the province. The foreigners were getting money. The government was getting money. Even other Iranians who moved to Abadan were getting money. Wealth underneath the soil of Arab Iranians' land. But they were prevented from sharing the benefits of their own country's resources.

As Bahram sat in his bed in the cell, he was happy that no one could hear his thoughts. These rebellious ideas could jeopardize his freedom. He found himself dwelling on these vivid memories of Talib more often so that he wouldn't have to think about Hesam too much.

He didn't want to examine his feelings for Hesam. He genuinely liked him and enjoyed his affection. But he also knew that seducing Hesam was important to his future. This way, Hesam would liberate Bahram from prison, before anyone had a chance of finding out Bahram's real political positions on issues of minority rights or such. And, he told himself over and over, if it were merely seduction, a clever strategy, then it wouldn't really be cheating on Talib. He had surrendered his body to various guys since Talib left, but he had never surrendered his heart.

A sound of a wounded animal disrupted Bahram's thoughts. The sound slowly got closer. It sounded like a dog. But why would there be a dog in prison? Unless the guards brought it to harass the detainees. Were they going to put a wounded animal in their ward? Bahram hoped the animal didn't have fleas. Or rabies.

It sounded as if the dog was stuck in a trap, its metal edges sinking into the flesh of the animal. As the sound got closer, Bahram realized there was a human dimension to the voice.

"Shut up, stupid Beast," Bahram heard a guard say.

The door of the ward opened and a haggard guy was thrown into the ward. The door was swiftly closed and locked behind him. Dark circles under his eyes made him look unearthly and his unkempt hair flew in every direction.

The Beast scanned the ward with tangible fear.

Bahram looked around to see the reaction of the other detainees and prisoners. No one moved. One man whispered something to another.

Vargha looked at the Beast and stood up, went out of the cell and brought the guy inside. "Glory to God, see what crime they've committed against this boy."

"He keeps screaming like crazy," another prisoner complained.

"Maybe he just saw a scorpion and it scared him," Vargha responded. He took a plastic cup from the window ledge and walked back to the Beast. "Come, my son. Drink some water. It'll help you calm down."

The Beast clenched his hands into paws and swatted Vargha's hand, spilling some water on the floor. The Beast shouted, "*Aoufni.*"

Vargha probably didn't understand what that meant. He bent over the Beast and held his hands so he couldn't punch. The Beast tried again to push him away but quieted down after a moment. Vargha picked up the cup and gently poured some water into his mouth. The Beast swallowed and roughly wiped off his face.

"Good job. What's your name, son?"

The Beast looked around as if surprised that Vargha talked to him.

"Are you in pain? Did something frighten you?"

"Waleed."

"Who is that?" Vargha was confused.

"Me."

Vargha looked embarrassed. Bahram slowly walked closer so he could observe the interaction better.

"A rat was about to bite me. It was huge, as big as you. And its tail was a snake that enveloped my body."

"Is that a nightmare you keep having?"

Waleed's eyes glazed over Bahram.

"Did you always have nightmares, or only since you came here?"

Waleed reached for the cup and drank some more. He didn't speak again. Bahram guessed that silence only indicated that Waleed had a lot to say.

Hesam inserted his index fingers into his ears to muffle the howling that came from the political prisoners' ward. He walked faster toward the office and hurried to shut the door. Mansoor had buried his head into a folder. But Naser was standing by the window looking outside and seemed to not be bothered by the screaming.

"This is so annoying," Hesam said. "What's wrong with this guy?"

"The Beast?" Naser suggested.

Hesam looked at Mansoor, who ignored the exchange. He waited for Naser to offer an explanation.

"You know who's to blame for that one?" Naser asked, then pointed to Mansoor.

Hesam didn't know what to make of it.

"It wasn't my fault," Mansoor protested.

"You should have shot him. That's what an execution means," Naser scolded. He turned to Hesam and continued, "A mishap during an execution last month. Our little Brother here missed the target."

"Missed the target at an execution? I thought there'd be a firing squad," Hesam commented.

"You'd think so," Mansoor observed sullenly.

"Our resources are limited, Brother," Naser said defensively. "We had only one guard to do the shooting. And he missed. So the convict wasn't shot and we didn't know what to do with him. And so the Beast was born."

"So he started having seizures after the incident?"

"We don't know exactly what's wrong with him," Mansoor said.

"He's not gonna get better," Naser insisted. "He was already sentenced to death. Why keep the poor thing suffering? And those unbearable noises make us all suffer. There's no hope."

Saeed walked into the room and objected. "If God spared his life, how can we take it away?"

"I'll ask Haj Agha again what to do," Naser offered with a shrug of his shoulders.

Mansoor looked at Hesam apologetically. "It wasn't my fault. I'd never shot a gun before."

Hesam didn't answer. He alone couldn't solve all the unbelievable problems Karoun faced. He wondered how to make the best out of this situation. Should he obey the orders until he was promoted and gained real power? If he were to fight unjust policies now, that might delay his advancement. Would it be better if he helped out this one prisoner somehow, or if he waited and gained the authority to help many prisoners in the future?

"Maybe he was already crazy. How can you get crazy if you're not even hurt?" Mansoor said, thinking out loud and fishing for someone to agree with him.

"We have other things to worry about now," Naser snapped in impatience. "As our support from Tehran leaves, we need to work harder to make up for fewer guards. We need to conversate about handling our additional duties."

Hesam looked at Saeed in confusion. Did Naser just say "conversate"?

Saeed avoided Hesam's eyes. The howling of the Beast peaked again.

"What should we do with him until Haj Agha makes a final decision?" Hesam asked Naser.

"I don't know, Brother. One problem at a time." Naser left the room.

"It wasn't my fault," Mansoor insisted again, but the others ignored him.

Hesam didn't know what he could do for the Beast. But he *had* made an important decision about one of his detainees. A decision that wouldn't endanger his career. A decision that would save a life. He decided he would talk to Naser about it tomorrow. Hesam needed his boss on his side for this plan to work.

Karoun Prison, Ahwaz

Hesam stood in front of the bathroom sink and stared at the mirror. He had grown stubble so as to not irritate Naser. To win him over further. He patted his hair. He fixed his shirt and inspected his teeth. He took a deep breath and wondered if there was anything else he had to do. Anything to make his request seem more appealing to Naser. Nothing came to mind. He had written down and memorized exactly what he was going to say. He had even prepared responses to Naser's likely objections. Now, it was time to go.

Hesam walked into the office. Naser was alone, going through files. "Good morning. How are you today?"

"Brother Hesam. Good morning." Naser looked up briefly and then continued to read the file in his hand. "I'm fine, praised be God. How are you?"

"Good. Would you like some tea?"

"No, thank you."

"I…" Hesam rubbed his hands on his pants. "I investigated one of the detainees. Vargha Mobasheri."

"Good, good."

"Yeah. Thanks. I…umm…I've talked to his family, coworkers, neighbors, friends…"

"Good work. What did you find out?"

"Well…there's nothing to tie him to SAVAK or a foreign country."

Naser continued to go through his file. "Go to their center. I think the Bahá'ís have a center in Amanieh. It has a big conference hall and everything."

"Well…yeah, I've done that. There's really nothing there."

"Dig deeper."

"But Naser…" Hesam lowered his voice to conceal his objection. "Brother Naser, I couldn't find anything wrong with him."

Naser looked up. "Did you not find evidence that he sent money to Israel?"

Hesam shook his head. "It seems the donations they collected were either given to the needy here, or sent to Tehran."

"What happened to the money in Tehran?"

"I don't know but I don't think we can hold Vargha accountable for whatever they did in Tehran."

"They are all part of the same organization. Haven't you heard the saying 'Follow the money'? You can't stop investigating after the first transaction and say the rest is not his fault."

"I don't really think it was a conspiracy against the revolution."

Naser crossed his arms. "So what are you saying?"

Hesam took a deep breath. "I couldn't find anything illegal. The prosecutor is not going to have a case."

Naser gazed into Hesam's eyes. "So what are you saying?"

"I think we should let him go."

"Let the Bahá'í go?"

"He hasn't done anything illegal."

"Do you know anything about their wayward sect, Brother Hesam? They have satanic beliefs and try to mislead the Muslim nation into believing their perverse ideas. The Constitution of the Islamic Republic of Iran recognizes the people of the Book. That doesn't expand to all these sects, devil-worshippers, and sorcerers."

"We also have socialists…" Hesam realized he shouldn't have said that. There was no need to aggravate Naser further. "They fought the Shah's monarchy and support the government right now. I don't think the constitution means we have to imprison everyone whose religion is not recognized."

"You mean the Socialist Party of Iran? Yes, they support us, but their ideology is still questionable. They're still pagans in an Islamic country."

Hesam took note of Naser's opinion and for a second felt thankful to Saeed for keeping his secret. "I think we should free Vargha Mobasheri."

Naser paused for a minute.

"Is there anybody else you'd like to free?"

Was he implying that Hesam hasn't been working hard enough? Or just questioning why he'd started with Vargha? "I haven't had a chance to complete my investigations into other detainees. So, just Mobasheri for the time being."

Hesam thought of Bahram. He hadn't had the chance to investigate Bahram yet, since he lived in Abadan. Hesam hadn't had the time to travel there. Plus, if he freed Bahram, he may not have another chance to see him. To tenderly hold his hand in those brief moments together that he had scheduled.

Naser started reviewing the files again. "OK. I will talk to Haj Agha about that."

"Are you serious?"

"You seem to have investigated him well. If we're gonna work together, we have to trust each other."

"Thank you, Brother Naser."

Despite the one awkward moment, that hadn't seemed all that difficult, Hesam thought as he exited the room. He'd expected more resistance, more pushback. When he'd freed Najeeb on his first day, he felt like he had crossed a line—that Naser would find out and reprimand him. He had gotten off with a mild warning. But freeing Vargha felt different. He didn't act out of fear or even compassion. His actions were guided by evidence and facts.

Hesam went back into the bathroom and looked at his image in the mirror. *You are a noble man*, he remembered Umberto saying. He smiled.

Naser looked repeatedly at the papers in the folder, but he couldn't make sense of them. Somehow his mind refused to comprehend the writing. He didn't want to disappoint a young Brother who was fulfilling his duties in good faith. But he didn't have the time to reinvestigate the detainee. Plus, that would be unnecessary. He knew Haj Agha would not approve. So he had to think of a solution.

He used to know someone from the Revolutionary Committee of the Kampolo neighborhood. He picked up the phone and dialed the number. His friend Abdullah had left Ahwaz and was now fighting the Kurdish rebels. But there was a new head of the Committee, some guy by the name of Gholam Asadi.

Ahwaz

Esmat was walking back home with a bottle of fresh milk and a pack of sweet crackers when she saw it. More than an act of vandalism, the fresh graffiti was a specific threat to Naser. The excess white paint was already bleeding down the gate. In this heat, it would quickly dry into permanent drops, as if the gate was weeping.

"Death to the mercenary Revolutionary Guard," it read.

Esmat bit the sides of her *chador* so it wouldn't fall as she approached the house gates. The smell of wet paint stung her nose. Someone had spray-painted the threatening slogan after she'd left the house in the morning, which meant this person, whoever it was, observed her comings and goings. She frantically reached into her purse to get the key. Her hand suddenly covered her mouth to cage the scream about to break free. She leaned against the wall and took a deep breath to collect herself. Then she opened the gate again and peeked outside. She saw a young boy, around five, kicking a blue and black ball down the alley and running after it. He noticed her, stuck out his tongue, and then kept going.

She wondered at what exact age children grew up to become monsters. Would they just wake up as teenagers one random day and realize that playing soccer no longer interested them? That they needed to take up some political cause and begin to fight their neighbors? Write graffiti threats on their gates?

Esmat looked at the message again. With all the current political upheavals, the note could have originated from a number of sources. Any group with a particular dislike of the Revolutionary Guards. She'd expected some ups and downs when she married Naser, but she didn't expect anything like this.

An old lady entered the small street, walking slowly toward her. The tattoos that accentuated her eyebrows attracted Esmat's attention. "Rafat *Khanum*? Hello." Esmat tried to hide her surprise.

"Esmat, dear, hello to your beautiful face." The woman she had met at Karoun Prison gates slowly walked toward her, as if wading through waves of heat. "Could you please get me some water, dear?"

"Sure. Come in."

"I'm so sorry, dear." Rafat noticed the graffiti. "We have all sorts of idiots these days. Your husband can clean it up with some paint thinner."

But Esmat wanted to spare him this sight, hoping to wipe away the graffiti before Naser came home. She invited Rafat in. "Come in. Have a seat."

Rafat entered the living room, sat on the rug, and leaned against the Persian cushion. Esmat emerged from the kitchen with a tall glass in her hand.

"May God reward you, dear."

"How are you doing, Rafat *Khanum*?"

"Thank you. Not too bad. I went to the prison. They said they have Waleed. But he's banned from having visitors."

"I think they'll keep him incommunicado until after the court hearing."

"No, no. He had a court. They…they told him they'd execute him."

"God take my life. For what?"

"I don't know. I think they realized it was a mistake. My Waleed wasn't involved in politics. He wasn't. But you know how it is. When the oil pipelines are blown up, they say it's the Arabs who did it. Just being Arab is bad enough to get you killed."

Esmat swallowed. "Do you want more water?"

"No, dear. This was good. Thank you. I'm not saying all Persians hate Arabs. After all, we have lived side by side for centuries. But someone must have scapegoated him, my Waleed."

"But is he all right?"

"I don't know. My hope rests on God."

Esmat could now guess why Rafat had come over. "Is there anything I can do?" She felt obliged to ask.

"May God grant you a long life. I don't mean to bother you. I know you're a new bride."

"It's no bother. Please!" She had to be polite.

"Esmat, dear, can you please speak with Naser *Agha*? Let me see my son. He's done nothing wrong. I'm sure they took him by mistake."

"Rafat *Khanum*, I'm ashamed but Naser doesn't talk much about work." Esmat looked at Rafat. Her eyes projected a deep sense of sorrow.

The visitor looked down. "I understand, dear. It's all about men and their work. They get mad, and we have to calm them down. They get injured, and we have to nurse them back to health. They fight, and we have to pick up the pieces and make peace." Rafat grabbed her *chador* and planted her right hand on the ground and tilted her body.

"I'll talk to him," Esmat found herself saying. "I'll ask him to look into it."

"May God protect you, my dear." Rafat began her effort to get up.

Esmat imagined the woman's knees hurt. "Don't go now. Wait and rest a bit."

"No, Esmat *jan*, I don't want to bother you."

"It's no bother. I haven't had lunch yet. Let's eat something simple."

"My dear, you're a new bride. You should have good healthy lunch. God willing, you'll be expecting soon."

"I just want something light. I have yogurt and cucumber in the fridge. I'll grate the cucumber and serve that with some bread."

"I'll help you dear. Shame on me, I invited myself for lunch."

"No, Rafat *Khanum*. Feel at home. I didn't know married life would be so lonely."

"You are not lonely. You have your husband." Rafat looked at the picture on the side table. "He's a handsome man. Soon you'll have children. There'll be so many people here, you will miss these quiet days."

Esmat smiled and led Rafat to the kitchen.

"My Waleed should soon get married too. God willing, he'll be out of prison. I'll slap him if he hangs out with the neighborhood boys again. They're nothing but trouble. I'll get him married. He'll be so busy with a wife that he won't have time for trouble."

Esmat opened the fridge and took out some cucumbers and radishes.

"Let me wash them, dear." Rafat grabbed the bags and went to the sink. "He hasn't done anything, you know. But just having the wrong friends these days is bad enough to get you detained. God knows I'm tired of these fights between Arabs and Persians."

Esmat nodded. She got the yogurt from the fridge and thought of a way to change the topic. "So why call him Waleed?"

"It's just a nickname we call him. His Arabic name. But the name on his birth certificate is Saleh Moghadam. Maybe Naser *Agha* knows him by that name."

"OK, I'll remember that." Esmat wondered what else to say. "How was he as a kid? Boys can be naughty."

"You don't know the first thing about it. My God, this child was a handful. He'd stand behind the wall and jump everyone. Scared the hell out of me, once. I dropped and broke a jar of pepper. He and I were sneezing for a while that day. He'd go to play, and every day he would come back with a new injury. I don't know how his knees didn't give in. One day, he hid a frog and let it loose on his sister during lunch. His father chastised him that day. Maybe if he'd been punished more, he'd know better than to hang out with the neighborhood kids. I'm sure that's how he ended up in prison."

Esmat placed the washed cucumbers on the cutting board.

"I'll bake some cookies," Rafat said. "Next week, I'll take them to prison for him."

Esmat wondered if Rafat imagined she could obtain visitation rights. But she didn't want to upset her. Rafat finally had a smile on her face.

"Cookies with raisins and date molasses. My mother-in-law's recipe. Her cookies were legendary. May she rest in peace."

"Maybe you can teach me."

"I'll bring you some, my dear. Baking takes too much time. Soon, you won't have time to even think about it. The first pregnancy is not always easy. But God willing, it'll be easy on you. I'll bring you as many cookies as you want."

"Thank you, Rafat *Khanum*. You're very kind."

"You're very kind, my dear. You keep my son safe, I'll do anything for you."

Esmat mixed the cucumbers in the yogurt.

"Esmat *jan*, do you know a good girl? I soon will have to marry my Waleed. His brothers already snatched the best girls I knew. I need to find a bride for him. Beautiful like yourself."

Esmat blushed and lowered her head. "I have to think about that one."

"You do that, dear," Rafat said, her eyes shining with the hint of tears. "You do that."

MAY 21, 1980
Kampolo, Ahwaz

As much as Naser wanted to help build Hesam's confidence and train him to be a deserving Revolutionary Guard, he couldn't tolerate freeing a Bahá'í. Not while Muslim prisoners with much lesser crimes were kept in jail. Naser suddenly remembered that boy, Bahram. His charges seemed much less severe. No matter how thorough of an investigation Hesam thought he'd completed, he was wrong, Naser felt. Hesam was new and he didn't know better. Naser would teach Hesam the difference between the guilty and innocent at the appropriate time.

Naser parked the car behind a white van associated with the Committee and double-checked the address. He walked in through the side entrance. The Brothers of the Committee wore plain clothes but didn't hide their weapons. Many were in their late teens. They wore sandals and short-sleeved shirts. The top button kept their collars closely wrapped around the neck.

"I'm looking for Brother Gholam," he said to the teenager closest to the door.

"Who do you want?"

Naser noted the casual juvenile tone. This would not be accepted at the Corps. But in the Committees, anyone could serve the revolution, even if unfamiliar with the etiquette of the armed forces.

"Brother Gholam Asadi," he explained. "He replaced Brother Abdullah."

The teenager stared at him for a moment, then turned to another. "What is he talking about?"

"What do you need, Brother?" The second teenager approached Naser and extended his hand.

Naser reciprocated.

"Brother Abdullah is gone to Kurdistan to fight the infidel Kurds," said the second guy.

"I know…" Naser tried to keep cool. "I know that, Brother. But I heard that Brother Gholam replaced him."

"I don't know. We just joined recently. I need to go find out."

"No worries. I can wait." He wondered if there was even a list of who served the Committee and who didn't. The teenagers didn't look any different than high school children. They could easily escape detection in a crowd of young men. The perfect method if you wanted to do something without leaving telltale tracks.

"What's going on?" A third guy approached carrying a Kalashnikov.

"He says he's here to meet Brother Gholam."

He shook Naser's hand. "Sure, come with me," he said.

Naser followed. At least the newest teenager knew whom he expected to see. He could guess that the guy had no training in using the gun he was casually carrying, as if it were nothing more than a book bag.

The teenager knocked on a closed door, then opened it. "Brother Gholam, you have a visitor."

The guy was sitting on the floor in the center of a circle of young men. He stood up and walked over to Naser. He had a buzz haircut and facial hair. His olive green uniform gave him a somber look. "I've been expecting you."

Naser leaned in to discuss the matter at hand.

The meeting didn't last long. Naser was soon in the car, going home. He would receive a piece of blue paper containing the details of the operation. It seemed rather easy. Naser exhaled with relief. This way, he would do the right thing without humiliating Hesam and his naïve miscalculation. He had just come back from abroad to serve the revolution and didn't understand the nuances quite yet. Naser had to guide him. He needed all the men who wanted to serve, especially since the backup support would soon return to Tehran.

Naser remembered what Gholam had told him: "You need to figure out why this guard wanted to free a Bahá'í dog. The Revolutionary Guards Corps is not immune to anti-revolutionaries." He'd cautioned Naser that the Corps may need to be purged, just like the universities.

Karoun Prison, Ahwaz

Nosrat waited with the rest of the family members at the gates. Thursday was visitation day for the residents of Karoun Prison. At nine in the morning, the temperature was already ninety-five degrees and, according to the forecast, it was going to reach one hundred eight by midafternoon. Nosrat wiped his forehead with his handkerchief and put it back into his shirt pocket. He saw no trees in the vicinity to provide shade. He was grateful when the guard soon opened the gate.

"You can come in now. But orderly," a guard instructed. "In a single line. If anyone makes any trouble, everybody's visit will be canceled. Only members of the nuclear family are allowed visitation."

Nosrat noticed that many visitors entering were holding their birth certificates. That was the first problem with his plan. He needed some documentation to prove he was related to the prisoner he wanted to visit. Detainees under investigation were not allowed visitors. He had to come up with a backup

plan. And he had to do it fast. Maybe he could tell the truth…
partially.

He approached the guard who looked most personable, wearing glasses. "Brother, good morning. My name is Nosrat." He extended his hand.

"Saeed…but if you are not here to visit, you have to—"

"I'm here to visit—"

"OK, you can go in then. Have your birth certificate ready."

"The thing is…"

"Yes?"

"My birth certificate doesn't… see, he was an orphan boy when I took him in."

"OK, then adoption papers will do."

"See, the thing is…"

Saeed shook his head. "Brother, if you don't have any documents, you won't be able to visit your boy."

"Can you make one exception? For a helpless orphan boy?"

"Brother, if we agreed to make exceptions, there'd be no end to the line at the gates. This is not a hotel. It's a prison. I'm sorry. You just have to—"

"At least let me send him some money. So he can buy some snacks, food…"

"From the prison store? You could easily just bring him the food and snacks."

"Please, I beg you. I kiss your hand. His mother is sick. Let her have peace of mind that her son won't go hungry in prison." Nosrat put his hand on his chest and lowered his head.

"OK. Go in and ask for Mansoor. He'll help you. But the prison shop doesn't really have good food."

"God bless you, my son," Nosrat murmured, eager to advance forward. He followed the crowd up a few steps and entered the building. He passed a few guards and went inside a large waiting area. Visitors had started to line up by the desk of a guard who verified their documents.

He approached one of the guards in front of the room. "Good morning. I'm looking for Brother Mansoor."

"Your name?"

"Nosrat."

"Does he know you?"

"Of course. He's waiting for me."

The guard surveyed the room and told Nosrat to wait. A woman nearby was showing her birth certificate to the guard. He wondered what she would find once she saw her son. Behind her in line was an elderly man, leaning on his cane. The guard went through a large book, searching for the name of the prisoner. He told the woman something. She argued. The guard's body language got more agitated as he threw his arms around and raised his voice. Nosrat could now hear the guard.

"How many times should I say? He's not here. Why don't you understand, *khanum*? Go! Don't waste other people's time."

"He was here. He was here! Where did he go?"

"You need to get out. Your son's not here."

The woman started to scream. "He was here. They told us he was here. I know he is."

"Go to the police. Say your son's missing."

"He is here…"

The guard waved his hand at another guard standing next to Nosrat. "Come, *khanum*. Let's go."

The woman continued to yell, "I've gone to the police, gone to the hospitals, gone to the morgue. He was arrested by the Revolutionary Guards. He was here. Brother Naser knows."

"How do you know him?"

The woman hesitated a bit. "His wife told me. She's a God-fearing lady. She knows how a mother must feel."

"Come, *khanum*." The guard pointed at the door.

Nosrat wondered if there were female guards who could take her out. Men shouldn't be pulling on her like that.

The woman started walking toward the door where Nosrat was standing, but she continued to protest. "His name is Saleh Moghadam. But everyone calls him Waleed. He's here. Please, I beg you. Ask Brother Naser."

The guard walked next to her. "Your son is banned from having visits. You can't see him."

"But he's here, isn't he? When can I see him?"

"After the court hearing."

"He already had a court hearing. When is his next hearing?"

"You have to ask that of the Revolutionary Court."

Nosrat imagined Bibi doing the same thing. Looking for Bahram everywhere. He watched the woman being escorted out. Then his eyes caught a young man who approached. "Brother Mansoor?"

"Yes. And you are?"

Nosrat extended his hand. "Brother Saeed told me to ask for you. I'm Nosrat."

"How can I help you, Nosrat *Agha*?"

"I brought a small amount of cash for my stepson, Bahram—" Nosrat thought that sounded more logical than *my adoptive cousin.*

"Stepson? Where is his real father?"

"He doesn't…he's an orphan."

"Do you have his adoption papers?"

"His adoption papers…I have them but I've misplaced them. I'm a simple farmer. I don't know much about papers."

"What has he done?"

Nosrat had to think on his feet. "He hasn't done anything. He was arrested by mistake. There was a petty theft in the neighborhood."

"An orphan and a thief! You are a lucky stepfather."

Nosrat looked down.

Mansoor tapped him on the arm. "I guess I better give him the money before he robs a prisoner."

Nosrat reached into his pocket and gave Mansoor a 10-*toman* bill.

"All this trouble for just ten *tomans*? The prices inside prison are higher than outside, you know!"

"What can I say? I'm one of the dispossessed. I don't have a luxurious life. Didn't we revolt against the Shah to help people like me?"

Mansoor took the money. "What's his name?"

"Bahram. Bahram Karimi."

"OK. Let me see what I can do."

"May God bless you. And grant you health and a long life."

Mansoor walked out into the yard and then entered the office building. He sat down behind the desk and opened a tall green book to look for the letter K. He reviewed the page a few times, then compared it against another list.

"If he's accused of petty theft, why is he in ward three with the political prisoners?" Mansoor mumbled. He didn't realize Naser was passing by.

"You call me?" Naser appeared at the doorway.

Mansoor stared at him for a minute. "No."

"OK. My bad! I'll wait in the hallway." Naser walked away.

An orphan, a thief, and a liar, Mansoor concluded as he picked up a blank receipt. He exited the office, walked across the yard and went inside the political prisoners' section. He opened the door and went to ward three.

"Bahram Karimi."

A teenager with eyes the color of caramel and long, curly eyelashes stood up. He looked clean and the bed he was sitting on was tidy. He didn't look like a common criminal.

"Your stepfather is here. He brought you some money."

Bahram edged tentatively forward.

Mansoor gave him the cash and the receipt. "You need to sign that."

Bahram held the bill in his fist. "You got a pen?"

Mansoor checked his pants pockets, and then his shirt pockets. He found one. Bahram signed the paper and handed it back to Mansoor.

"Describe your stepfather."

Bahram looked up oddly at Mansoor. "What?"

"He says you're here for petty theft but you're with the political prisoners. So either you lied to him. Or he lied to me. If he's your stepfather, describe him."

"He's like…my height. He's got a belly, almost bald, gray mustache and beard…"

"What does he do for a living?"

"He's…umm—"

"Speak before he joins you in the cell."

"He's a farmer."

Mansoor studied Bahram's expression. He looked at the receipt and walked away.

That was a close one. Bahram shuddered. He felt relieved. The man who'd visited, he had guessed, must be Bibi's relative who lived in Ahwaz. He'd come to Abadan once or twice. He was probably completely bald by now. And probably there's more gray hair in his beard than before. What was his name? Nozar?

Bahram looked around. None of the detainees cared to ask him about his "stepfather" who came to bring him money but couldn't visit him. They were probably banned from visitations or else they'd already be in the visiting hall. Ah, yes—Nosrat, Bahram remembered. His name was Nosrat.

Bahram looked at the 10-*toman* bill. It was half the amount of money that caused so much trouble about three years ago. That trouble occurred in another lifetime, but the memory remained vivid in his mind.

Back then, a 20-*toman* bill had created a commotion in the neighborhood. But it had also been good luck for him. The bill had established his reputation in the new city.

The day his teacher had beaten his feet with the *falak*, the whole class witnessed how Asadi had humiliated him. So several weeks later, after Talib had taught Bahram how to fight better, he planned to get even with Asadi. He also planned to teach everybody else a lesson not to mess with him again.

Bahram found Asadi not far from the tea house. He watched Asadi walk alone and turn into a quiet alley. Bahram followed him. He knew Majid and a couple of his friends, alerted beforehand, were walking behind. They were excited to watch the fight that was about to ensue.

"Hey, you!" Bahram yelled from across the alley.

Asadi turned around. "Shut the hell up, boy."

"Wait up."

"The hell you want? Go home. This is not a place for children."

Bahram ran to catch up with him. "I saw you have 20 *tomans*."

"What?"

"I saw it. It's in your pocket."

"It's none of your damn business what's in my pocket."

"Give it to me. I want it," Bahram demanded.

"The hell is wrong with you? You wanna get beaten up?"

"I wanna treat my friends to some ice cream from the tea house. Give me the money."

"You want money, go to your father. Oh yeah, you don't have one. Go to your mama. She must've made some money at the cabaret last night. Isn't that how she made you?" Asadi smirked and turned around to leave.

"Hey, face me when I'm talking to you."

"Who the hell do you think you are?" He looked at the guys behind Bahram. "Majid, put the leash back on your neighbor boy before I kick him and break his jaw."

Majid ignored the comment and Asadi looked worried about what was happening.

Bahram shoved Asadi with both hands, propelling the boy backward a few steps.

"Psychotic boy. Get lost before I tear up your behind." Asadi grabbed his crotch and yelled, "Freaking butt-boy."

"What did you call me?" Bahram lunged forward and slapped Asadi on the face.

"What the—"

Before Asadi could react, Bahram slapped him again. Enraged, Asadi threw a punch at his head, but Bahram dodged the blow. Bahram flexed his abdominal muscles as he struck Asadi with his fist. The boy shielded his face with his left forearm and jabbed Bahram in the stomach. Asadi's eyes widened to see his opponent didn't fall to the ground. Asadi kicked out his right knee but it just brushed between Bahram's legs. Bahram jumped back and bent his body a little, taking a moment to catch his breath.

"Oh, you got a boo-boo?" Asadi mocked.

Bahram waved his left hand in front of Asadi's face to block his vision and then gathered all his strength to punch him in the gut. As Asadi fell to the ground, Bahram jumped forward and kicked him in the stomach. Asadi folded his knees into the fetal position. Bahram grabbed his hair, refusing to let go even when Asadi punched him on the arm. Bahram delivered a series of smacks to the bewildered boy's face, alternating his blows between the left side and the right.

Bahram then kicked Asadi in the side, causing him to roll on the ground. In a final triumphant gesture, Bahram rested his foot on his nemesis's chest. He pressed his foot and looked around.

Suddenly Bahram noticed Majid was accompanied by a large crowd of high schoolers watching the commotion. And his friends were holding back two guys who were hoping to stop the fight.

Bahram returned his attention to the boy still squirming under his foot. For a moment, Bahram didn't see the body of his rival Asadi on the ground. Instead, he saw Daniar. The reason for all of Bahram's misery. The reason he had lost his family and his home. Daniar probably had married Atefeh by now.

"I'm gonna show you who's in charge," Bahram shouted at Asadi, loud enough for the spectators to hear. With his back to the crowd, he unzipped his pants and began wetting his tormentor. The spectators gasped once they realized what was happening. Asadi yelled out expletives but shut his mouth when Bahram threatened to change his angle to direct the stream into his mouth.

Bahram stepped back to avoid the splash back. He felt good to defeat his enemy. "Who's the butt-boy now?" he taunted.

Asadi whimpered something and tried to move away from the final drops.

Bahram shouted at him, "Who?"

"*I* am!" Asadi was practically weeping. "I'm the…butt-boy." He rolled over and reached into his pocket. "Take the money and go," he pleaded, sniffling back tears of anger and humiliation.

Some boys in the crowd began cheering for Bahram.

He snatched the bill, paused for a second, and then tore it up, dropping the pieces on Asadi. "I don't want your money," Bahram said as he walked over to Majid in the section cheering.

Bahram liked the way the boys looked at him, with this strange combination of fear and respect. It was a little scary, but he was determined to enjoy it.

"OK guys," he said with a forced casualness. "Let's get out of here before the police show up."

The gawkers all scattered in different directions. "I feel bad for Gholam," Majid told him as they walked away.

Bahram was startled. He had forgotten Asadi's first name. He smiled as he remembered his day of glory. After the battle, there were rumors that Asadi wanted to recruit some others and take revenge. But word grew about Bahram's aggression and victory, and it became legend. So no one dared mess with the new thug in town.

No one ever called Bahram Karimi a butt-boy again.

Bahram crumpled the 10-*toman* bill in his hand and looked around the prison cell. He saw that Vargha was humming while packing his clothes.

"Good news?"

"They told me to pack my stuff. I think they're letting me go."

"You're lucky." Bahram imagined Hesam had recommended Vargha's release.

"You want to me contact anyone in your family? Call anybody?"

Bahram didn't trust Vargha enough to give him a phone number. Plus, Nosrat had just brought him some money. "I'm good. Thank you, though."

"You sure?"

"Yeah. Bibi sent me some money."

"Your day will come too, my son. Take care of Waleed for me."

"Who?"

"Waleed. The boy with the tantrums."

"The Beast guy?"

"Don't call him that."

Bahram scratched his head. "I'll try to watch him."

"Thanks."

Bahram extended his hand. But Vargha gave him a tight hug.

After Vargha left the cell, Bahram was caught up in a swirl of emotions. Of course he was happy for the man. And perhaps this meant he would also be released. But what was the holdup? Bahram brooded. If Hesam could let Vargha go, why not him?

Bahram wished Hesam would call him in for another interrogation. That would bring him closer to freedom, he reasoned. But there was a part of Bahram that secretly liked these meetings—even if he was reluctant to admit it to himself.

The intimacy was nice. While he was letting the guard touch him and hug him so he could get released, there was something more, he had to admit. Which caught him by surprise. After Talib, he hadn't allowed anyone into his heart.

Was he beginning to develop feelings for Hesam now that he didn't have a choice of pushing him away? He had to admit that Hesam, while uptight and regimented, was also sexy, with his meticulously waxed boots, and the smoky and sweet cologne that Bahram breathed in during their embraces. He was getting accustomed to the meetings, but it was still strange and exciting. Hesam would hold Bahram's hands, not too strongly to cause discomfort, but not too softly to easily let go. And the prisoner would let him do it, while pretending it didn't really matter all that much to him. But it did. Was he charming Hesam…or was it the other way around?

Karoun Prison, Ahwaz

Hesam couldn't wait for his next chance to interrogate Bahram. This meant he could stay with him and talk, possibly for hours, and no one was going to interfere.

He missed Bahram. He often spent nights thinking of him, the feel of his strong hands and the depth of his beautiful brown eyes. He'd thought of Bahram most of the previous night, and didn't get much sleep.

He thought of their future. They could be together. He could totally see it now. Hesam and Bahram. Bahram and Hesam. Could it really happen? How could he make it happen?

Hesam still had to pass a few hurdles. After he succeeded in freeing Vargha, Naser ordered that he could not free anyone in the future without a repentance letter. Hesam would have to talk Bahram into that. Not that he was in a hurry to free the guy he now adored and obsessed over. He was the only thing that brightened Hesam's boring days as a prison guard.

Before he set Bahram free, Hesam needed to make sure that their bond was strong enough—that Bahram would agree to keep seeing him even outside prison. He couldn't imagine no longer having the chance of spending hours with the beautiful detainee. He had to make sure Bahram would want to see him even if he didn't have to. So the release date could wait. There were many other prisoners to free first.

Hesam greeted Mansoor in the hallway and walked into the office. He almost tripped on his shoelace. He bent and quickly tucked it inside his boot. As he raised his head, he wondered if he was in the right place. There was a woman in a black *chador* standing by Naser's desk. Her back was to him so he couldn't see what exactly she was doing.

"Excuse me, may I help you?" Hesam wondered why a woman was in a men's prison office.

She put something on the desk and quickly turned around. "Hello, Brother. I'm sorry to bother you."

"It's not a problem. Do you need something?"

"Me? Oh no! My name is Esmat. I'm Naser's wife. Naser Atri."

Hesam tried to hide his surprise. "It's nice to meet you."

"I brought him lunch. But I couldn't find him."

"Oh. I'm not sure where he is right now. But I'll make sure he gets it."

"It's right here on the desk." Esmat shuffled some papers on the desk and walked away. "I should be going now. Thank you, Brother…?"

"Hesam."

"Brother Hesam. May God protect you."

"Have a good day," Hesam said, wondering why she was looking through the papers.

Hesam had expected Naser's wife to be more traditional. Yet she'd brazenly asked Hesam's name. Maybe she wanted to remind him that her husband was his boss. And she was brave enough to stay in the prison's office. Alone.

He scanned the desk to figure out what Esmat was searching. The clock showed only 10:53, too early for lunch. He picked up the food containers in order to transfer them to the little fridge in the corner. As he did, a folder fell on the ground. The writing on the cover said: "Saleh Moghadam, organizational name: Waleed."

Hesam set down the food and opened the folder to skim the pages. Waleed was an Arab guy charged with sabotage through blowing up oil pipelines. There was little else in the folder. *Good luck investigating,* he thought. There were no leads in the file. As he was about to close the folder, Hesam saw the last page. "The Revolutionary Court of Khuzestan Province hereby sentences him to death." *With what evidence?* Hesam wondered.

"I thought you'd be in the interrogation room by now," Saeed said as he walked in.

"Oh…yeah. I'm going." Hesam thought for a moment whether he was being teased. Was his time with Bahram becoming too obvious? He put the folder on the desk and picked up the food containers.

"Well, the detainee is alone waiting," Saeed added.

"I'm going. I just need to put these in the fridge."

"What's that? You cooked for us?"

"Don't flatter yourself. Naser's wife brought it for him."

"He can't possibly eat that much. Let's see what it is."

Hesam hesitated.

"What, you think he's gonna sit here and eat all of that alone and not offer? We're all Iranians, you know. We have manners. Not like you and your Italian buddies."

Hesam laughed. "If you really had manners, you wouldn't be stealing someone else's food."

"Who talked about stealing, genius? Especially when we don't even know what it is. We have to see it first. I bet the new bride doesn't know how to cook yet."

"Here. You inspect the food. I'll question the detainee."

"Inspect the pretty boy," Saeed said as he adjusted his glasses. "Maybe you'll find something you like."

Hesam froze. Had Saeed found him out? Hesam felt a panic inside, but had to play it cool. He took a piece of paper from the desk, crumpled it and threw it at Saeed. "You think you're funny?"

"Excuse me. You need to stop wasting the public property," Saeed said with a sarcastic edge, then bent and picked up the crumpled paper. "This is the property of the dispossessed nation. Don't be wasting it," he chuckled.

Hesam put up his hands. "Fine. Whatever you say."

"I wish I could get more people to say that."

"What are you so happy about, today?"

"God is good."

"OK. You take Naser's food. He doesn't seem dispossessed."

"I hope I don't like the food. Otherwise, I may take Naser's wife as my personal cook."

Hesam shook his head. "Man, you're crazy."

"It's just a joke."

Hesam walked down the hallway to the interrogation room. He hesitated for a moment, still nagged by Saeed's comment. Then he slowly opened the small window in the door and watched Bahram through the bars. He was sitting on the chair with a table arm, blindfolded and with his hands tied. But his back was straight and his shoulders touched the chair's backrest. He looked beautiful, even if Hesam couldn't see those honey-brown eyes.

Hesam entered the room. He wanted to say, "Dear Bahram" but settled for "Bahram." He was afraid if he pushed too much, he'd scare him off. He took off the beautiful prisoner's blindfold and removed the handcuffs. "How are you doing?" Hesam leaned forward.

"OK."

"Great. I'm glad to hear it." Hesam wanted to tell his captive that he couldn't sleep last night. That he was thinking of him, imagining kissing him, yearning for this moment to be next to him. But he just stood and watched him.

"You freed Vargha. When are you gonna let me out?"

Hesam felt a knot in his stomach. "Good to see you too." He tried hiding his hurt.

Bahram averted his eyes as if he wasn't worth a glance. Was he disdainful of Hesam's love: boundless, fragile, and hopeful?

Hesam had words stuck in his throat, words he wished to say: *I'm no less of a prisoner than you. I'm helpless and dependent on the actions and feelings of a young man I have fallen for. I'm afraid I could say the wrong thing or make the wrong move and all this could end at any moment.*

But he just kept quiet. He placed his chair in from of Bahram's. He sat down and softly grasped Bahram's hand, touching only the fingertips. They were warm but not sweaty. Hesam felt Bahram's fingers pressing against his palm. He swallowed. He gently put his hand behind Bahram's neck and drew himself closer. He now sensed Bahram's breath on his lips. He wanted to take in his scent, his essence. Embarrassed by his own longing, he looked down, his forehead on Bahram's.

The Enthraller stroked him on the arm for a second, and then pulled back.

Happy that his bicep was flexed, Hesam hoped Bahram would find it appealing. "Bahram, I…" He didn't know how to finish his sentence without baring his soul.

Their eyes locked for a moment, but then Bahram looked away, prompting Hesam to release his fingers from the guy's neck.

With his eyes, Hesam begged him for a sign.

"Maybe if we were out of here…" Bahram finally murmured, "we could be together."

Unable to stop himself, Hesam reached out tentatively but withdrew before making contact with Bahram's skin.

"It's not going to be here, where you have everything to gain and I have everything to lose," Bahram explained.

"This will take time," Hesam said. "We have hundreds of prisoners. Most were arrested in the last month or so. Releasing everyone is going to take some time."

Bahram leaned back in anger.

"But if you want your file to be prioritized," Hesam added, "you can help me with one thing."

"I'm not sleeping with you," Bahram spat out. "I'm not using my body as collateral."

"Was that even an option?" Hesam teased.

"I'm not in the mood for jokes."

Hesam took a breath before sharing the next piece of news. "See, there's been a policy change. From now on, we only release prisoners who sign a repentance letter. That's Naser's new requirement."

"A repentance letter?"

"Just denounce your organization and pledge to support the government."

"I'm not a member of any organization."

"Then just sign the letter."

"Why should I do that? Why don't you just walk on the streets and ask everybody to sign your letters?"

"Because we have no reason to believe they don't already support the government."

"Your guys had no reason for arresting me, either. So just let me go."

"If you support the government, why can't you just sign the letter?"

"Because it's stupid that I have to sign it when millions of people outside the prison don't."

Hesam noticed the circular argument and didn't want to continue. Plus, he didn't really want to free Bahram anyway. Not quite yet. "I'll prove to you that I'm trustworthy," Hesam said, reaching to touch the prisoner again.

"Good. Start by letting me go," Bahram said, backing off.

"I want to…sleep with you."

Bahram snorted. "Forget it."

"I won't do anything. Just lie next to you."

Bahram glared back at him. "You are something else."

Hesam worried he had overstepped the line. Maybe if they talked more, he could win him back. He wanted to just hold Bahram's hand and talk. About life. Bahram's life. Italy. Not Italy, because then he would have to mention Umberto. Too complicated.

"If you recall, sodomy is punishable by death," Bahram fired back. "You should know. It's your revolutionary law."

Hesam frowned. Sodomy. What an ugly word for such a beautiful thing. He'd suspected that committing it could lead to execution, but he had been too afraid to verify. "I like you, Bahram."

"I like you too, Hesam but—"

"I'll prove to you I'm worth it," Hesam interrupted. "Just give me a chance."

"But do you love me enough to give me my freedom?"

Naser smiled as he thought of his beautiful bride, bringing him lunch. Then he suddenly stopped on his way to the interrogation room. He didn't want all these single young men to see his bride. What if any of them had some vile thoughts about her? Although Esmat always dressed properly.

Naser had to have a talk with Esmat. A men's prison was no place for a beautiful young woman. As he walked forward, he noticed that the small window to one of the interrogation rooms was half-open. Someone must have forgotten to close it. He walked up to the window and peered through. He suddenly recoiled.

Brother Hesam was holding a detainee's hand. The detainee was not wearing the blindfold. Hesam was speaking gently to him, not yelling at him. What was more, he was looking tenderly at the man.

Naser felt repulsion. He quietly closed the small window of the interrogation room's door and walked away, his stomach still sickened. He knew he had to address such a despicable act.

Ahwaz

As she sat on the chair, Esmat kept shaking her leg. She pressed her hand on her leg to force it to stop. But then the jerking resumed. It was nerves, pure and simple. She was in a panic.

Naser had come home right after work, as he usually did. But unlike a typical night, she had a serious matter to bring up over dinner.

Last week, he had surprised her by coming home late one night. He had to visit some friend in the Kampolo Revolutionary Committee, he told her. That was the first night since their wedding that he'd come home late. And in a strange mood. That night he didn't compliment her as he entered the house. He didn't even say thank you when she brought him dinner. Esmat remembered it exactly. In her new role as a bride, she noticed every move Naser made.

As she sat this evening, she could smell the dry-lime and prunes boiling in the pot. She had cooked Naser's favorite split-pea beef stew with French fries and rice. She had planned the evening right down to her appearance: She was wearing some pink and light-blue eye shadow. More than the simple eyeliner and lipstick that was her usual makeup. She wanted Naser to be in the best mood possible when she asked her questions.

She heard him come into the living room. He had changed into his home clothes, a white T-shirt and gray pajamas. He looked different without his camouflage uniform, as if he left the guard personality at the door. When he was in the house, he was barefoot and relaxed, a husband freshly in love. He turned on the TV and sat down on the floor, holding the day's local paper in hand.

Esmat poured two cups of tea and replenished the small bowl with sugar cubes. She walked into the living room and placed the tray next to Naser.

"Could you turn it off, please?" Naser asked her.

"You just turned it on." She was taken by surprise.

"I'd rather talk to you." He smiled as he put aside the newspaper.

Esmat turned off the TV and sat next to her husband.

He handed her a cup. "So how was your day? Do you still get bored sometimes?"

"Praise God. Good day. I fill up my day with housework. I'm starting to get to know the neighbors."

"We can go and visit your parents. Next Friday maybe. I don't want you to be lonely here."

"It's all right. I can't complain. I ironed your uniform."

"Yeah. Thanks." He put his hand on hers. "I'm lucky to have you."

Esmat smiled to cover her nervousness. "I came to the prison to bring you food." She held the cup but didn't drink.

"Something bothering you?" Naser inquired.

"No, no. Not at all. I saw this old woman, looking for her son."

Naser put his cup back on the tray. "Esmat, maybe it's not a good idea to come to the prison," he preempted. "We live in dangerous times. There are all types of anti-revolutionaries. Violent groups. I don't want—"

"Don't worry about me, Naser. But if you don't consent, I won't come. I'm not an unruly woman." Esmat wanted Naser to feel in charge. Then he'd let his guard down and she'd be able to ask about Waleed.

"No, no, no!" Naser protested. "You're an educated smart woman. I love that about you. You don't have to bring me lunch, though. I'm only concerned with your safety. That's all."

"Whatever you say. I'll cook earlier in the morning."

"No need. I can take leftovers from dinner. You don't have to cook lunch every day."

Esmat took a breath to continue her agenda. "That old woman I saw…she was looking for her son. She's been trying to find a trace of him for weeks. Months maybe."

"A detainee can't have visitors during interrogation. Tell her to be patient."

"Do you know him? His name is Saleh Moghadam. But she calls him Waleed."

Naser looked away and took a long sip from his cup.

Esmat let the silence hover over them.

"Esmat, I can't really talk about work."

Esmat felt dejected and dropped her head.

Naser put the cup aside and sat closer to her. "You're so beautiful."

"Whatever you say," she pretended to comply.

Naser exhaled and leaned against the wall. "Now you're upset."

"It's just that…the old woman was bawling like a hungry baby. Her son's missing. Just hard to see. Poor thing."

Naser rubbed his beard. "I know her son. That guy is a saboteur. He's charged with exploding the oil pipes. He's sentenced to death."

"May God have mercy on his soul. Is he dead?"

"No…he was supposed to be executed a while ago, but… one of the Brothers didn't how to shoot and he missed."

"Oh! So God has forgiven him," Esmat proclaimed, then regretted immediately making such a pronouncement. She had seen Waleed's file and found nothing that could have led to a capital punishment verdict. But Naser didn't have to know that. She placed her hand on Naser's lap. "I'm sorry. I don't mean to meddle in your job."

"I told you I can't talk about work," Naser repeated apologetically.

Esmat nodded and withdrew her hand from his lap. But she couldn't keep silent. "But if God spared his life, they need to let him go."

"I know he probably should be out," Naser agreed. "The problem is…he's gone crazy. He screams like an animal, bothers other prisoners, and he…he can't be released like this. Even in prison he's so much trouble. Someone has to decide what to do with him—the head of the prison, or the judge, or somebody. But he's under a death sentence so no visitors until his situation is cleared."

Esmat persisted. She'd promised she would. "I think it's clear that God has spared his life. The Court is here to do God's command."

Naser looked away. His silence ended that conversation.

"Maybe we can bring my sewing machine from my parents' house…you know?" She capitulated. "If we visit them next Friday."

"OK. Yeah. That will keep you busy. You don't have to worry about the detainees."

Esmat felt she had made some progress. She suppressed a smile and lifted her teacup.

Karoun Prison, Ahwaz

Hesam stood uneasily in the long hall and watched. Prisoners behind the glass divider were talking to family members through the wall phones. He looked at his watch. It was only 10:25. Five and a half hours remained of the visitation day, and it wasn't going to become any more interesting. He'd learned to offer a firm nod but nothing more when family members approached and insisted that their loved one was an angel and had been wrongly accused.

He and Saeed made a list of family members who had come to visit prisoners. Mansoor and another guard would bring the prisoners into the hall and then bring in the visitors.

The cycle would repeat, again and again, throughout the day. The monotony was impossible. Hesam leaned against the wall and bent his knee to anchor his foot on the wall. He folded his arms and stared into space.

To ease the boredom, he recalled his last encounter with Bahram a few days ago. It nearly caused him to salivate. He remembered feeling Bahram's hands on his forearm. Hesam took a deep breath and closed his eyes. In his mind, Bahram was pressing his fingers into Hesam's flesh, pulling him closer. Their lips would touch…

Suddenly, a voice jerked him back to reality.

"No, just take a nap. No need to watch the visitors. I got it!" Saeed was standing right in front of him.

Hesam looked up and frowned. "I'm sorry."

"Genius," Saeed shook his head.

"Is visiting time over?"

"Awhile longer. But there's something else."

"What's that?"

"An old woman. She's here for your detainee. What's his name, Bahram something?"

"Is she his mother?"

"She says he's an orphan, but lives with her."

Hesam shifted uneasily as he considered the information. "But he's still under interrogation."

"I know that, genius. But she traveled a long way. From Abadan."

Hesam lost the excuse for failing to investigate. "Abadan?"

"Yeah. Did he never mention that?"

Hesam didn't want to look incompetent in his interrogation. "Maybe. I don't remember. He said a lot. I have quite a file. But how does she know he's here?"

"Well, her story is a bit strange. About two weeks ago, a man came here saying that he's Bahram's stepfather. He learned that he could send money to him in prison. But he's from Ahwaz and this mother of his lives in Abadan. She says she has the receipt for the money that was sent."

"Sounds like a very organized, older divorced couple," Hesam said, trying to appeal to Saeed's offbeat sense of humor.

"Who ever heard of such a coordinated older couple?"

"People in Abadan are…you know, progressive."

"A bit too westernized if you ask me. But either way, the poor woman is out there, under the burning sun. She came all the way from Abadan. It's your call, since it's your prisoner."

Was Saeed really letting him decide? Should the old woman see Bahram even though he was being held *incommunicado*?

Naser suddenly barked out. "Brother Hesam. I need to see you when you have a moment. Saeed will watch the visitors."

"Yes, Brother Naser," Hesam said as he prepared to follow him. At that moment, Saeed looked at Hesam and shook his head. It was a signal that it was unwise to bend the rules regarding Bahram, especially with Naser watching everything.

Naser was sitting behind the desk. "Tell me, how many repentance letters have you gathered?"

"Umm…I'm working on it, sir."

"You don't have to call me sir."

"Yes, Brother Naser." Hesam adjusted his terminology.

"I presume you don't have any repentance letters. Is that so?"

"Yes, Brother. Still working on them."

"You don't work on the letters, Brother Hesam. You work on the detainees." His voice got louder and more authoritative as he leaned forward. "With the right balance of force and persuasion, they will sign them. They sign them, they get released. They get released, we won't have so many visitors."

"I understand."

"Good. I wanna see half of your prisoners freed by next week."

"Pardon me?"

"We don't have the resources to keep these prisoners

forever. The backup support from Tehran is leaving. Many were detained because they seemed suspicious. But we can't justificate their detention for much longer."

Justificate? Hesam wondered. *He means 'justify.'* But Hesam kept his mouth shut in the midst of Naser's obvious anger.

"We get the repentance letters, we let them go. And if they're arrested again, we have concrete evidence that they broke their own pledge of support for the government."

There was a pause and Hesam realized it was time to agree. "Yes, sir."

"Brother, you don't have to call me 'sir.' I would appreciate it if you obeyed me and called me Brother, instead of disregarding my orders and then calling me sir, like some Western movie."

"Yes, Brother Naser."

"You're dismissed."

"Yes, Brother Naser." He started walking toward the door.

"And Brother Hesam?"

He turned around.

"That detainee, Bahram Karimi…has he signed the letter?"

"No, not yet, Brother."

"He's going to need some convincing." Naser showed Hesam his fist.

"Excuse me, Brother?" Hesam tried to pretend he hadn't understood.

"Beat him up. He's a cocky one, and we need to break him. Let me know if your arms get tired. I'll help."

Hesam nodded and headed for the door. Why was Naser taking special notice of Bahram? Why the suggestion to beat him?

"One more thing," Naser yelled before Hesam could exit. "You live with Brother Saeed, right?"

Hesam nodded.

"You should use him as a role model. I know you lived abroad. I think you forgot our traditions. Remember, there's no shame in learning how to pray again. Ask him. Go to the mosque. Stand behind as he prays and learn."

What's up with this holier-than-thou attitude today? Hesam wished he could ask.

"You can go now," Naser barked.

Hesam walked out. Walking back to the visitation hall, he ran into Mansoor. The guard told him that Saeed wanted to talk to him and to meet him at the gates. Hesam exited the building and reached the gates where he saw Saeed.

"The lady refuses to leave," Saeed announced.

"Who?"

"Your lover, genius! Who do you think? Your detainee's mother. Stepmother. Whatever she is. She says she's not leaving until she talks to someone."

"But we can't let her see him," Hesam said with discomfort. They had agreed on that point, given Naser's excessive supervision.

"Give her some water or something. She's old. I don't want her to have a stroke here. But then send her away."

"If I can't let her see him, I can at least take her back home," Hesam concluded. "After visitation, that is." He went to the building to get some water.

"And Hesam."

"What now?"

"If Naser asks, tell him you are investigating Bahram's case. And that you are close to completion, so we can let him go already."

Hesam didn't want to let him go. Not yet. But he just nodded and walked away.

After the visitation hour, Hesam helped Bibi into the passenger seat of his Jeep. As he began driving, Bibi launched into the same questions as before. "Why was he arrested? He hasn't done anything, no. I know my son. He wouldn't assault anyone. He wouldn't carry a knife."

"Nobody says he assaulted anybody. He's in prison for suspicious political activities."

"What suspicious activities? Long time ago, he read some magazines. That's all. But I had him stop that. He never took part in any activities. Everybody reads magazines. But he hasn't done anything."

"What was he doing in Ahwaz? Don't you all live in Abadan?"

"He came to visit his cousin."

Hesam thought back to his conversations with the prisoner. Bahram had insisted he was in Ahwaz to look for a job. He specifically remembered that because he thought Abadan had better employment opportunities than Ahwaz.

"I didn't give birth to him," Bibi volunteered. "But he's my son. He has lived with me for several years."

"How...did you find him?"

"He came to me as a young boy. So beautiful. Those eyes! I took him in, raised him."

Hesam still wondered how many years ago that was. But Bibi was talking too fast to interrupt.

"He asked if he could stay. Probably, he'd come from the streets. He asked to stay with me. He said he'd work. My heart fell for him. I asked him what happened to him. Who'd put him out? He just stood and stared at me like a scarecrow. I asked him so many times that my tongue grew hair. He refused to say any more. So I gave up asking."

"You're very kind."

"I'm not rich. I had to wash people's clothes and dishes, clean houses to give him some food and raise him. I became his Bibi."

Hesam stopped abruptly and reversed the Jeep. "I missed the turn," he explained.

"You don't pay attention to the road signs, no," she criticized. "Just follow the one sign that says Abadan. I can tell you all you need to know about Bahram so you can let him go."

"Uh, OK," Hesam said, both irked and impressed by her presumption.

Bibi rattled on. About how Bahram worked after school, mowing lawns, to pitch in. He mowed the lawns for Americans and the other employees of the National Oil Company.

"He worked. Wasn't a lazy boy, no. He didn't let me wash his clothes. I'd say, 'Bahram, son, don't wash clothes. You're a man. Men don't wash clothes.' He said, 'Bibi, I'm young. How can I let you bend over the bowl and get backache washing my clothes?' I realized he was right. Men should help women. He was smarter than me. You let him go, officer. No need for arresting innocent youth, no."

"Don't worry, Mother," Hesam said out of respect. "He'll be out soon."

"Oh, now I can breathe. Now that you promised."

I didn't promise to let him go, Hesam thought. *Not until he likes me more.*

"You guarantee he would be freed unharmed?"

"I promise. We just need to finalize a few things."

"Why don't you finalize these things already? He has been inside so long."

"We just have to ask a few more questions." Hesam repeated the official line. He couldn't have Bibi argue with him the entire way to Abadan.

"Ask your questions and let them go. Don't the Revolutionary Guards have anything better to do?"

"Don't worry, Mother. He'll be out before you know."

"God bless you, young man. He will reward you."

Hesam looked at the road sign. It was eighty miles to Khorramshahr and six more miles to Abadan. Underneath the word *Abadan*, someone had written with spray paint *Your very own Brazil*. The people of Abadan were particularly proud of the soccer team of the oil company, comparing it to the team from Brazil.

Hesam had never been to Abadan before. The city was the symbol of modernity and progress. People wore the latest western fashion and danced to the newest European songs. He had heard of luxurious swimming pools and decadent nightclubs. Hesam pushed down on the accelerator as he was growing weary of Bibi.

Abadan

The road to Abadan followed the Karoun River. Where the river wound and twisted, the road moved in a straight line and the distance between the two ebbed and flowed. It reminded Hesam of a love affair: falling in love, making love, and then taking a breath of separation that would make you miss what you fell in love with in the first place. Hesam preferred when the river came back into view, hugging the road again, as it gave him hope that Bahram would love him back.

As much as he wanted to get information from Bibi, Hesam eventually tuned her out just so he could enjoy the ride.

He was more interested in seeing where Bahram lived, where he spent the nights. He wanted to understand him better, so he could get closer to him.

Farther away, Hesam noticed a small fishing boat and palm trees by the river. He saw the Old Bridge and crossed the Karoun at the eastern edge of Khorramshahr, approaching Abadan.

Hesam slowly pressed his foot on the brakes. He wanted to slow down so he could see the sights better, rather than have them speed by. The distance between the road and the two rivers on both sides widened. The palm trees enjoyed the company of other types of trees and Hesam saw various hues of green. He saw cars that shone under the sunlight: BMWs and Iranian Paykans, newer and cleaner than the ones in Ahwaz. He saw a sign that marked the road to a dairy farm and a restaurant on the right. He slowed down, considering a visit to the restaurant, when he heard the loud horn of a Mercedes-Benz convertible as it passed on the left.

"Don't slow so suddenly, no. You'll cause an accident," Bibi advised.

Hesam passed a roundabout and the road that led to the Abadan International Airport as well as to a golf and horse-riding club. This was a westernized city. He touched on the accelerator, pivoting on the heel of his foot as he hesitated to pick up speed. The road was smooth and inviting. Maybe he should catch up with the Benz and show that his Jeep was just as good.

"I'm old, but I can reach my own death without your help, son. No need to start racing like that," Bibi complained again.

He confronted more cars as the traffic intensified. He passed several hotels, taking a mental note that he might have to come back to one of them to spend the night, although they were so large, he might not be able to afford them.

"This is the Braim neighborhood." Bibi pointed to the left side. "That's where the employees of the oil company live. They have everything. From soccer fields to swimming pools. You name it, they got it. My Bahram is going to end up there someday. I know he will. He works hard. He's driven. I used to think that's just a dream, until I realized he will be able to reach it."

Hesam admired the houses, each with a green lawn in front, separated only by trimmed evergreen shrubs. They had small wooden gates. The green was ornamented with the pink and red of oleanders and bougainvilleas. There were smaller plants Hesam hadn't seen before, even in Ahwaz with a similar climate.

"Men and women sunbathe here on the front lawns. God bless them. I'd be too ashamed to take off my clothes like that," Bibi announced. "One of these men helped Bahram get a better job."

On his right, Hesam saw the top of masts and topsails of boats. Bibi explained this was the Small Ships Harbor, a space for cargo ships and tourist sailboats. He could smell the wet sand.

A few blocks later, they passed the refinery: large structures with pipes and tall chimneys, painted red and white, emitting smoke high into the sky. It wasn't pretty. But it paid for the rest of the city's beauty.

"Make a left," Bibi instructed as they reached a fork in the road.

They went deeper into the city, away from the river with the controversial name. The Arvand River, Hesam concluded quickly, aligning with fellow Persians, as opposed to its Arabic name.

He was still thinking about the reasons that justified calling it the Arvand when the Jeep jolted over a pothole.

"From here, you need to pay more attention. We're reaching the poor people's neighborhood."

Adjacent to City Park, the face of the city changed into a slight frown. Hesam had to maneuver the Jeep to avoid an increasing number of potholes in narrow streets. Yard shrubs gave way to brick walls and metal gates. Bibi said this was Ahmad-Abad. The streets had numbers, as if no one could be bothered to think of names. She directed him to park in front of her gate.

"Thank you my son. God bless you. I had no power to take the bus again."

"No problem. I'm sorry you couldn't see Bahram."

"I ask you only one thing. Let him out. Let him come home. You already promised. A man should keep his word."

"Bibi, I—"

"You won't earn respect by aiming your gun, no. Only by keeping your word."

"I understand, Bibi *Khanum*."

Bibi got out of the Jeep. Hesam was curious to see where Bahram lived, but he didn't want to seem too eager. "I think I should be heading back soon."

"Are you crazy? You just drove for two hours. You need to rest. Stay here overnight. In Bahram's room."

Hesam looked away, entranced by the notion of sleeping where the Enthraller once slept.

"Why are you hesitating? You're not afraid of me, no?"

"No, Bibi *Khanum*. Are you sure I won't be bothering you?"

"You are no bother. Ask the neighbors about Bahram. Then, let him go. Come." Bibi opened the gate and led him in. There was a small courtyard covered with pavers. A few pots of geraniums and stock flowers were placed next to the glass door with metal bars that opened to the house. Hesam untied his boots' laces and followed Bibi.

"It is right here." Bibi led Hesam into Bahram's room. There was a bed, a desk and a chair. A poster of a building was pinned into the wall. The writing on the façade of the building read "Abadan Museum."

Bibi offered Hesam tea, but he said he preferred water. Bibi walked away and gave Hesam more time to inspect the room. On the other wall was a small poster of the singer Dariush, with long hair and full-grown beard. Underneath was a picture of Bahram in the middle of two guys. One guy with dark skin and curly hair had his hand on Bahram's shoulder. On the other side, Bahram had his hand wrapped around the waist of a guy wearing a *keffiyeh*. Bahram looked younger, hinting that the picture was taken a year or two ago. Hesam thought, *Well, he definitely hung out with good-looking guys.*

Bibi returned with a glass of water and saw Hesam peering at the photo. "These are his friends. All are good boys. Nothing illegal you will find here. Here are his clothes." Bibi opened the closet door.

"Thank you, Bibi *Khanum*. No need to look into his clothes."

"I thought you came here to investigate."

"I really don't want to bother you. I can leave."

"You won't do anything like that. Stay. I will make some dinner. But I have to go and finish a chore. You need nothing else?"

"No. Thank you very much."

Bibi walked out of the room. Hesam sat on the bed. He contemplated smelling the bedding but decided against it. He saw a *keffiyeh* scrunched on the chair under the desk, not dissimilar to the one in the photo. He lifted the *keffiyeh* and found a few booklets made up of photocopied papers.

He read the title and immediately got goosebumps. *Official Publication of the Socialist Organization to Alleviate Laborers' Struggles.* Hesam unbuttoned the first button of his uniform. He tried to remember all he knew about SOALS. It was a radical socialist organization that openly opposed the government. It sided with the Kurds who had rebelled against the government since the latter's inception.

Hesam had come back from Rome hoping to join the Revolutionary Guards Corps in its fight against the Kurds. And Bahram, this sweet guy who claimed no political activity, read the publications of the most radical socialist group. That explained why his story didn't add up. He said he was in Ahwaz to look for a job. But Bibi said he was there to meet up with his cousin. He was arrested near the city hall, right after clashes broke out between the Revolutionary Guards and the socialist students who had defied orders to close down their campus offices. Judging by the evidence, Bahram was probably a supporter of SOALS and had taken part in confrontations with the Revolutionary Guards at the university.

Hesam picked up the glass and noticed his hand was shaking slightly. He drank the rest of the water. He was, he realized with melancholy, in love with a guy who could have killed him if they'd met in Kurdistan. Why would anyone support the separatist rebels? Why support them after they aimed to chop up the country? And why fight against the Revolutionary Guards in the university? Bahram wasn't even old enough to study at the university.

Hesam suddenly began punching the blanket he sat on. All the while when Hesam was sleeplessly in love, Bahram was lying to him. Hesam wished Bahram were there. He needed the guy to explain himself. But even after explaining, would it be enough? Could Hesam forgive him?

He felt his veins constrict and his breathing become shallow. He left the room and entered the courtyard just so he could breathe. He tried to calm his mind to assess the situation. What had just happened? He had a crush on a guy who only fed him lies, and, judging by the evidence, was an enemy. It occurred to Hesam that Bahram had never liked him. He was just using him to get out of prison. He felt shame, outrage, self-pity at this unrequited love and betrayal. The thoughts clouded Hesam's head, forming a fog of confusion and hurt.

What do I do now? Should I tell Naser about these magazines? Reading SOALS publications was not illegal. Or was it? They did fight along with the Kurds against the government. Bahram was a nonbeliever, a socialist. And therefore, he could be called an infidel, a label that could cost him his life. *He definitely has to stay in prison until he signs the letter of repentance. Even if he doesn't love me, even if he lied to me, am I ready to take his life?*

Hesam felt a strange weakness in his spine. Maybe he should confide in Saeed. He always knew what to do. After all, Saeed suggested that Hesam meet with Bibi. He did his job but never lost his humanity.

Bibi. Hesam hoped she would not show up in the front yard while he was in such a state. He needed to collect himself. He could use some more water.

Taking in deep breaths of hot air, he noticed he was still holding the magazines. He looked at the first headline: "Genocide in a Kurdish village by the Revolutionary Guards." *What a pile of garbage! This propaganda is not worth reading.* He wrapped the magazines in the *keffiyeh.*

"Bibi *Khanum*?" Hesam heard a young man's voice from behind the gate. "It's Majid. Did you find Bahram?"

Hesam walked to the gate and opened it.

"Who are you? What are you doing here?" Majid demanded an answer.

Hesam recognized the guy from the wall photo. Hesam had to find a way of extracting information about his prisoner.

"You're a Revolutionary Guard," Majid said, recognizing Hesam's uniform.

"Be quiet. I'm a socialist too," he declared in a hushed voice, surprising himself with his candor. "And stop yelling."

"Where's Bibi?" Majid walked in boldly with his chest pumped up.

"She's inside. There's no emergency. Calm down."

"Who are you? What do you want?"

"Shhh…lower your voice. My name is Hesam. I'm a friend. I came here to help Bahram."

"Help him? How?"

"I need to find out what evidence there is against him."

Majid didn't budge.

"And then destroy it." Hesam surprised himself with the impromptu fabrications.

"What are you talking about? There's no evidence—"

Hesam showed Majid the magazines in his hand.

"You're from SOALS? Rubbish! I've never heard of you." Majid took a step backward. He had just exposed himself as a supporter of SOALS.

"I told you. I'm one of us," Hesam consoled him.

"Why are you wearing the Revolutionary Guards uniform?"

"The Organization needed someone on the inside. I was doing my own thing until I came across Bahram. If they find out who he is, they'll name him an infidel and execute him." Hesam was not sure of this, but had no time to think of a better story.

"How do I know I can trust you?"

"Here! If you take these magazines, there is no evidence in Bahram's room." Hesam handed Majid the magazines. "I'm surprised you didn't get rid of these already."

"I don't go through his personal stuff."

"What else can be used against him? Who are the witnesses I should know of?"

Majid stood in silence.

Hesam imagined that this meant Majid was Bahram's only link to SOALS. *Should I arrest this guy also?* He quickly decided against it. He already had one problem to deal with. "What about his personal life?"

The question hung in the air for a moment. Majid looked wary but finally responded. "What do you mean?"

"What evidence is there that can be used against him?"

"I don't know what you're talking about."

"I know he has certain…inclinations. Would his…" Hesam searched for the right words in his head. "Would his sex partner testify against him?"

Majid leaped toward Hesam and shoved him against the wall, angrily pressing his elbow into Hesam's ribcage. Majid looked to the gate and then to the house door to ensure no one was looking. "What on earth is wrong with you?" he hissed. "Shut your mouth."

Hesam was surprised by the forceful gesture. "I'm only being cautious," he justified his question. "If there is someone who knows, I have to make sure they don't talk."

"I don't know where the hell you're from, but no one Bahram knows would say a word. One guy mentioned it once and Bahram almost beat him unconscious."

"You don't have to choke me. I'm not the enemy here."

Majid lifted his elbow and took a step back. "You don't look like a friend either."

"I am clearly on your side. Didn't I just give you the evidence to destroy?" He adjusted his uniform.

Majid still looked skeptical. "No one will speak."

"You're scared of him. That's why you didn't get the magazines out of his room."

"I'm not. But everybody else is."

"What happened? You just said Bahram beat someone."

"Yeah, he beat him up. And humiliated him in front of everyone. No one else will say anything. You can trust that."

"What about his—"

Majid raised a finger in warning. "Bahram's…friend no longer lives in the country and the others…they have their own reputation to worry about."

Personally, Hesam wanted to ask how many other lovers Bahram had—but he had to think of a delicate way of asking.

"Are there any possible third-party witnesses? Who didn't participate but might have found out."

"Are you listening to yourself? You think they'd gather an audience for that sort of thing?"

"Well, how do *you* know all this?" Hesam barked.

"I'm his best friend. I'm the one who covered for him every time he missed Talib. His…friend."

"What happened to Talib?"

Majid took a breath and glared at Hesam. "I'm getting tired of your questions."

"I gave you the evidence to destroy. I told you I'm also a socialist. What else do you want me to do?" he pleaded.

Majid reached into his pants pocket to extract a pack of cigarettes. "So…what is this mission that you infiltrated the Revolutionary Guards for?"

"Ah, I can't tell you, man."

"Well, whatever it is, you better accomplish it fast and get out before you get purged." Majid exhaled the smoke insolently into Hesam's face. "And you like him?"

Hesam didn't reply, but tightened his jaw.

"I thought so." Majid smiled briefly. "I like him too. But just as a friend." He continued, his voice rising. "I went through a lot of trouble to make sure he's safe. He's a bit too impulsive. Stupidly courageous sometimes."

"I'll make sure he's safe," Hesam insisted, his heart swelling with the words. "He just has to sign a repentance letter."

Majid rolled his eyes and exhaled another cloud of smoke. "He's never gonna do that."

"He has to."

"I thought you said you're one of us. Why force him into doing that rubbish?"

"I can't blow my cover."

"Is your cover worth his freedom? Anything he signs can be used against him."

"Well, I want him to understand the extent of the danger. He needs to adjust his actions or he'll be back in prison before you know it." *I also need him to love me back before I let him go.* "Next time, I may not be able to save him."

"Majid *jan*. You see who brought me home?" Bibi walked out of the house.

"*Salam*, Bibi *Khanum*. So you went to Ahwaz after all."

"I did. And see who drove me back. He already promised to let Bahram go free."

"Yes, he told me."

"Majid *jan*, what is that in your hand? No more political magazines in this house. I can't have it. I'm getting old."

"Yes, Bibi *Khanum*. Comrade Hesam came to destroy any evidence against Bahram."

Hesam's gaze darted back to Majid. Hesam mouthed "shut up." Although it was nice to be called a comrade, even if by a socialist who disagreed with him. Hesam remembered how his lover Umberto would call him Comrade Hesam when he talked about his political activities in Rome, especially the demonstration outside the Iranian Embassy. He both winced and smiled at the memory.

"For real? Why didn't you tell me?" Bibi walked toward Hesam, arms outstretched. "May you live a long life for bringing me such good news. God bless you, dear. Oh, how I prayed for my Bahram to be safe! God sent you to me. You're like my son too." Bibi took Hesam's face in her hands and kissed him on the cheek. "Why didn't you tell me earlier? I worried so much my heart was about to stop. I'm not like you young men, no. I can't live in danger and worry all the time. But it's all good now."

Majid smiled and continued to smoke.

"Oh God, look at the youth these days. They smoke like chimneys. God, give me patience. Go ahead, smoke. Today, I already won one battle. My Bahram's coming home.

Tomorrow, I'll have another battle, until you stop smoking. I should be looking for wives for all three of you. Sisters maybe. Oh, I can't wait for Bahram to come home."

"Bibi *Khanum*, let us enjoy a little smoke. No need to pick wives quite yet."

"It's not too early, no. It's never too early. You're not getting younger, Majid *jan*. I wanna see my grandkids. A wife and kids will give you some structure. You won't be standing in my yard, smoking, and reading all this nonsense. Take them out of my house, Majid *jan*. No more political stuff in this house. I put my foot down."

"Yes, Bibi *Khanum*. I'm going. I'm taking these with me." Majid walked to the gate. He stopped and looked back at Hesam. "You coming?"

Hesam looked at Bibi.

"Go. Go with him. I have something to finish. I expect both of you for dinner."

"No, I don't want to trouble you," Majid protested.

"I expect both of you back for dinner. I wanna hear no other words."

"Yes, Bibi *Khanum*," Majid replied.

"Yes, Bibi *Khanum*," Hesam echoed. He walked back toward the door to put on his boots.

"Go. May God protect you." Bibi said goodbye.

Hesam got out of the front yard and Majid closed the gate behind him.

"Where are we going?"

"Is this your first time in Abadan?"

Hesam nodded.

"Let's go to the river. If we're lucky, we should get there before sunset."

Hesam would have preferred to enjoy this romantic evening promenade with Bahram. But he felt betrayed. Bahram had lied to him. He agonized that Bahram only faked affection to get out of prison. He needed some time to think. This was all so damned complicated.

"Have you read the latest SOALS magazine?" Majid asked.

Hesam shook his head.

"How can you help the organization if you're not in the loop of what your Revolutionary Guard 'Brothers' are doing?"

"What did they do?" Hesam feigned interest.

"What they did in the city hall in Ahwaz. You should track down your comrades and help them get out."

Hesam was careful not to make any promises. Bibi had already misinterpreted his words.

"Wait here, I'll go get it. You must read the latest issue." Majid walked away and went into one of the houses down the street. A few moments later, he emerged with another magazine. He wrapped it in the *keffiyeh* and gave it to Hesam.

"Thanks. I'll read it later when I can better concentrate." Hesam threw it in the Jeep, unhappy that he still had a magazine in his possession even after getting rid of a pile of them a few minutes earlier.

"Not like that. You act like a rookie." Majid opened the door and placed the bundle under the passenger seat, hidden from view. Then, he sat down.

Hesam and Majid drove to the river shore, passing through Bowardeh. On the river banks, people enjoyed watching the sun set on the Iraqi side. Hesam imagined walking hand in hand along the river bank with Bahram. Despite the deceptions and lies, he still loved him.

They could be fishermen. He would live here with Bahram, away from the inconveniences of politics and the revolution.

He and Majid looked out on the river and saw a raft made of tree logs. One man was tying it to a pole on the shore.

"Before the revolution," Majid grumbled, "fishermen

could easily go back and forth between Iran and Iraq. Not now. Any movement is scrutinized by the Revolutionary Guards."

Hesam noticed two armed guards walking along the shore, patrolling the area.

"Your Brothers," Majid mocked. Then, he saw a street vendor. "You must try the real *sambusa*. Bahram's favorite." He urged Hesam to follow as he quickened his pace.

Majid taught him to dip the *sambusa* into red hot sauce that was a lot spicier than he expected. Majid got him a bottle of Coca Cola to soothe his burning tongue.

"Stop," someone yelled.

Hesam turned around. The two Revolutionary Guards were pointing their guns at another raft approaching the shore.

"Stop," the Guard yelled again and pulled the trigger. The bullet was merely a warning. The raft veered back to the Iraqi side.

"Told you," Majid said. "It's no longer safe attempting to cross the border. Maybe we should go now."

Hesam agreed.

Road from Abadan to Ahwaz

Hesam woke up early in the morning and changed into his uniform. As he buttoned up his shirt, the reality started to sink in again. This trip to Abadan felt like a dream. He had met with Bahram's best friend, eaten his favorite food, and slept in his bed. Now, he was back to reality. A reality of prison and prisoners. He obsessed over what he now knew: He was in love with someone who had told him nothing but lies. And he was under the command of a boss who demanded he mistreat the young man he loved.

What to do with Bahram? He didn't know if he could trust him anymore. But if not, then why was he still in love? He was a fool to risk his career and his new life for Bahram. Could he truly love someone who supported SOALS? If they had met in Kurdistan, they would shoot at each other. In Abadan, away from the politics, they could be lovers. But they were in Ahwaz, and here they were prisoner and prison guard.

As he drove back to Ahwaz, Hesam could only think of the irony of his life: a socialist employee of the Revolutionary Guards Corps, in charge of a detained radical socialist teenager, the son of a poor illiterate woman, from the class that the revolutionaries aspired to support. All these groups had come together to remove the monarchy for the betterment of regular Iranians. Now, they were in conflict with each other and the only thing they still had in common was that they all harmed regular people, the group they all wanted to support most.

He drove closer to Ahwaz and saw the torches. Further on, he noticed a herd of goats being led by several men. He slowed down to avoid hitting the goats that were now crossing. One of the men suddenly waved his arms to flag down Hesam.

He pulled over. "Good morning. What's going on?"

Several men began talking at once. Hesam made out the word "murder."

"Say what?"

"A man's been murdered." One young man spoke up.

Hesam followed the young man, who shooed a goat out of his way. Hesam saw a man on his back. Blood stained his T-shirt and pajamas and pooled beneath him on the ground. He had a slipper on one foot and the other slipper was on the ground.

"We should call an ambulance," announced someone from the back.

"What ambulance? Call the coroner," another responded.

"Who found him?" Hesam inquired.

"I did."

Hesam turned around and saw a boy around fifteen, wearing a white *kufi* and *dishdasha*.

"I was herding the goats. Maybe one hour ago."

"Has anyone called…the coroner?"

"Some guy went to call. But maybe you can inform the Revolutionary Guards on your wireless."

Hesam wasn't sure if he should be collecting witness testimonies or if this was for the city police to do. "Does he have identity papers?" Hesam asked as he squatted by the body.

"Where? In his pajamas?" the boy sneered.

"Be quiet." The young man hit the boy on the side of his head. The boy adjusted his *kufi*.

Hesam glanced at the body, which had visible stab wounds. The smell of fresh blood under the sun reminded him of a butcher shop. A vile butcher shop. Hesam looked more closely at the face.

Suddenly, Hesam felt his stomach coming out of his mouth, tasting like a thousand cups of vinegar. He paced away from the body. The others noticed his nausea pool on the ground.

"What a delicate Guard," someone mocked.

The boy handed him a cloth handkerchief. Hesam wiped his mouth and got on his feet. "Does anyone know this man?"

No one spoke up.

"His name is Vargha. Vargha Mobasheri. He was released from prison not too long ago. Does anybody know him?"

"We don't know him." The young man spoke as others shook their heads.

"He's obviously a criminal. With a prison record and now getting himself killed like this," announced another man.

"He's a Bahá'í," Hesam shot back to stop the slander.

"What's that?" the boy inquired.

"It's his religion."

"What did he say?" another man wondered.

"He's a Wahhabi," the boy answered.

"No—" Hesam attempted to clarify as another man interrupted him.

"In our village, we're all Shia. We don't have any Wahhabis."

"He has to be from Ahwaz or something," the young man protested.

Hesam tuned out the confused chatter. *How did Vargha get himself killed? Who would kidnap him while he was sleeping in pajamas? Why bring him here?*

"Here they come," the boy called out as an ambulance pulled up and parked next to Hesam's Jeep. Two paramedics jumped out.

"Unfortunately, he's already gone," Hesam explained to them.

One of the paramedics went back to the ambulance and returned with a white cloth and stretcher. They moved quickly. Hesam felt sick. He said he had to go back to Ahwaz.

Hesam couldn't wait to get in his car and speed away. What had he done to his life? He had fought to release a detainee—and now he lay dead by the road.

This was just part of the overall pattern, Hesam thought. He let people down. They got hurt. He abandoned Umberto and broke his heart.

Hesam drove back to Karoun Prison in a daze. He went straight to the office and found Naser. Uncharacteristically, he wasn't wearing his uniform. Hesam spoke in broken sentences about Vargha's death, but was met by no emotion from his boss. He insisted they start an investigation. Naser was unconvinced.

"I told you, you shouldn't free him," Naser said coldly. "He should have been here in prison. It would have been better for him."

"What should I do now?"

"Forget it. You freed a Bahá'í. A cancerous cell. And you let him back into our society. Our Muslim Brothers couldn't live with an infidel among them. So they carried out justice because you, their Revolutionary Guard, failed to do that."

"I don't understand."

"It is better this way. The shorter his life, the less time he has to commit sins."

"What about the murderers?"

"Brother Hesam, I've told you before: you need to purificate your own soul. There's no murder here. The man was an infidel. So shedding his blood is permissible."

"Permissible?"

"I really don't have the time to explain everything to you. Next time you go to the mosque, ask the cleric. Now, get back to work. I want to see a pile of repentance letters signed by detainees. I already gave you the order before. I'm losing my patience with you."

Hesam wanted to punch him in the mouth. But he had to stay on Naser's good side—at least as long as Bahram was still in prison.

Hesam left the office. But he couldn't face Bahram right now, or any other detainee for that matter. He climbed into his Jeep and closed his eyes. He felt sweat roll down his chest. Hesam wished his whole body would melt away so he wouldn't have to continue his prison work.

Then it dawned on him. Hesam needed to investigate the murder on his own. Vargha's address was on file. But wait. If he showed up so soon, would he be the first officer to inform the family of his death? And him being a Revolutionary Guard, would family and neighbors think he was involved?

Hesam pressed two fingers between his eyebrows. Being too impulsive could implicate him in the murder, or attract the attention of the real murderers. He had to keep a low profile for the time being.

JUNE 3, 1980
Ahwaz

Esmat rubbed her eyes and looked at the clock on the nightstand. It was 8:44. She jumped out of the bed and looked around to see if Naser was still home. His uniform was still on the chair. But he should have left more than an hour ago. She ran her hand through her hair and called Naser's name, just to be sure. No answer.

She sat at the dresser to brush her hair. Just then, she noticed a blue paper peeking from her husband's camouflage uniform pocket. On it was scribbled an address in Amanieh and a time: four o'clock. She looked at the clock again. She pondered what to do with this information.

JUNE 5, 1980

Karoun Prison, Ahwaz

Bahram looked around his cell. Waleed was sitting on the floor and, thank God, he was quiet for the time being. When he threw his frequent tantrums, he'd punch and kick the air and scream like an animal. It was best for the other prisoners to stay away until the episode passed. If these were seizures, then Waleed needed medical attention. If he were mental, Bahram wondered if he was always like this or if he became crazy inside the prison. There was nothing Bahram could do. But at least he could call him by name, rather than the Beast, thanks to Vargha.

Bahram wished he had talked more with Majid and his political comrades. They could have given him some pointers on how to navigate prison life. Was it the right choice to deny everything? Or should he just sign this repentance letter Hesam wanted? And what was Hesam's deal? One day he would offer love, the next day he would tear up his interrogation forms. Was he really Bahram's ally—or did he just want to use him as a convenient sex partner?

Although he liked Hesam, if he slept with him he'd lose all leverage. It didn't help that he found Hesam sexy.

Bahram needed to think of something else. He looked at another detainee. An old Arab guy. Why had he ended up in prison in the ward for political detainees? It was generally the younger generation that got involved in political activities. That was fashionable. Most youth supported one organization or another.

Bahram knew he had few supporters among the various political groups. Even the most liberal organizations would condemn his sexuality. The organization Bahram disliked the least was SOALS. They opposed the government categorically, supported the Kurds and the Arabs. Majid supported SOALS, so Bahram wanted to side with him.

The old Arab guy started coughing, then wiped his mouth with his sleeve. His *keffiyeh* was a bit crooked and Bahram felt tempted to fix it.

Talib's *keffiyeh* was always immaculate. Bahram had made it a habit of wearing Talib's *keffiyeh* since it made him feel closer to Talib. One summer day in 1978, he also wore the *dishdasha* but didn't button it. Talib stood behind him. He slid his hand under the *dishdasha* and pressed Bahram's chest into his.

"You make everything so sexy," Talib murmured as he kissed Bahram on the cheek. "What am I gonna do with you?"

Bahram smiled and tenderly rubbed Talib's forearm. He thought Talib wanted to move to the bed.

"I have something to tell you."

"I see." Bahram kissed Talib's arm.

"It's serious," Talib protested as he pulled his arm away. "You would be in serious danger if you were really in love with me."

Bahram wondered what he meant by *if*. Talib's smile was gone. His voice now had a harsh tone. He hated that his lover was questioning Bahram's affections. The tenderness of his touch had disappeared.

"Bahram?"

Bahram was afraid of what was coming. He felt as if his body was shrinking in Talib's arms. As if Bahram was growing smaller, turning less significant, as Talib withdrew his love. He closed his eyes and persisted in touching Talib's arm, even as he felt the man's muscles tense up. Bahram pretended he did not notice.

"Foad," said Talib sharply.

Bahram was taken aback.

Talib knew his real name but had never used it before, honoring his wish. Talib put his hands on Bahram's shoulder and forced him to turn around and look at him. "Are you in love with me?"

Bahram wanted to say, "Yes, since the first moment we met." But he couldn't.

Talib's gaze penetrated Bahram's eyes, but the younger guy did not say a word. The long pause lingered. Finally, Talib's Adam's apple moved as he whispered, "I love you too, Foad."

Bahram got goosebumps all over his body. But he wasn't fully comforted by the confession, since the words lacked any trace of warmth. This was not a joyous declaration of love. Bad news was to follow. The silence made his heartbeat sound so loud. He felt emotionally naked.

"I just don't know what to do with you. You've been...so loving, so loyal. Too loyal! At my feet any time I want you."

At my feet? Had Bahram been too available? Too willing? So much so that Talib now took him for granted? *At my feet?* He suddenly felt disposable, as if he was a sock with a hole on the big toe. Once a sock is worn out, you throw it away. Was he nothing more than an accessory?

"I don't know how else to say it, other than to just say it."

"Say it, already. I'm a man. I can take it."

"Foad, I'm taking a woman."

Bahram felt an avalanche crash into his body.

"Nothing has to change between us. I'll still see you."

Bahram was now trembling. But he was outraged enough that he wanted to mock the pronouncement. *You'll still see me? You mean I won't be invisible to you? What a great pleasure!* Bahram couldn't say any of this. All of his energy was concentrated on holding back a scream from deep down in his soul.

"I'll still see you but maybe not as often," Talib corrected himself.

"So…what do you want me to say?"

"I'm not doing this to hurt you. We're growing up. We can't keep doing this…full time."

Bahram searched for something to say. Something that didn't put his heart on display. He couldn't think of anything. "When is the wedding?" he asked, even though he didn't want to know the answer.

"In a few months."

My man is marrying a woman. Bahram felt a tenderness in his nose as his eyes began to get watery. But he didn't want Talib to see him cry.

"Soon enough you will get married too. Our wives will be friends. They can gossip about who's bigger down there."

I don't want you to get married. You are mine. I want you all to myself. Bahram was screaming these words silently. He tried to force a smile at Talib's attempt at humor. "Why all of a sudden?"

"What do you mean all of a sudden?" Talib frowned at the accusation. "I'm a man. I'm healthy. I'm hot…you knew that already though."

Bahram ignored the second attempt at humor.

"I'm the oldest son. They've been looking for a proper girl for me since…forever."

Bahram couldn't hold back anymore. His eyes welled up and, as soon as he blinked, a teardrop rolled down his face. "Congratulations, Talib."

Talib wiped away the tear with his thumb. "Don't cry. Nobody's dead."

"Our love is," Bahram said with more force than he expected.

"Our love isn't dead," Talib tried to console him. "It's just taking a new shape." Talib leaned closer and kissed Bahram on the lips. The longest and the most fragile kiss they'd ever shared. But it made everything even worse because Bahram would lose him soon.

"I don't want it to take a new shape. I don't want it to change at all."

"I know." Talib dried Bahram's face with the back of his fingers, then hugged him. "But we both knew this wasn't going to last forever."

We did? Bahram wondered.

"It was just a break from reality. But we can't hide forever." He looked into Bahram's eyes and smiled. "Some things don't change, though." Talib winked as he ran his hand down Bahram's spine and grabbed his butt. "No matter how old we are, you're still available for your Talib, right?"

Bahram felt offended, like a piece of meat. He hadn't felt so hurt since being banished. But Talib held onto him. Bahram relented and hugged him back, placing his head on his chest.

"It's gonna be alright." Talib kissed his head. "My lovely Foad."

Bahram took off the *keffiyeh* and handed it to Talib.

"No. You keep it." Talib returned it. "And don't you dare forget me. I'll be back on top of you as soon as I get my wife knocked up."

"You wish." Bahram pushed him away.

"Yeah. My wishes come true when you're with me."

All this charm and flirtation was only temporary. Within weeks, it would evaporate. The sincerest love he'd ever felt would soon turn into dust. Everything was lost.

Bahram felt a wave of immeasurable sadness descend on him, as he sat on his prison bed. He had to stop thinking of Talib before he broke down in tears in front of all these detainees.

Bahram never did return Talib's *keffiyeh*. Not even when he left. It was still in his bedroom.

His eyes had already gotten watery. If Hesam were there, he would've kissed his eyes. Bahram wished he were there, not entirely sure if he really missed Hesam, or just wanted a distraction from a painful memory with Talib. Like the guys he had sex with after Talib, with no emotional attachment. Was Hesam's persistence starting to break loose the lock on his heart?

JUNE 6, 1980
Amanieh, Ahwaz

Esmat paid the cab driver and got out of the car. She knew the address. She had already gone there three days before. She was there at four o'clock, hoping to discover whatever Naser was doing there. But no one had shown up.

So today, she'd come back. Naser had gone to the Friday prayer. She'd feigned a headache so she could investigate the apartment and learn what her husband was up to. Maybe she'd have better luck on the weekend. If she were lucky, really lucky, she hoped to discover something she could use as leverage against Naser so he would free Waleed.

She turned right on Boo-Ali Street and walked toward the four-story building. She could hear kids behind her, arguing.

"You had your own cotton candy. Leave mine alone."

She pushed the front door to the building. Unlike Tuesday, it was locked. She studied the resident directory callbox. Apartment C belonged to a Mobasheri household. She rang the bell.

No answer.

The kids' noise got closer. She rang the bell again and listened carefully for a voice.

"That's not fair. Mine fell on the ground."

"If you were less clumsy—"

"Both of you be quiet." Their mother scolded them. She separated the quarreling boys and addressed Esmat. "Are you looking for someone?"

"I'm looking for a friend of mine. We've been out of touch for years," Esmat lied.

"What's her name, dear?"

"Soheila. Soheila Qaisar."

"No one here is named Qaisar."

"I can see." Esmat pointed to the callbox. "She was supposed to be in Apartment C, but I don't see her name here. I was wondering if someone recently moved or something…"

"Give it to me," one of the boys suddenly screamed.

"'Be quiet,' I said." The woman snatched the cotton candy out of his hands. "Neither of you will get it."

"Mom," one of the boys nagged.

"Shhh!" She reached into her purse and got her key. "Go inside. Not a word," she ordered as she opened the door.

The boys pouted as they entered the building. One of them hit the other lightly on the head and ran away. The other chased after him. When they disappeared, the mother looked at Esmat. "I'm sorry. There's no Soheila Qaisar in this building. Someone gave you the wrong address."

"Apartment C. She's supposed to be in Apartment C." Esmat pretended to be confused.

"I wouldn't ring their bell if I were you."

"Why not? They may know where I can look for Soheila."

"They're grieving. The husband…this is terrible…he was murdered," she said in a lowered voice.

"What did you say?" Esmat lost hold of her *chador*. It made small waves as it fell, like a sailcloth with a broken mast. As she stooped to pick it up, she dropped her purse. Her cheeks reddened.

The woman crouched down to help Esmat pick up her purse. "His name was Vargha Mobasheri. He was murdered early in the morning, a few days ago."

Suddenly, Esmat understood Naser's note. It referred to four in the morning, not afternoon. On Tuesday, when she'd come here for the first time, she had been twelve hours late. She tried her best to stop the rest of the thoughts from forming, before she panicked or sickened.

"I didn't wake up that day." The woman explained. "With these boys, I'm so exhausted that nothing can wake me up unless it's a screaming boy next to my bed! Which happens more than you'd think."

"May God watch over your boys," Esmat said as the truth returned to her head. Naser's note was the address of a murder scene. With the exact date and time. She gripped her *chador* and pulled it over her face as she stood up. She hoped it would help mask her shock.

"I'm sorry, I shouldn't have told you."

"May he rest in peace."

"Well, at least your friend is not here."

"Yes."

"OK, well, I must go. I can't leave the boys alone."

"Of course not. Thank you."

"Do you want some water?"

Esmat's mouth was dry but she had to get out of there before she broke down. "No, thank you. May God have mercy on us all."

"Goodbye."

Esmat realized she was biting the inside of her mouth. She pulled her *chador* and bit on it instead. She rushed away toward the street corner. She needed to catch a cab.

JUNE 8, 1980
Sanandaj

Atefeh made a small opening between the two panels of lace curtains to see the street. She smelled the dust on the curtains. They used to be white, part of her dowry. She always wanted white lace curtains, with embroidered flowers on the edges. But they didn't make her happy. She didn't even care about them anymore. All she hoped for was that her husband, Daniar, would come back home. Alive and unharmed.

They had been happy for some time, Daniar and Atefeh. Banoo the matriarch was good to her. Daniar filled the absence left by Banoo's son, Foad. But after the revolution, that tribal hierarchy meant that Daniar had to lead their group against the Revolutionary Guards when the civil war broke out. They wanted autonomy. They wanted their children to learn Kurdish at schools. And they wanted to administer their land. They didn't want Persian rulers from Tehran.

If Atefeh hadn't caused Foad to be banished, Daniar wouldn't have to lead the group in armed conflict. Maybe he would be home with her now. Maybe they would have gone to Tehran when the war began.

Atefeh pushed her face into the curtain to distract herself from painful thoughts. But she inhaled a mote of dust and felt a sneeze come on. She used her sleeve to muffle the sound. She had heard gunshots earlier in the morning, so she had to be careful not to attract attention. She always had to be careful. At any moment, the Revolutionary Guards could pass by her house.

Someone knocked. "Atefeh! Open the door. It's me."

She opened the door and let out a shriek.

"Be quiet." Daniar hobbled into the house, his left leg wet with blood. "Do you want them to find us?" He put his arm around her shoulder. "Help me get to the couch."

Atefeh pressed her lips together and felt her husband's weight on her shoulder. He sat down and she bent to unlace his boots.

"It's not too bad. The bullet didn't hit me, just grazed my calf."

Atefeh pulled off the boots and rolled up the left leg of Daniar's pants. A piece of his flesh was missing and blood had clotted around the area. She pulled off the sock and started to sob.

"Don't cry. I'm alive. Go, get Mercurochrome."

Atefeh hurried to the bedroom closet. She returned with a roll of gauze bandage and a bottle. She sat next to Daniar.

"It's gonna really burn," she apologized.

"Better than getting infected."

She brought the open bottle to the wound.

"Hold on." Daniar grabbed a cushion, then nodded.

She poured the red liquid on his wound. Behind the cushion, he screamed with pain. Atefeh put the bottle on the floor and wiped her tears with her wrist. She begged in her head, *Please Foad, lift this curse. I suffered enough. I beg you.*

She continued to cry quietly as she rolled the gauze bandage around her husband's calf.

Karoun Prison, Ahwaz

Bahram pressed the pillow over his ear. It didn't help. Waleed had already had three episodes that night. Earlier, Bahram had tried to calm him down, but to no avail. Waleed had punched him in the mouth. Bahram was afraid of needing any dental care in prison so he had left him alone. He touched the inside of his mouth with his tongue. It was sore.

Now, Waleed was screaming again. Bahram saw him squatted on the floor, punching the air. He tried to kick and fell on the ground.

"Make him stop already," yelled another detainee.

Mansoor arrived and spoke sharply to Waleed. "Shut up."

"We could have told him to shut up, ourselves," the detainee said. "The Beast is crazy. You need to take him to an asylum."

"Don't tell me what to do," Mansoor barked back.

Waleed screamed again.

"Didn't you hear what I said? Stop it," Mansoor ordered.

"What a smart guard! No one ever thought of that solution before."

"Hey," Mansoor shouted. "One more word from you and I'll send you to solitary for a week. No food or water."

Waleed moaned in response to the yelling.

Mansoor unlocked the door and stepped in. "Shut up." Mansoor bent over and slapped Waleed. He screamed. "Why do you howl like that?" Mansoor asked as he slapped him again, then kicked him lightly in the chest.

Waleed's eyes opened and shifted between Mansoor and some unknown object that Bahram couldn't see. Waleed was quiet for a bit.

"Good boy!"

Waleed put both palms on the ground and crawled backward. He hit the wall and howled.

Naser, the angry guard, showed up at the cell. "Brother Mansoor, what's going on?"

"I'm trying to shut him up." Mansoor suddenly waved his pistol at Waleed. "Cut it out, now."

"Mansoor, stop this," Naser yelled.

"I'm tired of this Beast."

"Mansoor, out of the cell."

Waleed screeched at the arguing of the two guards. Naser squatted next to him, causing Waleed to attempt to punch and kick the guard. Neither made contact.

"Be quiet!" Naser tried to hold him still, but Waleed pushed him on the side.

Then, Bahram heard a bang. He saw smoke coming out of the pistol in Mansoor's hand. Waleed was silent, shocked by the sound. The shot echoed in the small space.

"The next time," Mansoor boomed, "I'll shoot you."

"Get back to your desk, Mansoor. That's an order," Naser threatened.

Waleed uttered some indistinct moaning. Naser put his

hand over the prisoner's mouth, but Waleed kicked Naser in the chest. He went flying backward.

Bahram heard another shot. Waleed hit the wall. Blood started to soak his shirt.

Bahram felt as if he was out of his body. His ears still ringing from the bang. And then he felt as if a thousand scorpions stung him on every hair follicle. His entire body began to shake. Waleed was now eternally peaceful.

"What the hell?" Naser lunged at Mansoor.

"What is going on?" Saeed materialized out of nowhere, followed by another guard.

"Isn't it me who missed the target?" Mansoor barked at Naser. "Weren't you all blaming me for this? Well, you can calm down. I fixed it myself!"

Naser pushed Mansoor against the bars and placed his forearm heavily on his neck.

"Brother Naser," Saeed called out.

Naser paused, then lifted his arm. "Take him out of here," he ordered.

Saeed approached Mansoor and pulled on his arm.

"Watch out, you all," Mansoor glared at the detainees as Saeed pulled him away. "If you talk back to me...you'll be next."

Saeed pulled Mansoor out of the cell.

"Don't touch me. I can walk," Mansoor objected.

As Naser turned around, Bahram could see that blood had splattered all over his uniform.

"Are you alright?" one of the detainees asked him.

Naser was breathing heavy. He nodded slightly at the detainee. "Have someone collect the body," Naser instructed the other guard. As he left the cell, Naser noticed Bahram staring at him.

"What are you looking at?" he snarled. "Sit your ass down."

Bahram obeyed. The smell of blood nauseated him and he could already feel his stomach acid rising in his throat.

Hesam saw Mansoor approach, trudging angrily, and followed him into the office. "I heard shots."

"I killed the freaking Beast. You're welcome."

"What?"

"I'm tired. Tired of you all blaming me," Mansoor spat out his words. "He was a goner anyway, from the day I missed him. He lost it. He wasn't going to get better. I just took care of it. I was the only one with the balls to do it."

Naser entered the office and slammed the door. "Mansoor! I swear to God, I wanna shoot you right now."

"I'm not scared of you."

"Mansoor," Hesam cautioned.

"You think you can kill any detainee you want?"

"So only the Tehranis can? They killed a young woman last month. Did you reprimand them?"

"Shut up," Naser yelled so loudly that the walls shook. "Go home and don't come back until you're rested. You know what? Take off the rest of the week."

"With pleasure!" Mansoor began to walk away.

"And leave your pistol here."

Mansoor gave Naser the meanest look, then took the pistol off of his belt and put it on the desk. He walked out of the office.

"Naser, you have blood on your uniform," Hesam observed.

Naser took off his shirt, checking his white undershirt to see the blood had seeped through. It was stained too.

"The Brothers are overwhelmed," Naser said to Hesam, sighing. "We don't have the capacity to hold so many detainees. We need to let them go. How many times do I need to remind you of those damn repentance letters? That will release half of them. But you just drag your feet."

"I'm working on it," Hesam said, offering the same excuse.

"Well, get it done already." Naser was red as a beet, as red as his T-shirt's bloodstains. "I told you, you need to convince some of them. What have you done? I saw your detainee, Bahram. Not a bruise on his face. How are you trying to convince him? By kissing his cheeks?"

Hesam suppressed the desire to ask Naser what he meant. He felt his pulse elevate quickly.

"Either find some evidence against your detainees so we can submit them to the court, or get them to sign the damn letters and get them out."

Hesam felt his belly tighten. He had already discovered evidence against Bahram. His ties to SOALS could earn him a hefty imprisonment sentence.

"And the next time I see Bahram, he better have bruises on his face."

As Hesam stood there, Naser snapped, "Don't stand there staring at me like a statue. Go and help Saeed collect the body."

JUNE 11, 1980
Ahwaz

Esmat put the colander on the table. Since she had come from Mobasheri's apartment, she couldn't concentrate. She needed distraction, so today's plan was to cook some *ghormeh sabzi*. Earlier she'd gone to the market and bought chives, spinach, cilantro, fenugreek, and parsley. Then she separated the leaves from the stems and washed them. She now had to chop them up and sauté them. Then, she would get started with the meat. Esmat hoped that cooking would take most of her day and keep her focused.

Esmat had no one to confide in, no one with whom to discuss the murder of Mobasheri and the note in Naser's pocket.

She lined up a bunch of herbs on the cutting board. As she prepared to chop, Esmat noticed that the water from the drainer had flowed onto the table and was now dripping on the floor. She had forgotten to put a plate under the drainer.

She snorted and left the kitchen to get the kitchen towels from the washing machine. She emptied the washing machine and put the clean items into the basket. Now that the washing machine was empty, she spontaneously decided to do another load. She reached into the dirty laundry basket and put the clothes into the washing machine. Shirts, undershirts, uniforms.

Just then, her hand touched something foreign on the surface of the fabric. She pulled it out from the rest of the laundry to see what it was.

Naser's uniform was stained with blood. Esmat felt like screaming but her throat wouldn't produce any noise. She touched her throat to see if something was suffocating her, constricting her breath.

The shock loosened the leash she had carefully attached to her thoughts. She couldn't control her mind anymore. Had she done the laundry after she found the blue note? That was last Tuesday. She did laundry every Thursday.

She dropped the uniform on the floor. She went to the bedroom. She looked at her bed. Her marital bed. Then it dawned on her. Her hands moved to touch her belly.

She tried to take small breaths. But her lungs felt as if they were made of cement. They would not move. They would not allow any air in. Esmat ran into the yard. The hot humid air slapped her. She glanced at the sun so maybe her eyes would forget the blood stains on Naser's shirt. She could only think of one thing now: If she were already pregnant, then…

She felt something dripping down her face. Was it tears or sweat?

Her little innocent baby would have a murderer for a father.

Esmat fell on the ground and covered her face with her hands.

Karoun Prison, Ahwaz

Hesam took Bahram's file and held it in front of his pants pocket so no one would notice how it bulged with secret contents.

He wasn't sure if he could pull off this scheme. But this was his best chance of keeping Bahram safe. He didn't want to make Naser any more suspicious than he already was, assuming that his guard was going too easy on the prisoner. Why did Naser insist that he should beat up Bahram? They held many detainees. Why all this emphasis on Bahram?

Hesam hoped he could remember Umberto's techniques enough to carry out his plans.

Saeed had brought Bahram into the interrogation room.

Hesam opened the door and entered. "Bahram! It's me." Hesam removed Bahram's blindfold. Before he untied Bahram's bonds, Bahram held Hesam's hand and squeezed.

"Hi," Bahram said. He had a hint of stubble on his face.

Hesam felt bare before Bahram's gaze. He felt his muscles tighten with desire.

"Mansoor killed Waleed. Right in front of my eyes," Bahram whimpered.

Hesam looked down. He heard Bahram exhale.

"I'm scared. And I missed you." Bahram held on to Hesam's hand. "Comrade Hesam."

"Me too. Should I say, 'Comrade Bahram?'"

Bahram's eyes widened. He could not hide his surprise.

Now they were even. Hesam and Bahram knew one another's secrets.

Hesam tried to pull his hand out of Bahram's grip. But Bahram held on hard.

"Although I'm not so sure you're a comrade, Bahram. You're on the enemy's side."

"You don't know what you're talking about. I'm not part of any political organization."

Hesam yanked his hand from Bahram's. He couldn't stand the lies anymore. "Really? Well, the SOALS magazines in your bedroom say otherwise." He sat on the desk in front of Bahram. "I went to your house."

"What?" Bahram blurted.

"Your Bibi came here to visit you."

"What?! When?"

"She came here to find you. She said you came to Ahwaz to visit your cousin."

"So you decided to not let her see me."

Hesam wanted to explain Naser's increased surveillance of Bahram. He ignored the comment instead. "I drove her back to Abadan. I saw your room. And your stash of SOALS magazines."

Bahram looked away and started shaking his leg.

"Oh, and your *keffiyeh*. No, your boyfriend's *keffiyeh*."

Bahram shook his head. "Whoever told you these things is lying."

"So you're calling Majid a liar?"

"What have you done to Majid?"

"I told him the truth. You should try that sometime."

"What did you tell him?"

"I can't even…you betrayed me."

"Then go ahead and shoot me like Mansoor murdered the Beast—I mean, Waleed." Bahram's voice cracked at the memory. "Can I have a cigarette? Please?"

Hesam thought about refusing him, but the guy was clearly shaken. He produced a pack of Winstons.

Bahram lit a cigarette and inhaled. "Is Majid alright?"

Hesam nodded.

"Don't hurt him. Please." Bahram closed his eyes as he allowed his lungs to fill with tobacco smoke. "You're upset with me. I get it. Just don't take it out on him."

Hesam watched the sudden transformation with intrigue. The beautiful and defiant seventeen-year-old was gone. The wall of strength and pride Bahram had built around himself had crumbled. The person sitting before him was a defeated child.

"So what happens now?" Bahram's voice still trembled.

"If I show the magazines to Naser, he'd want me to start preparing your file for…" Hesam hated the cruelty in his words. "Did you take part in armed resistance on the university campus?"

Bahram opened his mouth.

Hesam interrupted. "Tell me the truth, this time." Hesam tapped Bahram's hand with his boot, not quite ready to let go of his position of power.

Bahram shook his head. "I didn't."

"Then tell me what really happened."

"I didn't come to Ahwaz to see my cousin. I didn't even come to look for a job. I came to help protect the SOALS office in the university." Bahram paused. "Can I have another cigarette?"

Hesam noticed that only the filter remained of the cigarette in Bahram's fidgety hand. He offered the nervous prisoner another.

"By the time I got there, I couldn't get onto campus," Bahram continued. "Your Brothers had already barricaded the place. My friend had been taken into custody. I heard he was taken to the city hall. So I went there—and got arrested."

Hesam's eyes narrowed as he listened. Bahram noticed the gesture. "It's true. I swear."

"OK."

"Please just do one thing for me."

"You're not in the position of asking favors right now."

"Please, Hesam, please don't hurt Majid."

"Do you have a crush on him, too?"

"Majid is not like me, or you."

Hesam had finally broken Bahram. But he regretted it. He wanted the confident Bahram back. "I gave your magazines to Majid. Told him to get rid of them." For a second, Hesam remembered that Majid had given him another magazine that now lay under the passenger seat in his Jeep.

A spark appeared in Bahram's eyes, distracting Hesam from the memory. "What?"

"If Naser finds out you're a sympathizer of SOALS, detention is going to be the least of our problems." Hesam noticed he'd just called it "our" problems.

"You gave the magazines back to Majid?"

"I did."

Bahram inhaled from his cigarette. "Why?"

Because I love you. Hesam wanted to yell it. But he knew Bahram didn't reciprocate. "You're still in love with Talib."

"Talib broke my heart."

That makes two of us—isolated, brokenhearted, defeated.

Bahram kept dragging hard on the second cigarette. The end of the cigarette soon sizzled closer to Bahram's lips. After another puff, the flame was gone and only the filter remained. Bahram threw it on the floor. "How's Bibi?"

Hesam thought of Bibi's chatty, scheming ways. "Didn't you think she'd be worried, no?" He imitated Bibi's cadence as best he could.

Bahram broke into a smile.

"And she wants to find girls for us all to get married."

"Who's 'us?'" Bahram wiped his face.

"You, Majid, and me."

"Well, congratulations, Comrade Hesam! It took you just a few hours to be welcomed into the family. But brides? We're more likely to marry each other."

Hesam fought the temptation to respond to the comment, even though it thrilled him. But he didn't, fearing Bahram would revoke it. "'Three sisters,' she said. Can you think of a bigger disaster?"

"I can." Bahram turned cold again. His smile vanished. "Mansoor killed Waleed right in front of my eyes. He shot him like a dog, as if his life didn't matter." Tears flowed down Bahram's face.

Hesam jumped up and took Bahram in his arms. He rubbed his back to extract the pain from his body. "I wish I'd been there to stop him."

"I'm scared."

"I know."

"What should I do now?"

Hesam broke the embrace. He could ask him to sign the repentance letter. In this weakened position, he was confident, Bahram would sign it. But what if Hesam freed him and he was also killed like Vargha—found slaughtered on the side of the road? Hesam shuddered. He sat on the desk and put his foot on Bahram's chair's table arm. He had to think.

"Your bootlace is untied," Bahram remarked and then reached out, pulled on the lace, and knotted it. Maybe his way of saying thank you for not giving him up to Naser. For a cocky guy like Bahram, tying another man's shoelaces was a big deal. An act of love, Hesam wanted to think.

"Bahram, do you know why Naser is so interested in hurting you?"

"What?"

"Naser wants me to beat you. He mentioned you by name."

"The nice gentleman who used me as his punching bag before you took over the interrogations? He's evil. That's why."

"I have a plan. It's a bit unusual so don't freak out. I brought these…" Hesam stood up to reach deep into his pockets. He took out a couple of boxes of makeup.

"You want me to be his bride for the night?"

"Shut up, silly! I have to put makeup on you so you look beat up."

"What?"

"It'll buy me some time to figure out why Naser has developed this weird interest in you. Figure out how to get you out of here *safely*." Hesam paused to let his words sink in.

"How's that gonna work?" Bahram was puzzled. "Are you a makeup artist or something?"

No, but I've watched Umberto get ready for his drama class. "Making you look bad does require an artist!" Hesam smiled. He put the boxes on the chair's table arm.

He picked up an eyeshadow applicator and brushed it in the brown slot, then mixed it with red. "Close your eyes." He rubbed the applicator lightly over Bahram's eyelid.

"So after this, are you gonna let me go?"

"When the time's right."

"What do you mean? You let Vargha go. Why not me?"

"Vargha got killed."

"What?!" Bahram jerked his head at the news and Hesam's applicator smeared color on the side of Bahram's face.

"Damn! Be careful."

"When? When did this happen?"

"I found his body when I was coming back from Abadan."

"Poor Vargha. Damn, they'll come for me too," Bahram said, and fresh tears appeared in his eyes.

"Bahram, get it together. I'll figure it out. I'll protect you. I just need some time."

"You can't even protect yourself. You think you're so invincible. They can come after you too. In the Corps, you don't have Brothers. To them, you're just an infidel, socialist, fa—"

"Don't say it."

"Just like me. There's no way out."

"You're in shock. I understand. But trust me. I'll find a way. All is not lost. Just give me time." Hesam shook his head. "Just don't irritate the guards." Hesam removed the cover of the lipstick. "I'm gonna use this. The eyeshadow is not enough to make you look beat up."

"You think it's a game."

"Remember who you are. You're Bahram. You're strong. You're confident. This is not the time to give up. I will protect you. Trust me, this time." Hesam rubbed the side of Bahram's face. "I'll leave you the makeup kit. In a day or so, you need to use a lot of blue, so it looks real."

"I don't know how to wear makeup."

"You have to learn really quickly if you want to fool Naser. You can do this." Hesam stood up to leave the interrogation room.

"Hesam?"

He turned around.

"Thank you. You're a noble man."

Hesam shivered. These were the exact words Umberto had told him. Perhaps this meant that Bahram loved him, too. Just like Umberto.

Hesam was content that Umberto would never find out that he loved Bahram so much more.

JUNE 14, 1980
Karoun Prison, Ahwaz

Rafat had received no new information about Waleed from the prison authorities. All she knew was that there was a mass amnesty and some prisoners would be released. Who was going to be freed, or when, she didn't know, but she'd found out from other families that today was the first day of the scheduled releases. So she arrived at the prison gate at 6:30 in the morning so she wouldn't miss Waleed as he exited. He had to be set free. They probably finally figured out he wasn't involved in any crimes and decided to let him go.

She hadn't seen Waleed since his arrest in mid-April. At the time, the officials had charged him as an anti-revolutionary and he was sentenced to be executed. Upon learning the verdict, Rafat went to different mosques and clerics, begging them to intervene. One of the clerics coldly said to her: "Don't worry, my sister. If he's innocent and is executed, he will go to paradise. If he's guilty and executed, at least he had a shorter life to sin."

If it wasn't for the cleric's turban, Rafat would have slapped him on the face.

The sun was already up. This was the sun that was going to bring her back Waleed. She wouldn't have to worry about clerics. She had her cookies in her purse. With raisins and date molasses. She didn't wake her older son, Jamal, to join her. He had his own kids and wife to worry about. The gates were opened and four additional guards joined the other two. This had to be the moment of freedom.

She had stared at these gates before. She could sketch them from memory. The façade resembled an eye. Rafat hated this eye, ominously staring back at her every time she arrived. She thought of all the long hours she'd spent here, sweating and thirsty under the burning sun, hoping for news about Waleed.

This was not going to be one of those days, Rafat reminded herself. She would see Waleed walk out of those gates. Any moment now.

Naser entered the cell to take the detainees scheduled for release. He was proud of his men. They had reached a landmark. They'd had big challenges: from the banning of political activities in universities, to the confrontations on the university campus, to the unfortunate events of the city hall. But they had proven to be able to do their job, despite all the stress and overcrowding. And now, releasing detainees who'd been arrested as a precaution would prevent further unrest in the city. The riffraff had been separated from the reformable. The latter were to be freed soon. This was going to lessen the burden on the Brothers. They had been overworked, watching over so many detainees, much more than the capacity of Karoun Prison.

Naser felt he was making a positive impression on Hesam, who needed better training. Freeing Vargha was a bad decision. But at least Hesam was learning. He now carefully followed Naser's instructions. A few of his detainees were being freed and, Naser noticed, the stubborn one had been badly beaten. Naser smirked as he recalled the bruises on Bahram's face. He even had a black eye. Hesam had done his job and roughed him up during interrogation to extract a repentance letter.

Naser reviewed the list of detainees who had signed the repentance letter. Today was the day they were going to get rid of tens of detainees. They wouldn't have to be working around the clock anymore. Saeed and Hesam were going to bring groups of five out of the wards and escort them to the gates. Even Mansoor was back from his assigned leave, much calmer.

But Naser still had to come up with an explanation about the detainee Mansoor had shot last week: the Beast. His body had already been sent to the morgue. Naser needed to talk to the records keeper to create the alibi, but that could wait for a couple of days.

Karoun Prison, Ahwaz

The trick had worked. Saeed had confronted Hesam about Bahram. "He's pretty banged up. Are you sure you wanna continue like this?"

Hesam smiled inwardly. Saeed's voice kept echoing in Hesam's head, as he slowly walked into the hallway of the solitary cells. With so many detainees freed, space was no longer such a big problem. Still, he insisted on moving Bahram. Perhaps he had become paranoid, but he was afraid of another detainee killing Bahram in the cell.

"I'm not beating him anymore," Hesam reassured Saeed. "Solitary is gonna be enough."

Mansoor had offered to "take care" of Bahram but Hesam had politely declined. He'd determined that solitary confinement was a good excuse to not physically hurt Bahram anymore. Well, at least pretending to. He had to keep the story believable until he could figure things out.

Hesam looked into the first cell. It was empty. He looked into the cell on his right. The man inside wasn't Bahram.

Hesam looked into the cell on his left. Not Bahram.

Tonight, he was going to take a break from it all and just be with Bahram. He had no intention of initiating intimacy. Bahram had made it clear he wouldn't accept it. Tonight he was going to prove to Bahram that his love was more than just physical. If Bahram trusted him, maybe together they could think of a way out of this predicament.

He moved up to the next cell. Bahram was sitting on the carpet in the corner, leaning against the wall. He was wearing striped gray pajamas and a V-neck sky-blue T-shirt. Hesam felt his stomach tighten. He looked so sexy.

The detainee sensed Hesam's presence and looked up. The makeup black eye and cheek bruise had been touched up convincingly.

"Hey, Bahram. Great job," Hesam whispered as he unlocked the door and stepped in.

Bahram's only reply was a smile.

"How are you?"

"Happy to see you," Bahram said and tapped his hand on the carpet, signaling Hesam to sit down. Hesam sat and slipped his right leg behind Bahram and the other in front of him. He folded his knees. Bahram wrapped his arms around Hesam's leg and laid his head on his captor's knee.

"Let's clean up your makeup."

Bahram pulled a fresh T-shirt from under Hesam's foot. "You're not taking off your boots?"

"I need to pretend I'm harassing you. Can't look like I'm just chilling." Hesam picked up a red plastic cup of water and gave it to Bahram, who poured a bit of water on the T-shirt. Hesam took the damp cloth and rubbed the side of Bahram's eye.

"Just make sure you don't rub everything away. It would take time for the marks to heal."

"Yeah. I know." Hesam put his palm on Bahram's face

and caressed it with his thumb. "You shaved."

"Nosrat brought me clean clothes and a razor and stuff. Saeed allowed it."

"He's a good guy."

Bahram nodded.

"I'm sorry you couldn't see Nosrat. A detainee under interrogation can't have visitors. Otherwise, Naser would become suspicious."

"He's such an ass, this Naser."

"Can you think of why he singles you out?"

"Hell knows what's wrong with him! I don't."

"We have to be careful."

"I'm scared, Hesam."

"I know. But I'll protect you."

"They can just shoot anyone they want. With impunity." Bahram sounded defeated. "Do you know why he was after Vargha?"

"I'm not entirely sure it was him."

"Who else? Mansoor can't plan big things like that."

"Maybe it's someone outside the Revolutionary Guards."

"How would they know he was freed and where to find him?"

"I don't know. Some neighbor?" Hesam took Bahram's chin in his hand and scraped some stubborn makeup off his face.

"Easy, man," Bahram complained. "This is my face. Not a piece of lumber to sand."

"I'm sorry, baby," Hesam teased. "Forgot how fragile you are."

"I'm not fragile," Bahram protested. "I'm a thug." He playfully tapped Hesam on the face.

"Oh, I'm sorry, dear thug. I was confused by you sitting between my legs."

"Shut up, Hesam." Bahram put his head on Hesam's knee again. "Thug doesn't mean…antagonistic. Believe me, they're not all hostile."

"I guess not. Majid said you were with several…"

"Oh, nice try. Why do you care so much about the number of my sex partners?"

"Because I'm not one of them. Yet."

"You won't become one of them tonight," Bahram said as he lifted his head.

"I'll just lie down next to you," Hesam declared. "No funny business."

"It's just that I'd lose my self-respect if I do it under the condition of…coercion."

"There's no coercion. And I won't do anything. Not until you want me to."

"OK."

"You have to beg for it at that point," he joked.

Bahram laughed. "Your penis isn't all that special."

"It is too. I can prove it," Hesam teased.

Bahram kissed Hesam's knee. "What's special is your personality."

Hesam stroked Bahram's hair. "I'm in love with you. I can wait till the end of the world if that's what it takes."

"You're a good guy, Hesam. How did you end up in the freaking Revolutionary Guards Corps?"

"I wonder myself. I guess to find you."

"Get us out of here, Hesam. So we can have a normal life."

"Yeah, Bibi is already looking for three sisters to marry us."

Bahram chuckled. "We'll give all three to Majid."

Hesam lifted Bahram's hand and brought it to his lips. "I wanna marry you."

"I used to dream of that."

"Well, we can now dream together." Hesam playfully stroked Bahram's hair, shaking his head. "I challenge God to not fall in love with your beauty."

"I thought you don't believe in God, Mr. Socialist."

"I believe in my love for you."

"I love you too, Hesam," Bahram whispered.

Hesam pulled his detainee closer.

Naser kept driving. He hadn't wanted to get into an argument with Esmat, so he'd left the house. She hadn't been herself for several days. Naser spent most of his time with men. At work, at mosque, in family gatherings. He wasn't sure how to react when a woman was distant but denied there was anything wrong. Esmat still went through the motions of their daily routine, but something was different. She wouldn't say. He didn't know what else to do. So he made up some excuse and got out of the house.

As he drove, Naser realized that his muscle memory had led him to drive to the prison. He looked at his watch. It was only 9:37. Too early to go back home. He aimed to return around 11 or 12. By then, Esmat would be in bed and he could avoid another argument.

Naser rarely came to the prison at night, so this was an opportunity to oversee how the night guards operated. He sat in the office and skimmed the local newspaper, *Khuzestan*. He used to buy the paper every evening on his way home and go through it after watching the TV news. But since his wedding, the newspapers had piled up in the corner, unread.

Naser put the paper aside and started reviewing the lists of prisoners. With the mass amnesty of detainees yesterday, he had to update it. But the two sets of records didn't match.

He took the lists and walked toward the political prisoners' ward.

"Peace on you, Brother Naser," said the guard. "Can I help you with something?"

"I need you to cross-reference these lists. I'm missing the location for two detainees."

"Sure, no problem."

Naser gave him the lists. "Who's over there?"

"The solitary ward? I think one detainee was moved today. Bahram Karimi. I'm…I haven't had a chance to…"

"It's fine. I'll look into it. It'll take a couple of days until we update the records."

Naser walked into the hallway of the solitary ward. He waited for his eyes to get used to the darkness. The first cell was empty, contrary to his records. The next two cells were occupied. Naser walked over to the next one. It was darker. He looked, then rubbed his eyes. He still couldn't make out what he was seeing. He blinked a few times.

There was a young man, lying on his side, fetus-style. He was wearing nothing but a pair of boxer shorts. It looked like Bahram. Spooning him was another man. His arm was wrapped around his bare chest.

Seeing two men lying together turned his stomach upside down. Naser resisted the urge to spit. He wondered if he should call the guards immediately. But he decided against it. Bahram would stay the rest of his imprisonment in solitary. But Naser needed to know who else was involved and how he'd gained access to the solitary cell.

He stepped closer to the small window in the door. The second man was wearing boots. Military boots. And the dark clothing was the uniform of the Revolutionary Guards.

He had to severely punish whoever this was. This was an Islamist institution, not a house of corruption. Naser wondered which of the night guards was the dirty animal in front of him. As the man moved his head, the dim light shined onto Hesam's face.

Naser jolted. He reached for his gun. Then stopped. No. He had to think of something better. He had suspected Hesam had a strange relationship with Bahram. The way he held Bahram's hand. Maybe Hesam couldn't control his needs. But to lay with a man, in prison…this was a crime against nature, against everything Naser believed in.

This was not going to continue. Not under his watch. He needed to get in touch with Brother Gholam at the Kampolo Revolutionary Committee.

JUNE 16, 1980
Ahwaz

L ast night, Esmat hadn't been able to eat dinner again. Everywhere she looked, she saw blood—even on her dinner plate. Naser noticed and asked her why she hadn't been eating properly for the last few days. But Esmat didn't know what to say, so she kept quiet, offending Naser to the point that he left the house. He came back late at night. She pretended to be asleep, so she wouldn't have to hear more questions. It was not good that Naser had started to notice the change in her behavior.

As soon as Naser left for work in the morning, Esmat went to the corner store and purchased the day's paper. Once back home, she dropped her *chador* in the living room and spread the newspaper on the floor. She went straight for the incidents page, covering local news. She was looking for one particular event.

Today's coverage included a missing blind man, some car accident on the way to Shush, and someone declaring he didn't believe in the "wayward sect of Bahaism." None of those interested her. Just like the days before, she found nothing. She had to find an explanation.

The doorbell rang. She wasn't expecting anyone. Then there was banging on the front yard gate. The doorbell rang several more times. A woman's voice called out.

She peeked out the door and yelled, "Who is it?"

The voice cried, "Open the door. My child is gone. Open the door." The banging continued. Esmat reached for her *chador* and rushed to the gate.

"Esmat *jan*, they killed my child! God help me. I'm overtaken by wretchedness."

Esmat recognized her right away. Rafat, Waleed's mother. Esmat had been so distracted these past few days by the blood on her husband's shirt, she'd forgotten to ask Naser about him.

Rafat started hitting herself on the head. "They killed my Waleed," she repeated over and over.

"Rafat *Khanum*. Come in. You're not in good shape."

"I'll never be in good shape again. They killed my son. May God grant me death too."

Esmat pulled her in and quickly closed the gate, hoping none of the neighbors saw such a visitor at her gate. "They're lying. God's spared his life. They're just finishing some paperwork before they let him go."

"What are you saying?" Rafat protested. "I waited outside prison for the mass amnesty. They said they'd release him. But they killed him. I'm coming from the morgue."

"What?"

"I saw him with my own eyes. Shot in the stomach."

That can't be true, Esmat told herself.

"May God take my life. I can't. They gunned him down. Butchered him like a sacrificial lamb."

Esmat brought Rafat into the house.

"Oh God, oh God." Rafat screamed at the top of her

lungs. "What have I done? Why did you take away my child? Take me also."

"You saw him?"

"In the hospital morgue. He'd lost so much weight. Just bones. His skin all gray. God! Oh God, what will I do?" Rafat fell on the floor on the newspapers and started to sob. Esmat knelt next to her.

"They gave me his death certificate. They took him all alive and healthy. And gave me this in return." Rafat opened her fist and Esmat took a crumpled piece of paper.

She opened it and began reading, "Waleed Moghadam, politically active under the organizational pseudonym, Saleh."

"They didn't get his name right. His name is Saleh. That's on his birth certificate. We called him Waleed. He wasn't part of any political organization."

Esmat kept reading. "…is pronounced dead as a result of being shot by a bullet on June tenth, 1980."

"They executed him, the Godless murderers."

"There was no execution on the tenth. I've read the…" Esmat stopped herself before she could finish her sentence.

"They executed him! I saw my baby in the morgue with my own eyes. They killed him. They can't call themselves pious when they kill the innocent. Murderers, that's what they are."

Esmat hugged Rafat tightly. Maybe that would stop her body from shaking. She now knew the truth. Waleed had not been part of a legal execution in Karoun Prison. Not in the last two weeks. She had gone through the newspapers, page by page. No announcement of executions. Plus, executions were not carried out point blank. The blood would not have splattered on the uniform of the shooter.

Esmat felt tears well in her eyes. "Rafat *Khanum*. I'm so sorry."

"Now they want money."

"What?"

"They won't return his body unless I pay 100 *tomans* for the bullet and 100 *tomans* for storage in the morgue."

Esmat was horrified at the cruelty of the officials.

"I have to pay 200 *tomans* to buy my son's dead body. This is what the revolution has brought." Rafat sobbed.

Each word felt like a rope tightening around Esmat's ribcage, making it more difficult to gasp for air. "Where's your older son?"

"Jamal? At work. How can I say his brother was slaughtered? He's expecting him back home safely. My baby, Waleed."

"Let me get you some water, Rafat *Khanum*."

"I want nothing. God, oh God, what was my sin? Why did you take away my child?" Rafat kept hitting the top of her head. Her gestures echoed the religious mourning ceremony. "May God forgive your sins," Rafat cried. "He took my son for mine."

"I'm so sorry," Esmat suddenly stood up. She had to take her purse before she forgot.

So it was Waleed's blood that Esmat washed off of Naser's shirt. She would have to pay for her husband's sin. That wasn't a legitimate execution. Those appeared in the newspaper.

Esmat had to do something to make it up to Rafat. Otherwise, in twenty years, she would be in Rafat's shoes. She only prayed to God she wasn't already pregnant.

"Oh God, oh God! Take away my life." Rafat continued to bawl.

Esmat had to think. She had to add at least 200 *tomans* in her purse. And tell Jamal. "What is Jamal's number?" she asked Rafat.

Esmat thought the worst day of her life was when she found blood on Naser's uniform. But today, she felt even worse: spending the day mourning with the Moghadam family. In their grief, they didn't bother to ask how Rafat knew her. As she sat among the angry and weeping, Esmat reviewed the list in her head. She had many errands, logistics, and payments. That was the least she could do for them, to make up for the extrajudicial killing she was now complicit in.

Jamal, Rafat's older son, obeyed Rafat's demands. He yelled at the coroner and cursed the guards. He accepted Esmat's offer to pay for the fees to return Waleed's body, while making sure Rafat didn't find out. She wanted to see the body of her son one final time. He begged her not to, but finally gave in.

Esmat looked at the clock. It was about 4:30. She had an hour and a half before Naser came back. She hurried home, took a quick shower, slipped on her pink dress, then applied eyeliner, eyeshadow, and mascara. She donned a pair of large Ray-Ban sunglasses to conceal the makeup before going out. She headed to a little kebab restaurant and bought lamb kebab, fresh herbs, two bottles of Coke, and *noon-e sangak*, baked on hot pebbles.

Back home, she dropped her *chador* and ran back to her makeup dresser. Naser opened the front gate as she was applying the hot-pink lipstick. "Naser *jan*. Hello. How was your day?"

"I'm good. Praise God. You?"

"Good."

Naser looked his wife up and down. "You look amazing."

"Naser *jan*, please forgive me. I'm so sorry about last night. I just don't have a good appetite lately."

"No worries. Is everything all right?"

"Yeah. I'm…I'm so lucky to be your wife. I want you to know that."

Naser smiled. "You mean the world to me. I'm so blessed."

"I am too."

"Thank God, you're OK. I was worried." Naser started to unbutton his uniform. Esmat took it from him. "Prison is such a nasty place. I'm ashamed of what's going on in there. I have to…"

"What?"

"Please promise you'll never come back. I don't want you to be exposed to their filth."

"What bothers you so much?"

"I'm too ashamed to even say it."

"Naser, I'm your wife. I hope you feel you can confide in me. You are my everything." Esmat patted him on the shoulder. "And don't you ever be ashamed of anything."

"Well, they…umm…"

Esmat caressed Naser's arm.

"I saw something disgusting last night. Two men…lying together."

Esmat shook her head. "May God be the judge. You can't be ashamed of *their* sins."

"Yeah, but one of them…is a guard. He reports to me."

"I have no doubt you will find a way to discipline him."

"He's lived in Europe. I think that's where he learned it from."

"Yes, our people are more sensible than that. What filth! What are you going to do?"

"I'm thinking…I have to do it in a way that doesn't disturb the Brothers' morale. I mean…that's a grave sin. If it was between two prisoners, both would be executed the next morning."

"I'm sorry you have to work with such people."

"Yeah. I'll find a way. I'll consult with the Brothers of the Revolutionary Committee."

"You're not going there tonight though, right?"

"Umm…why?"

"The dinner is ready. I wanted to apologize for last night."

"Ah, OK. I'll go some other time."

Esmat put the uniform on the chair.

"Where are my pajamas?"

"Oh…I washed your clothes. Maybe I left it outside. Let me go get it."

"You know what? It's quite hot. Do you mind if I just stay in shorts?"

"Mind? I think nature is testing me when I see you like that!" Esmat said flirtatiously, and she was happy to see a playful smile on Naser's face. She had never talked to her husband like that before. "Naser, please allow me to confide in you, too."

"What is it?"

"The reason I was irritable last night…Naser, I think…I think I may be expecting." She didn't fully believe it, but it sounded like a good excuse.

"What? Oh, praised be God. Are you serious?"

"I think so…I hope I can give you a son. I've always wanted a son."

"We'll love our child, son or daughter. It doesn't matter, Esmat. Oh, this is the best news."

Esmat closed her eyes. Before she'd found the bloody shirt, a loving marriage and a baby on the way would have been perfect news. That was what she'd hoped for in a husband when she agreed to marry him. But what her husband had done to Waleed—playing God—had ruined everything.

"Your mom…have you told her you're pregnant?"

"No, not yet. I don't wanna tell anyone until I'm sure."

Naser hugged her. "So what is this special celebratory dinner?"

"Oh, you'll love it." Esmat pulled back gently from Naser's embrace, because she imagined she saw blood on his undershirt. "We have to eat before the food gets cold." She walked into the kitchen to get the plates and the tray of kebab.

"Esmat!" Naser called from the living room.

"Yes, Naser *jan*?"

"Is this today's paper?"

Esmat's hands began to shake as she tried to steady her nerves. "I got the paper for you. I know you like to read after dinner."

Naser frowned at the paper and placed it on the growing pile. He looked up as Esmat brought the food. "I think tonight I'd rather do something else!" He winked at Esmat.

"Naser, you are my world. But if you allow me, I think I must resist nature's temptations. I don't want our child to get hurt." Esmat kissed him on the cheek.

"Yeah. Oh, my God. I'm going to be a father!"

JUNE 17, 1980
Karoun Prison, Ahwaz

Hesam sat in the Jeep and looked at his watch. It was 5:49 in the evening. He should have gone home about an hour ago. But he needed any excuse to stay in the prison, so he could spend the night with Bahram again. What excuse could he come up with? He had already pretended to update the records of the solitary ward a few times. If he took Bahram to the interrogation room, he would be expected to beat Bahram to force him to sign the repentance letter.

He tossed up his car key absentmindedly and then snatched it in midair. If he wanted to keep seeing Bahram, he had to become very creative, very fast. He missed catching the key and it fell under the passenger seat.

Hesam cursed and reached under the seat. He touched something soft. He pulled it out. It was a *keffiyeh*, still wrapped around an issue of the SOALS magazine. He had completely forgotten about it. Majid had given it to him, insisting that Hesam had to know about the crisis at the city hall. That was where Bahram had been arrested.

Hesam untied the *keffiyeh* and pulled out the cheap photocopy. The ink was pale, but he could still find the article. As he skimmed the account, he shuddered. "City hall…shot…families of the student detainees…Guards shot her…detained professor confronted…three dead, twenty-six wounded." Hesam gasped and stuffed the magazine back in the *keffiyeh*. He threw everything back under the passenger seat.

How did he get into this position? How did life become so dangerous? A short few months ago, he was studying medicine. The closest he got to revolutionary fervor and bloodshed was through political magazines. He'd learned that back in Iran, executions were carried out, a civil war broke out in Kurdistan, and some suspicious characters created a hostage crisis. Meanwhile, Umberto was upset that Hesam was following Iranian news. He preferred that his lover spend every spare minute with him and discuss plays and art.

Maybe it was Hesam's ego that had convinced him he could have an impact if he returned. Maybe it was his fear of Umberto's growing adulation. Umberto adored him. But too much. So Hesam had used the Cultural Revolution as an excuse to get out.

And now, he was here, sitting in his Jeep, hoping he could spend some time with his love and keep him safe from random political killings.

Unlike Umberto, Bahram wasn't needy. If anything, Hesam had to work hard to prove that his love was worth receiving. He had to measure up to Bahram's exes and show that he was better than them. But Hesam also had power, and Bahram did not. Bahram's life was in danger. And only Hesam could protect him from being sentenced to imprisonment or worse.

Hesam looked at his watch again. It was 5:57. He wanted to see Bahram so much.

JUNE 18, 1980

Karoun Prison, Ahwaz

Two weeks had passed since Bahram had spent the night in the solitary cell with Hesam. But he could still remember the tenderness and the urgency of Hesam's touch. He wasn't sure how long Hesam had stayed on the floor with him. He had fallen asleep with Hesam's arm wrapped around his chest.

Talib never stayed in bed afterward. He wouldn't just lie down next to Bahram, even in the privacy of his own home. Hesam, on the other hand, was showing his love boldly. It was obvious he had risked his career, possibly his life, by spending the night lying next to Bahram.

Bahram wished Hesam were in his cell right now, holding his hand as he slightly squeezed his fingers and displaying that beautiful smile. Maybe he could tell Hesam everything. If he told him the truth, they would become closer. No one could tear them apart. Hesam would cut through the red tape and find a way to free Bahram. Then they would run off together to a better place where they could live freely.

Talib remained the only one to know all of his secrets. Bahram tried to push his saddest memory of Talib out of his mind, but failed. It happened in October 1978, a couple of months after his wedding. They saw each other less often but the marriage hadn't been the ultimate doom. He tried to hold Talib's hand, not a full palm-on-palm grip, but a mere touching of fingertips. Talib had hastily drawn away his hand and swatted a fly that Bahram didn't see. They walked two feet apart. The river flowed leisurely, as if at any time the water could change its mind and stop moving. At any fragile moment, as the air sank deeper onto the ground, the river could just turn into a lagoon. The Karoun began far up atop Zagros Mountains, originating with fresh water that formed from the melting snow. But by the time it reached Abadan, the water was thick and dark, more like heavy mud than water. Mercilessly dense and deep brown.

Bahram felt a heaviness of a whole other type that afternoon. Half an hour before, he'd been determined to tell Talib what weighed on his heart. Now, he wasn't all that sure. He wanted to first ascertain that Talib was on his side. He swallowed his saliva and managed to say, "Do you think you'd ever tell?"

Talib didn't look at Bahram. He looked at his feet as he kept walking on soil amid thorny plants. Bahram hesitated. Talib's cold reaction threw him off. Now he didn't feel he had the courage to continue. Maybe, Talib hadn't heard him.

Talib finally asked without emotion, "Tell what?"

Bahram noted the two words. Only two words. This was already less than what he wanted to get from Talib. He'd hoped for three words: *Tell what, babe?* This omission was unspoken, yet heard.

Bahram felt trapped by his own question. He wanted to

say, *Tell others that you love me.* But all that came out of his mouth was, "Tell others that you…"

Sometimes silence can be so loud. This was the perfect moment for a fisherman to sail by, some kids to run around, or the heavy hand of the wind to blow sand in their eyes. Anything to interrupt this quicksand of talk pulling both of them down. But no sounds came. Just a breeze.

Talib waited for an answer.

It was too late to backtrack. He tried again. "Tell others that…you like boys."

"You're crazy." Talib broke into a light chuckle, laughing at Bahram's naïveté. "You beautiful, crazy boy."

Bahram noted the word *beautiful*. He couldn't help but smile. Talib playfully shoved Bahram toward the river. A welcome touch for Bahram. He was emboldened to put his arm around Talib's waist. But Talib looked around nervously and took Bahram's hand off.

"What's wrong with you?" he snapped. "Haven't you heard of honor killing?"

Bahram had. "They wouldn't kill you," he offered.

"For bringing shame to my entire tribe? Yeah they would. Your family—" Talib caught himself before saying more.

Bahram's smile evaporated. He took a deep breath and muttered, "They didn't kill me." Bahram wished Talib would ask for details, so he could know exactly what had happened. He wanted to tell the whole terrible story.

They walked in silence. Bahram wondered if the sand felt sorry for him as it took the shape of his steps.

"You are just growing up," Talib consoled him. "Soon you'll dominate younger boys. And before you know, you'll get married. You can have a guy on the side if you choose to. Just be discreet, so you won't be the target of an honor killing. By *his* family."

Bahram wasn't convinced.

"You know what's funny?" Talib said in an upbeat tone.

Sulking, Bahram had no interest in responding.

"That you're more beautiful than my wife," Talib said with a chuckle. "If you were a female, I'd take you as my second wife. My current wife would hate you and make your life miserable. Me, I'd bring you gifts and sleep mostly with you."

Talib looked impressed with his own joke, oblivious to the outrage Bahram felt.

"Maybe she and I would be best friends, join forces against you. Teach you a lesson," Bahram countered.

"Chill, man. It was only a joke."

Bahram reached into his pocket and found his cigarettes.

"Look at me," Talib cooed. "Did I break your heart?"

Bahram ignored the question. How could Talib talk about his feelings so coldly? Bahram had never felt more fragile than this very moment, just walking by the river. He refused to look at the man rejecting him. He didn't want Talib to catch a glimpse of his vulnerability. He took the cigarette out of his mouth and exhaled. The smoke looked like a locomotive chugging away, carrying the love they once had. Dissipating into thin air.

Talib never admitted it, but Hesam tells me he loves me. For the first time, he loved a man who loved him back. Bahram wished he could brag to Talib about that. Just then, he remembered the eyeshadow. He had to reapply it to make sure he still looked injured.

JUNE 20, 1980

Ahwaz

Before the Friday prayer was over, Naser quietly stood up and walked out of the hall. As he slipped his foot into his shoe, he noticed that Gholam was already standing in the courtyard of the mosque with his arms crossed. Naser walked over and shook his hand. "Peace, Brother Gholam."

"How are you?"

"Praised be God."

"Tell me why you called me here," he said with a slight impatience to his voice.

Naser looked over his shoulder. No one else was around. The sermon was about to finish but this conversation had to end first, so nobody could overhear their talk.

"I know someone who…he's a…he needs to be eliminated."

"Who is it?"

"It's a sensitive case, Brother. Someone who may be… some of the Revolutionary Guards may think of this man… as a friend. I don't want to upset the Brothers' morale."

"We can take care of it. But we need more information."

"No…I have to do it myself."

"Then why come to me? What do you need from the Committee?"

"Help me clean up."

"Fine. So what's the plan? You want this man to have an accident?"

"I need something a bit more certain. He could easily survive a car crash."

"Do you know how to use a knife?"

"I'm good with guns. Plus, that way I can be sure he dies."

"Use a silencer. This way you won't attract unwanted attention."

Naser heard the collective sound of worshippers standing up. The sermon had just ended. He began talking faster to finish the discussion. "Just collect the body after I'm gone."

"Yes, Brother. We'll take care of it. So long as you are sure of your suspicions."

"I am. I saw it with my own eyes. Thanks."

"You'll find a blue piece of paper with information on your desk. Just like the last time. We'll collect the body."

The worshippers streamed into the mosque courtyard. Naser nodded at Gholam and joined the men leaving the mosque.

Hesam opened the folders he had brought from prison. He wanted to see if he could find any similarities between Vargha and Bahram's political backgrounds. Naser had opposed Vargha's release. With Naser's special interest in hurting Bahram, Hesam presumed Naser would oppose Bahram's release also. Hesam wanted to know why.

"I didn't know you started to bring work home." Saeed sat down, holding a book.

"Just trying to catch up on paperwork."

"Mansoor, could you make some tea please?"

"Certainly, your highness. Should I bake cookies too?" Mansoor sneered from the kitchen. "I'm tired of catering to you two. You want tea, make your own."

"I didn't realize he'd been catering to us," Hesam whispered.

"He's been edgy since…well, you know."

"Mhmmm," Hesam said, returning to his papers.

"No problem, I'll make it," Saeed said and got up.

Mansoor entered the living room and sat down. "Turn on the TV for me, would you?"

"What, your highness can't get up?" Hesam retaliated.

"Would you break a foot if you did something useful for once?"

Saeed returned, sighed at the arguing, and turned on the TV. "Anything else?"

"Thanks," Mansoor said begrudgingly.

"My book is not your ass warmer," Saeed yelled as he grabbed the book Mansoor had accidentally sat on.

Hesam put the papers aside. "Mansoor, do you wanna talk?"

Saeed jerked his head to get Hesam's attention and mouthed, "Not now."

"Talk? No, I don't wanna talk," Mansoor grumbled. "Just wanna watch the news in peace—without your interruptions."

Hesam looked at Saeed, who shrugged and left the room. Mansoor turned up the TV volume.

"Twenty-seven soldiers were arrested in Tehran today, and accused of having ties with the Baathist regime." The TV blared so loudly Hesam couldn't think. "This is as the Iraqi regime continues to violate the territorial integrity of our Muslim Nation. Last week, Baathist jets were seen in the Iranian airspace over the city of Abadan. According to the

Central News Agency…"

"Mansoor, will you turn it down a bit? I'm trying to read."

"Why don't you read in your room?"

Hesam closed the folder and stood up. On the way to his bedroom, he turned off the TV.

Mansoor's face turned red as he jumped up. "You want a beating? When I get finished, you'll look like that prisoner Bahram."

Saeed ran into the living room. "You are grown men. Act like it. Not like cats and dogs."

"I was watching TV. He turned it off."

"Whatever," Saeed said. "I'm so tired of this. I'm going for a drive." Saeed took his car keys and walked out.

Hesam looked at Mansoor. He wondered if this bad atmosphere would ever be fixed.

"What are you staring at?" Mansoor barked.

Hesam walked to his room, but allowed a smile to spread across his face. *So Mansoor believes Bahram's injuries. Good makeup job.*

JUNE 22, 1980
Ahwaz

Esmat couldn't push the image out of her mind: seeing Rafat hitting her own head over and over again, and then falling onto the living room floor and sobbing like a child. Now she knew everything. She had seen the bloodstains on Naser's uniform. She knew the officials had made Rafat pay a fee to retrieve her son's body. She learned that the officials didn't let the Moghadam family gather at the cemetery. They were denied the right to mourn publicly.

Esmat could face the graffiti threats written on her gate, calling for the death of her husband. She could even live with the fear that Naser might be taken away from her in his line of duty, making her a widow and outcast. But what she couldn't do was to bring a new life into this world, knowing that its father was a murderer.

She waited until she could hear water running. Naser didn't take very long in the shower. But she had enough time to search his uniform. She pushed her hands into the pants pockets, but only found some money. She grabbed the uniform shirt. Nothing in the right pocket. But in the other pocket was a piece of paper. She reached in and pulled out a square blue piece of paper. She gasped as she clutched the paper. It resembled the other one she had found.

The shower water was still running. She took a deep breath and opened the folded paper. Unlike Mobasheri's paper, it had no address, just a time and day. Esmat covered her mouth with her hand as if to prevent a scream. She read the note twice more, fought back tears, and folded it and put it back. She sat in front of the dresser and looked into the mirror. She couldn't deny anymore who her husband was. He was a loving man inside her house. But outside… he showed a different face.

She stared in the mirror at her own face and watched the mascara begin to run. She could already see herself as a widow. Pitied. Unwanted. Alone.

She heard the water stop running. She quickly wiped her tears and cleaned the running mascara. It was time to continue her plan. She went to the bathroom and opened the door.

Naser had a towel wrapped around his waist. "Esmat!"

"It's OK. You don't need to feel shy around me." Esmat stood next to Naser in front of the mirror. She combed his hair with her fingers. Drops of water trickled from his hair upon his shoulders and back. She kissed his shoulder. She touched his chest hair and could feel his chest expand and retract under her hand. She wanted to feel his heart, to reassure herself it was still there. "You are such a handsome man."

"You're beautiful yourself."

"Naser, let's get away from here."

"You miss your parents?"

"I miss you."

"I'm right here." Naser turned around.

Esmat embraced him tightly. "I'm so lucky to be with you." Esmat couldn't hold her tears anymore. She sobbed on his chest.

Naser broke the embrace. "Why are you crying?"

"Let's get away. We can go anywhere. I'll be a model wife. I'll dedicate myself to you. To you and our children. We don't have to be in this place. You can get another job. We can bake bread to make a living. I'll do anything you want."

"Esmat, what's going on?"

"I miss you all day. I want to see you more. I want to be out of this prison of a city."

"You really hate my job. What's wrong?"

Esmat looked at him and swallowed before speaking. "Someone wrote graffiti on the gates outside. Soon after the wedding."

"What did it say?"

"It's not important."

"Tell me. What did it say?"

"Death to the mercenary Revolutionary Guard."

"Why didn't you tell me before?"

"I didn't wanna worry you…back then."

"You're safe. I promise you."

"I'm worried about your safety. I beg you. Let's get away."

"I can't, Esmat. There are anti-revolutionaries everywhere. We have to fight, not run."

"But you don't have to be a Revolutionary Guard."

Naser kissed her hair. "Yes, I do. I need to make this city safe. For us and for everyone else. So that no one will be threatening a new bride."

Esmat held him tight.

He patted her between the shoulders. "You shouldn't be exposed to anything like that. You're too delicate, too precious…especially now." Naser put his hand on her belly.

"I want to get away from here," she whispered.

"I know. I'll send you to your parents for a couple of weeks."

"I want you with me."

"I can't leave my work right now. I have to take care of something."

"You don't need to take care of anything. Let God do his work. You can't do it for him."

"These anti-revolutionaries…their corruption needs to be stopped before it infects the whole society. We all have to do our part."

"You just don't hear me."

"I do. I do, my lovely Esmat. What I do now is going to pay off down the road. A sacrifice now is an investment in the future."

"I don't want to…"

"Imagine a generation who won't be exposed to corruption on earth. No more sodomites, and pagan socialists, and pseudo-intellectuals brainwashed in the West. I'm doing this for our child. For all Iranian children."

Esmat touched Naser's face and looked in his eyes. He no longer looked like her husband. His beliefs had a strange twist, uninfluenced by her logic. She couldn't change his mind. But she had to do something before she and her child would have to pay for his sins.

She thought of Waleed's older brother, Jamal. She knew his phone number by heart.

Karoun Prison, Ahwaz

By the end of his shift, Hesam was still unable to find the common characteristic between Vargha and Bahram. Vargha was a Bahá'í. Bahram was a socialist. But Naser wouldn't know that. Vargha was arrested because of his beliefs. Bahram was captured by the city hall for acting suspicious. Hesam now knew why Bahram seemed suspicious, but Naser didn't. Was he overthinking it? Was there no link between the two cases? He chewed on the end of his already dented pen.

Saeed entered the office. "Hesam, you look so melancholy—drowned in your thoughts. What's going on?" He took off his glasses and wiped them with a tissue from Hesam's desk, then peered closer. "What is that? Vargha Mobasheri's file?"

"Yeah."

"Wasn't he released a while ago?"

"Yeah."

"And yet you're investigating him? A closed case? Some genius. No wonder you're bringing work home."

"It's just that…I wanna see if everything is filed correctly."

"Yeah, you do that. I'm going home. Are you staying?"

"A little longer."

"OK. I'll see you at home."

"Hesam," Naser called as he entered the room.

"Yes?" Hesam closed the folder and put it on the desk.

"I need to talk to you in private." Naser looked hard at Saeed.

"Sure. I was on my way home anyway," Saeed said and left the office.

Naser sat on the desk in front of Hesam. "Good job with that detainee. He looks like you've been working on him."

"Who? That guy Bahram? Yeah. I put him in solitary."

"And gave him a black eye. Good."

"Thanks."

"I think I need your help for a special operation."

Hesam leaned against the back of his chair.

"I think you're finally ready, after months of training."

"Thanks, Brother Naser."

"I need you to come to the Torches."

"The Torches?" Hesam liked watching the flares of the excess natural gas that burned day and night, like giant candles.

"Yeah. Outside the refinery, on the Naft Boulevard."

"I know where they are."

"Good. Be there at ten. Tonight."

"I beg your pardon?"

"The Torches. At ten."

"For what?"

"I just said you were learning well. And you question your superior?"

"No, Brother Naser. It's just a bit unusual, that's all."

"It's a special operation. And like I said, I need your help." Naser stood up.

"I'll be there."

"And don't announce it to the world. It's a confidential operation."

"Yes, Brother Naser."

Naser nodded and walked out.

Hesam hadn't heard of special missions before. But if everything went well, he'd gain Naser's trust and would be able to free Bahram.

Driving fast at night in his Jeep gave Hesam a sort of relief. The speedometer needle moved up to 90 miles an hour. This was so relaxing. He took a mental note to do this more often.

He started to see the light of the flames.

The Torches were erected not far from the petroleum refinery. He had heard that the refinery of crude oil created the inflammable natural gases. It was simply cheaper to burn it than try to contain and use it. He wasn't sure if that was true or a myth. But the Torches flared into the sky, day and night, and were a tourist attraction in Ahwaz.

Hesam drove on the Fanni-Herfei Boulevard until it met the Naft Boulevard. He saw the Torches clearly now. He suddenly realized Naser had not given him an exact location. The Jeep tilted as he turned right into a two-lane road that led to the Torches.

He didn't see many cars around. This would make it easier to find Naser. He finally saw faint rear red lights of a vehicle ahead, probably a sedan. Then he saw a set of headlights positioned high coming toward him. Perhaps a truck. He felt giddy, reckless, and suddenly changed lanes to the left side so his Jeep was heading toward the truck at top speed.

Hesam laughed wildly and then changed lanes again to allow the truck to easily pass. But the truck moved into his lane, the wrong side of the road. Hesam honked his horn. The truck stayed on Hesam's lane.

The truck was directly in front of the Jeep. He could still see the sedan's red lights. It was parked on the shoulder. Hesam pressed his hand on the horn, but the truck kept speeding toward him. Hesam took his foot off the accelerator. At that speed, he was afraid if he pushed the brakes the Jeep would topple.

The truck got even closer. Hesam had to choose between colliding into the truck or getting on the shoulder and possibly crashing into the parked car. The truck was too close to ignore. A car passed him on the left lane. That was his last option. He just had to move to the shoulder on the left side of the road. He looked at the speedometer. His speed had fallen to 85, still too fast to hit the brakes.

Hesam shifted into the left lane. The truck honked. Hesam jolted at the thunder-like sound. As his body jerked, his foot pushed the brakes all the way down. He heard the tires squeak. The truck's headlights blinded Hesam. The Jeep began to spin.

Right lane, left lane. Hesam didn't know where he was. Everything happened too fast to process. The headlights. The dust. The dark. The spinning. He heard an explosion and suddenly felt a wall of heat. But Hesam couldn't see anything.

Bahram couldn't sleep. He felt so anxious. Something bad was happening, he sensed. Was Bibi OK? Did she make enough this month to cover the rent? Majid would surely check up on her. Unless he was also detained? What if he mentioned Bahram under torture? What if more incriminating evidence was discovered against him? What if Hesam got transferred? What if Hesam lost interest?

Maybe it was the heat that made him delirious. Bahram sat up in his bed, which was a thin blanket on the floor. He was only wearing a pair of boxer shorts but he was still sweating. He picked up his tank top from the floor and dried his chest. His nose took in a rotten smell. Was it the damp solitary cell—or his own body odor? He hadn't showered in a week. Since the night Hesam had stayed in his cell.

He wished Hesam were there. He felt safe when Hesam was around: He brought him food and water. He gave him cigarettes and news from Abadan. He'd hidden the SOALS magazines when he visited his room in Bibi's house. Bahram had started to believe that Hesam wanted to let him out.

He reached for the red plastic cup and drank some water.

A new fear settled over him. He hoped he wouldn't come across any scorpions. If Hesam were there, he could at least squeeze the life out of any scorpion with those boots. Bahram had only some plastic slippers. He wished Hesam were there.

Hesam would also let him use the shower to make him feel refreshed. Hesam could solve so many problems.

JUNE 24, 1980

Karoun Prison, Ahwaz

Saeed gulped down his tea when he heard that all guards had to report to the prison yard. This had to be something big. He found Mansoor in a corner. They shook hands.

"Do you know what's going on?"

Mansoor shook his head.

"Naser isn't here yet."

"Neither is Hesam. Where is he?"

"In my pocket," Saeed joked.

"Oh shut up. I don't think he came home last night."

"He did not."

"So…what's up with that?"

"I'm not his guardian."

They noticed a young guard they hadn't seen before standing on the steps to the building. He raised his hand to speak. The guards' chatter didn't diminish.

"Last week too, Hesam didn't come home one night."

"He's been working a lot," Saeed replied.

"Or maybe he found a girl of ill repute." Mansoor raised an eyebrow.

"That's it. Genius!" Saeed mocked.

Mansoor looked again at the young guard, still trying to get everyone to quiet down. "Who's that?"

"A new colleague?"

"I hope he's not one of those—"

"Brothers," yelled the young guard. This time, he got their attention. "I'm here to express my congratulations and my condolences after the loss of our leader and dear Brother, Naser Atri."

Mansoor elbowed Saeed. "What did he say?"

Saeed whispered, "Shhh, let me hear what he's saying."

"Congratulations because he was martyred last night while on a mission. He is guaranteed entry to heaven as he died while serving God. Condolences because we lost a leader and a stellar guard who championed the Corps during the riots in the University. I am Gholam and I will replace Brother Naser as your commander."

Mansoor slapped Saeed on the back in annoyance. "We're supposed to take orders from this mere boy? He hardly has a beard. He's like…eighteen or something."

"Be quiet," Saeed said.

"Brother in the corner. Are you having convulsions?" Gholam yelled out.

Mansoor put his hand on his chest, feeling embarrassed. "I'm fine."

"And your name?"

"Mansoor. Mansoor Bayat."

"Brother Mansoor, I've heard much of your bravery and unwavering decisiveness. I guess paying attention is not one of your strengths."

"I'm sorry, Brother."

"Call me Commander Gholam."

"Yes, sir."

Gholam paused and then resumed his address. "Even though I'm your commander, as my name suggests, I'm a servant here. God's servant, like all of you. And your servant who will do his best to help all of us accomplish our religious and civic duties here."

There were grunts of assent from the guards.

"Despite my age, I have years of experience. I have taken part in demonstrations with you against the corrupt monarchy. I have distributed leaflets of our leader's speeches. And most recently, I served in the Kampolo Revolutionary Committee. So think of me as a resource. We can all learn from each other and help each other fulfill our God-given obligations." Gholam gave the guards in the yard a sweeping look. "You are now dismissed."

The guards stomped their feet as they saluted their new young commander.

He parked the car in front of the house gate. He had come there only once before, but he was pretty sure this was the right house. He rang the doorbell and waited. Maybe nobody was home. He hoped she already knew. He rang again. Then he heard a set of footsteps approaching.

"Who is it?"

"I work with Naser. Open the gate...please."

Esmat opened the gate. "Brother Hesam?" she remembered him.

Hesam noticed her red eyes. Her hair was showing from under her headscarf.

"I'm sorry to bother...I...um...just wanted to make sure you're OK."

Esmat looked away.

"Naser was a good friend of mine. I'm so sorry."

Esmat fixed her *chador* with her right hand, and drew her eyebrows together. "Thanks. Can I help you?"

Hesam pressed his teeth together. He was hoping she would invite him in. He was still shaken. Everything had happened so fast.

Last night, when he came to, he heard the truck speed away. His Jeep, after so much spinning, was facing the direction he was coming from. Once the dust settled, he saw that the third parked car was upside down. He could now see it was Naser's Benz. The hood was completely crushed in. Hesam dazedly opened the door and tried to step out, but he had to wait for the vertigo to go away.

Suddenly, the Mercedes exploded. The heat of the blast slapped his face. Hesam stood wide-eyed, rooted to the spot. Even if Naser had survived the crash, he would have died in the explosion.

Hesam realized he had to get away before he was seen at the site. He sped off.

And now he was here at Naser's front gate, trying to figure out what had happened. Hesam realized he had been staring at Esmat.

She looked both ways before continuing, "Come in. It's not good to keep you at the gate." She led Hesam inside and invited him to sit down on the handmade rug opposite the television. "I'll bring some tea."

"I don't want to bother you."

"I could use some distraction."

Southerners never forgot their manners, Hesam thought. He heard Esmat turn on the faucet in the kitchen. He looked around. On a small stand, he saw a phone with a notebook and pen. Some pieces of paper were scattered on the stand. A pile of newspapers sat in the corner of the room.

"I put the water to boil," Esmat said as she entered the living room and sat.

"I really didn't—"

"It's no trouble. You're the first one to come by to offer your condolences. My parents should get here after lunch. I…I just found out a couple of hours ago."

"I'm so sorry. I can't imagine how you must be feeling."

"Naser had told me he worked with a foreigner."

"Why do you think I'm a foreigner? I'm not."

"A single man wouldn't come to visit a woman he didn't know, and a widow at that. Not when she's home alone."

He felt scolded. "I'm sorry. I'll leave."

"Nonsense. I'll go check on the tea."

Esmat went to the kitchen. Hesam could hear her opening drawers and clacking china cups. He leaned against a magenta hard cushion. A crumpled piece of blue paper attracted his attention.

Still in the kitchen, Esmat called out, "Naser liked tea. He had some before he went out last night. He said he'd be back soon."

Hesam picked up the paper just as Esmat entered the room.

"So you act like a guard and start snooping around."

"No, I'm sorry. It just looked like trash."

"You want to clean my house?" Esmat calmly set down the tray of tea cups. "Tell me what happened."

"Naser called me in for a confidential operation last night," Hesam explained. "When I got to the location, I saw a truck. It came to the wrong side of the road and wouldn't let me pass. I don't know what happened. I lost control of my vehicle. I may have blacked out. The next thing I know, I saw Naser's car…" Hesam didn't say the word *crushed*.

"So the truck…" Esmat didn't finish her sentence.

"I can't be sure, but I think the truck did it on purpose. If you have any information, you must tell me."

Esmat picked up a cup and brought it to her lips. Her hand was shaking slightly, making tiny ripples in the cup. She blew on the tea as if to hide the ripples.

"You know something," Hesam said slowly. The conclusion surprised him. "Had he been threatened before?"

Esmat placed the cup back into the tray. She inhaled deeply to give herself time to decide what her next words would be. "Naser was getting dangerous. Someone had to stop him."

"What do you mean dangerous? Was he abusive toward you?"

"If it were that easy, I would have just left."

"What then?"

"Fine, I'll tell you. The note you have in your hand… that's not the first note I found. The first one had the address of someone called Vargha Mobasheri."

"Vargha?" Hesam cried out his name, unable to control his emotions.

"You knew him? Did you know he was kidnapped and killed?"

"Naser arranged his killing? Oh my God, I found Vargha's body. I was the one who convinced Naser we should let him go."

"Well, he wasn't quite convinced," Esmat said in a strangely calm voice. As if she was in a trance.

Hesam covered his face with his hands. "And last night?"

"You have the note in your hand."

Hesam straightened the piece of paper to read the note. "This…doesn't prove anything."

"I found blood on his shirt." Esmat took a breath and continued. "He also killed Saleh Moghadam."

Hesam remembered the guy. The Beast. "He was sentenced to death, but the execution failed."

"Yet Naser took it upon himself to kill him anyway. You didn't even get his name right. His family called him Waleed."

"You knew his family?"

Esmat's eyes got watery. "It was retribution."

"An eye for an eye. And why do you think you have the right to seek retribution?"

"It wasn't *my* right. But it was the right of Waleed's family."

Hesam looked at the walls. They seemed to get closer. It wasn't Naser who'd killed Waleed. Did he have to explain that she killed her husband for a crime Mansoor had committed?

"Why…are you telling me all this? I can have you prosecuted," Hesam wondered.

"You wouldn't tell anyone."

"Don't be so sure."

Esmat gave him a look that frightened him. As if she was seeing right into his soul. "You wouldn't talk because you have more to lose than I do."

"Me? I have nothing to lose. I—"

"You're a homosexual," Esmat interrupted.

"What?"

"Naser knew."

"I don't know what you're talking about."

"Why do you think Naser wanted to get rid of you?"

Hesam realized he was digging his fingers, like claws, into his knees. His leg muscles felt like cramping. The whole room seemed to be getting smaller. He gasped for air. Sweat started to form on his forehead.

"He found out. The operation was meant to…"

"That's impossible. I'd never—" Hesam thought back to his times with Bahram. But they were always alone. Weren't they?

"Looks like you need a sip of tea." Esmat pushed the tray toward him.

Hesam tried to lift the cup but his hand wasn't strong enough. Naser. His boss and colleague. His mentor. That was why he was so determined to hurt Bahram.

"To Naser, being a homosexual is one of the greatest sins."

Hesam wiped his forehead and dried his hand with his pants. "And to you?"

"I just had my husband killed. Your sexual desires are the least of my problems." Esmat took a sip of her tea.

"I looked up to Naser. Meanwhile he was plotting my murder."

Esmat's headscarf fell on her shoulder. She ran her hand in her hair. Hesam realized the significance of this action. She didn't feel the need to observe her cover.

"I don't know what got into him," she said. "I thought he was a pious man. But turns out he liked to play God. He hated the anti-revolutionaries." Her voice trembled. "He thought you were a sinner beyond all redemption."

Hesam was lost for words. He felt the lump in Esmat's throat occupy his own.

"You must know that some of your other colleagues think just like Naser. They wouldn't blink if they had to..."

Hesam realized he was in more danger than he'd thought. But he also understood that he owed his life to Esmat. They shared a deep secret. Two secrets.

"And you know what makes it even worse?" she offered.

"What's that?"

"I loved him."

JUNE 25, 1980

Karoun Prison, Ahwaz

Bahram paced back and forth in his cell. It measured seven by thirteen feet, meaning he couldn't walk in any direction for more than a few steps. The prisoners in solitary received food twice a day and could use the bathroom only once. Earlier he had asked to use the bathroom but was told to wait. He banged on the door again. This time, no one even replied.

He wondered how he looked. Was he still good-looking? Would Hesam still find him attractive in this state? Had his facial hair grown too unevenly? He felt itchy and the beard felt strange to the touch. He also smelled. It had been nine days since his last shower. In this heat, he was sweating excessively. He had taken to wearing only his shorts. He couldn't bear to wear anything else. He hadn't retouched the makeup because his face was bathed in sweat. He hoped the guards would think his wounds had healed.

He picked up his tank top and dried his chest. Then he

dropped it on the floor and wiped his feet on it. The tank top was visibly damp. His bladder was hurting.

He wished Hesam were here. He would allow Bahram to take a shower. But he had to admit he also missed him, his smile, his touch.

Bahram couldn't hold it much longer. He banged on the door again. "I need to use the bathroom." No answer. His pacing no longer helped. He could try to pee in the gap between the bottom of the door and the floor, but the stream might just flow back into his cell. The guards would be angry and consider him an animal.

He had to do something but could think of only one other option. He held his red plastic cup low and relieved himself. He was humiliated. The acrid smell bothered him. And now he would have to use the same cup to bring drinking water back into the solitary. If there were a hell, he was already in it.

Bahram thought about his life. How did it lead him here? He was only fourteen when he surrendered his body and soul to a sexy teenager, back home in Sanandaj. It had been the most beautiful moment of his life, as he lay down next to the teenager, still panting, particles of sweat shining on his face. The next few days, he felt he'd been flying. The sun burned brighter and the wind felt more refreshing. The touch of warm water on his skin felt like Daniar's caress. But soon, his world crashed down. Someone found out and disclosed their secret. That fateful afternoon, his father's eyes were the color of fire. He didn't hit Bahram, as if his hands would get dirty. He simply locked him in his room. Bahram thought it would soon blow over. He could handle the initial shock and the ensuing punishment. He expected a good beating at some point.

After dark that night, he heard that Daniar had been summoned to their house. Banoo, his mother, the matriarch, had a conversation with Daniar, but from behind the locked bedroom door Bahram could hear only mumbling sounds.

Soon the door was unlocked so Daniar could enter. Bahram forced a smile. Daniar didn't. His face was the color of white plaster before a paint job. "How are you doing?" Daniar asked. After a long pause, he said, "Thanks for not telling them that it was," he struggled to find the right word, "forcible."

"I don't lie. My mom has taught me that," Bahram answered, recognizing Daniar's fear that Bahram would accuse him of rape. If Bahram were a victim, then he couldn't get punished. But he hadn't even considered lying like that. The experience with Daniar had been too amazing to be tainted with any negative and false description.

"You've saved my life," Daniar stated.

Bahram agreed.

"I did my best to do the same for you."

Bahram reassured him that his mom valued honesty and after a period of beatings and confinement, everything would go back to normal.

Daniar stared at his feet as if he'd discovered something new about them. "Your mom told me I was the one to do this to you, so I should be the one to fix it. She wanted me to defend the honor of the tribe, and…" He swallowed, unable to finish the sentence.

Not even for a second had Bahram taken the threat of honor killing seriously. He was the only child in the matriarch's family. He would grow up to be a leader in his tribe. His parents doted on him.

"I convinced them…a little. But they want me to send you away."

Daniar kept talking, but Bahram didn't hear anything else. He watched as Daniar, the boy he'd fallen in love with, the boy who'd made love to him just a few days earlier, tied his hands and informed him that he was banished to Tehran to live with a relative.

Bahram imagined his mother had wanted to teach him that men with whom Bahram fell in love would only betray him, and throw him out. But even after Talib did the same, Bahram still couldn't help but remain attracted to men.

That night, Daniar led him outside the house. An old man with a white beard and a gold tooth was waiting for him next to his dilapidated Paykan. Bahram lost it then. He screamed and pleaded and begged. But his mother didn't even come to see him go. His father just stood by and watched as if he were a ghost.

Daniar told the old man that he couldn't stop the car until dropping Bahram off at his destination. His words dug like a dagger into Bahram's heart.

Bahram cried and cried in that stinky, clunky car.

Several hours later, the driver had to stop to pee and eat a light breakfast. Bahram managed to put the gear to neutral, watching the car move downhill, causing a commotion on the road. By the time the driver ran back to the car, Bahram had already escaped. He hitched a ride and ended up at a bus terminal in Tehran.

After a moment of panic, a singsong call of a bus driver attracted his attention. "Abadan? Abadan!" he sang rhythmically. Bahram looked at the driver, with wrinkles that cut deep into his face. A young couple got on the bus.

"Abadan? Abadan! No more? Let's go!" the driver said as he climbed into the bus.

"Wait," Bahram yelled out. "I'm going to Abadan." He gave the driver all the change in his pocket, tears wetting his face. The man took pity on him. They passed through cities that Bahram had only heard of before: Boroujerd, Khorramabad, Ahwaz.

After arrival, he walked around the city in the dark. It was hot and the palm trees were taller than they looked in pictures. When hunger and fatigue overwhelmed him, he knocked on a door and begged the old woman to let him stay there. That was how he found Bibi. He also took a new name and told her what he thought was true in essence: that he was an orphan.

Abadanis were Persians, and Arabs, and Afro-Iranians, and Americans, and other foreigners. They had their dance clubs and swimming pools and bars. Spicy *sambusas* that Indians had brought with them. Music of the Persian Gulf with its upbeat drums. Foreign women sunbathed in their yards. Abadan was the most westernized city in Iran. The most decadent. Oil brought different peoples together.

But things fell apart again. Soon after Talib's wedding in August 1978, hundreds of movie watchers were killed in arson in Cinema Rex. Abadan was never the same. It was the last major city to take revolutionary fervor.

Before the Christian new year, unknown men assassinated an American engineer who worked at the oil company in Ahwaz. Hence the foreigners left. So did Talib, moving with his wife to Kuwait.

After the monarchy fell, Arabs hoped for autonomy: to speak their language and benefit from the oil, like Tehran did. The new government rejected these aspirations. Oil pipelines were blown up. Some Arabs were charged without evidence and executed.

Devastated by the departure of his lover, Bahram closed his heart. He had his brief affairs but never got emotionally entangled. And now, his own prison guard had fallen for him. A faint sign of hope. He missed Hesam. Where was he the past few days?

He ached to return to Abadan. Only then would things settle down. He would be able to go wherever he wanted, do whatever he wanted, and take as many showers as he pleased. He would throw away every red plastic cup he could find. He would be respected again.

He'd have to convince Hesam to move to Abadan with him.

JUNE 26, 1980

Karoun Prison, Ahwaz

Hesam hungered to see Bahram again. But he was afraid someone else would discover his feelings for the detainee. If Naser had found out so easily, he knew others could too. But Hesam had another plan. With Naser gone, no one was going to ask about repentance letters. So he prepared a list of six detainees he recommended for release. Bahram's name was among the six. He would submit the list and no one would suspect anything.

He went to meet Commander Gholam in the office. He handed Gholam the list to approve.

"What is this again?"

"The list we talked about. This is the list of prisoners we can get rid of."

"Execution?"

"No, Commander." Hesam almost yelled in panic. "The prisoners to be released," he quickly lowered his voice.

"Oh, OK. I'm happy you explained. We don't want to get that mixed up." Gholam glanced at the document from his desk.

"Is there anyone being executed?" Hesam tried to downplay his question.

"Oh yeah, a bunch of criminals, anti-revolutionaries, corruptors…so basically just criminals. Brother Hesam, you're assigned to the firing squad tomorrow."

"Sir?"

"The prison is still overcrowded and we have a few death sentences. We need to eliminate them. No need to wait."

"You're right, but I…I can't take part in an execution."

"Why is that?"

Hesam had to think fast. "I have a heart condition."

"A heart condition?"

"Yes, Commander. I have an irregular heartbeat. Stressful situations can induce a heart attack." Hesam hoped he sounded believable.

"How terrible! A dead Revolutionary Guard is no use."

"No, Brother."

"OK, fine. So…go ahead and tell Haj Agha to remove your name."

"I'll go right away." Hesam paced toward the door.

"Great."

Hesam started to walk out. But he stopped when he heard Gholam almost shout, "This can't be true."

Thinking the man was speaking to him, Hesam stopped.

"Brother Hesam," he called.

Hesam hesitated and then went back into the office.

"This Bahram Karimi, where is he from?"

"Ah…I don't remember. I have to look in his file," Hesam said, making a small performance of scratching his head in confusion.

"You don't remember?"

"He may be from Khorramshahr or something," Hesam lied, worried about this interest in his beloved.

"Any chance he's from Abadan?"

"Oh…umm…I guess. I mean the two cities are pretty—"

"I can't believe this," Gholam said, shaking his head from side to side. He suddenly had a sinister smirk on his face as he signed the list of detainees. "Here. I approved your list." Gholam held the piece of paper in the air.

Hesam reached to take it, almost ready to weep with joy.

"They can all be freed."

"Great. Thanks." Hesam started to walk away to hide the grin on his face.

"All but Bahram Karimi. He's gonna stay here."

Hesam looked at the list in his hand. Gholam had crossed out Bahram's name. "I don't understand."

"Karimi stays here. For a very long time." Gholam rubbed his hands together with odd relish. "Go and talk with Haj Agha about reassignment."

"Yeah. Sure."

Hesam left the office, his heart sinking in his chest. Why did Bahram have all these enemies? Naser wanted to hurt him because he found out he was gay. But what did Gholam have against him?

Hesam wished he had pushed harder to go fight in Kurdistan. At least there, it would've been clear who the enemy was. Maybe he should try to be transferred. He began knocking on Haj Agha's door.

He was invited in and offered a seat. He was unhappy about the conversation ahead. "Commander Gholam said I should talk to you about the executions tomorrow."

"Yes. You are a soldier of this country, a guardian of the revolution. I hear you were in Europe?"

"Yes, Haj Agha. I was in Italy, a student of biology."

"On your way to be a doctor?"

Hesam nodded.

"And what brought you here?"

"It was my duty to come back to my country. I wanted to serve the people." Hesam was careful to not say *the masses*. No, that would be socialist talk.

"Our country needs brave young men like you. You surely know how much the nation has sacrificed for this revolution. We must continue the revolution and honor the blood of the martyrs. The blood that the monarchist agents have shed on the streets. Do you have the willpower to defend the revolution?"

"Yes, Haj Agha. That's why I'm back." Hesam wondered how long this sermon would go on, fighting the urge to look at the wall clock.

"The revolution has been under attack from the start. There were hundreds of plots to destroy it. As we speak, some agent of the Great Satan or the Zionist regime may be plotting to undermine the revolution. It is our job to stop them. You must be courageous. You left your luxurious life in Italy to come here."

Hesam wanted to argue that his life in Rome was hardly luxurious, but he stayed mum. Why contradict the man in charge who was going to determine his role in the executions tomorrow?

"Haj Agha, I'm ready. When I joined the Corps, I was hoping to go to—" Hesam caught himself before he could say *Kurdistan*. If he planned to offer a heart problem as his excuse for not participating in the firing squad, he was disqualified from joining the war front in Kurdistan too. That would blow his chances of ever getting transferred there. "Haj Agha, I'm ready to do whatever is necessary, provided my condition allows," he began.

"Condition?"

Hesam cleared his throat. "Haj Agha, unfortunately I can't carry out executions. I…I have a heart condition. I may have a heart attack in…umm…"

"I see." Haj Agha leaned back in his chair. Hesam felt another sermon was coming. "Son, when I was a boy, a man could do anything, whatever his religious duties required. Nowadays, men are so fragile. So delicate. They place restrictions on God's commands. If we execute, it is to punish the criminals. It's to rid the nation of corruption on earth. You, my son, have to fulfill your religious duty. It's just like prayer."

"I assure you, I am ready. I honor my uniform. I only have to stay away from shootings."

"A soldier who can't shoot? A soldier's heart is made of iron. He's ready to face the enemy head-on, not retreat."

Hesam felt his temperature elevate, his armpits get damp. He would have to try harder to convince the cleric of his health limitations.

"If you have a strong will, you can deal with the weaknesses of the body," Haj Agha continued. "If you got involved in a confrontation on the street with the hooligans, you must use your gun to protect your Brothers. You can't just point to your heart and expect them to surrender."

Hesam remained silent, his head down. He could feel Haj Agha staring at him.

"Can you flog?"

Hesam was taken aback. "Sir?"

"You didn't hear me? Excuse me, my son. I am getting old and my voice trembles. Perhaps another sign that I need to relinquish my duties soon to the next generation. I was asking if you can flog the convicts for their crimes, in the name of God."

Hesam locked his fingers together and pressed them hard to hide the fact that he was trembling. He reassured Haj Agha he was ready to flog the enemy, knowing the situation was an unlikely one.

"Good. Remember, be kind to your Brothers and ruthless to your enemies."

"Yes, Haj Agha. I'll do as you say."

Haj Agha paused for a second. "How did you get along with Brother Naser?"

Hesam stiffened. "Very well." Had Naser told Haj Agha anything about Hesam before he'd died? "I learned a lot from Brother Naser. He was my mentor. This is a big loss for all of us."

"Martyrs go to paradise. God bless his soul. Now, Brother Gholam is your mentor. Learn as much as you can. I'll put you under his direct supervision."

"Yes, Haj Agha."

Haj Agha said no more, indicating the conversation was over. Hesam stood up and slightly bowed.

"The revolution needs men like you. Be brave. God will guide us all."

Hesam left the room. He paused in the hallway and took a deep breath. He'd gotten out of the firing squad. But he had made the absurd promise to whip the prisoners. He still had to find a way of freeing Bahram. He kept walking.

Hesam ran into Gholam in the hall and explained that Haj Agha had excused him from the firing squad, but that he had to flog someone.

When Gholam smiled at the news, Hesam immediately regretted it.

"Start with flogging Bahram."

"Pardon me, sir?"

"Just tie his feet and whip them as long as you can. Until you get tired. Then take a rest, and flog him some more." Gholam smirked.

"Yes, commander."

"It won't be his first time," said Gholam as he walked away.

Karoun Prison, Ahwaz

Saeed arrived late at work with the excuse that he'd over-slept. But he hadn't slept at all. He tossed and turned most of the night, questioning his life choices.

He had come to Ahwaz from Tabriz last winter, in the aftermath of clashes between forces of the government and the followers of one of the most prominent clerics in the country. The religious man had opposed a key element of the constitution. His faithful followers took to the streets, but the government quashed the movement. At one time, Saeed had thought both parties ultimately belonged to the same side. But he was no longer so sure about that. Saeed had fled Tabriz, hoping he could still play a role in the revolution if he hid his support for the cleric. He wondered if he could still be effective while following his own beliefs, even if they differed from the government's stance.

The main reason for Saeed's late arrival at work was to avoid the executions that took place early in the morning. Eight had been shot by the firing squad that day: three women and five men, including a respected doctor. They had been executed for charges ranging from prostitution to helping prisoners escape from the city hall. One was a sympathizer of SOALS.

The prisoners had been executed in the name of God. But Saeed felt a quiet objection in his heart. He believed in a God who would not approve the killings. Saeed believed God would be more interested in the well-being of souls than in killings for the sake of advancing the cogs in the massive state machine.

Saeed would refuse to participate in the execution of his countrymen. He had seen enough death last January in the streets of Tabriz, just before he'd fled. Although he wasn't high enough in the hierarchy to make major changes, he hoped this quiet rebellion would be somewhat effective. He would not take part in the firing squad. He would not have blood on his hands. Before, Saeed's prime interest had been in himself, in his promotion. Now, he wanted to do something positive, as if performing ablution on his soul. Besides, since the arrival of Gholam, a strict and regimented leader, any chances for promotion had been dashed.

Saeed busied himself by placing a few personal care products in the showers area. Shampoo, nail clippers, and a razor. Small gestures of kindness, humanity. He even put a bottle of rosewater there. He thought it was less pretentious than some fancy cologne.

Saeed was surprised to find Mansoor at the gate of the solitary ward. "Hi," Saeed said. "What are you doing here?"

"Farbod is sick. I'm just covering for him."

"OK. Open the door."

"You sure? They're being punished."

"For what?"

"I don't know. But they're not let out. Their movements are restricted."

"Who ordered it?"

"I don't know."

Saeed stared down the guard and pointed to the gate. Mansoor shrugged and opened it.

The first cell was empty. Saeed walked to the next one. A man was sleeping on the ground. Saeed walked by the third cell and then stopped at the fourth. He found a young man sitting on the floor. It took Saeed a moment to recognize Hesam's prisoner. His facial hair had grown and now resembled a rodent's whiskers more than a man's beard. He used to be handsome, this Bahram something. Now, his shirt was filthy and had yellow stains under the arms. Worst of all, he emanated a stale mix of sweat and urine.

"Good morning. You wanna take a shower?"

Bahram reacted slowly, as if dazed, but then a slight glimmer appeared in his eyes. "Can I wash my clothes?"

Saeed nodded.

Bahram bent to pick up his red plastic cup. The way he held it distastefully, away from himself, Saeed didn't need an explanation to know what it contained. He felt sorry for the teenager. *No one should have to be this humiliated*, Saeed thought. He wondered why Bahram had been arrested in the first place. He recalled that Hesam had been investigating his case for some time now. Maybe Hesam had found evidence that had landed the detainee in solitary. Maybe he wanted to force him to confess.

Bahram slowly walked out of his cell, still holding the red cup and not wanting to spill it. Saeed followed, giving him room because of the odor.

"Damn, you stink," Mansoor complained. "What are you, a pig?"

Bahram didn't reply.

Saeed opened the door to the showers. Bahram immediately noticed the hygiene products and looked at Saeed with a mixture of confusion and gratitude.

"You have half an hour."

The norm for shower time was five minutes. But Saeed wanted absolution.

"Thank you," Bahram mumbled.

"And throw away that cup," Saeed said. "I'll get you another one. A green one."

JUNE 28, 1980

Karoun Prison, Ahwaz

Bahram sat on the chair, blindfolded with hands tied behind the back. Hesam hadn't come to see him for almost two weeks. Bahram was kept in solitary, hungry and without access to a bathroom for long intervals and Hesam wasn't there to protect him. Yesterday, there had been executions. He could hear the shots. And yet, Hesam hadn't shown up. As he waited in the room, he wondered if he would ever see Hesam again. Had he given up on him because Bahram withheld his love?

He heard the door open and close. Someone approached him and gently lifted up Bahram's blindfold. Hesam, at last.

Hesam didn't smile like he used to. Neither did he immediately untie Bahram's hands. "How are you, darling?" Hesam asked solemnly.

Bahram looked around. This wasn't the same interrogation room. There was no desk. Just the chair he was sitting on and another chair facing him. There was a spring-bed to his left. He knew immediately what that meant.

"I missed you."

"That's why you came to visit me so often?" Bahram responded with a bitterness he had accumulated for the past thirteen days.

Hesam sat on the chair in front of him. "We need to talk."

Something attracted Bahram's eyes. He saw a piece of electric wire sticking out of Hesam's pants pocket. That confirmed what he'd already guessed. "You gonna whip me?" Bahram knew that guards would tie the prisoner to a spring-bed and lash him on the feet, or the back.

Hesam shook his head. "Something is happening and I need your help to figure out what it is."

"Why don't you just whip me until I talk?"

Hesam looked at the window in the door over Bahram's head, pressed his lips together and leaned forward. "Naser knew about us," he whispered.

Bahram couldn't believe it. "What do you mean?"

"Naser knew that I'm in love with you. He was planning to kill me."

Bahram tried to reach out to Hesam, but the rope restricted him.

"He died in an accident shortly after."

"He's dead? Wait, does anybody else know about us?"

"I don't know. That's why I didn't come to see you. I was afraid someone else might suspect something."

Bahram pushed against the ropes and grunted, hinting he wanted to be untied.

"We could be under surveillance. If anyone peeks in here, they need to see your hands tied," Hesam warned. "We have to be very careful now."

"You promised to free me."

"I was hoping to. I had recommended your name for release. But our new commander knows you. He has something against you. Something personal."

"Who is that?"

"Commander Gholam."

"I don't know him."

"Think carefully. Both of our lives may depend on it. He's from Abadan."

The name didn't remind Bahram of anyone. "I don't know a Gholam from Abadan."

"Would he know you're affiliated with SOALS?"

"Affiliated? I just read the SOALS magazines."

"Is that something someone would know? What about an enemy of Majid's?"

"How would I know?" Bahram was getting tired of the questions.

"Someone related to your…ex-boyfriend."

"Talib? No one knew about us except Majid."

Hesam covered his head with his hands and slouched forward. "I don't know how to help you if you don't help me figure it out."

"What do you want me to do? I don't know this Gholam guy."

Bahram thought back to school and the day when the teacher beat his feet with a wooden stick. Would a cable hurt more? Do more damage? Was Hesam really going to flog him?

"He recognized your name. He knows you're from Abadan. He personally wants to see you get hurt. Think. Gholam used to be in the Kampolo Revolutionary Committee."

Bahram couldn't take it anymore. "I've been in prison for two months. You had me in solitary for two weeks. How do you expect me to answer these questions?"

"I wanted to free you. I explained already. But Gholam crossed your name off the list. What does he have against you? How do you know him?"

Bahram looked at the metal bedframe. "So, why not flog me and make this Gholam happy? I'm not scared. Do it!"

Hesam put his elbows on his knees.

"Go ahead," Bahram taunted. "Whip me. It's not my first time. I'll be fine."

Hesam sighed. "This is not a joke, Bahram. A sympathizer of SOALS was executed yesterday…" He paused, frowning. "Wait. What do you mean it's not your first time? That's exactly what Gholam said."

It seemed pointless, but Bahram described, "A few years ago, they tied me to a *falak* and beat me with a wooden stick. At school."

"OK," Hesam exclaimed. "You must know him from school then. His name is Gholam Asadi."

Bahram felt his skin shrinking over his arms and chest. A hot shiver rippled over his body. His muscles tensed as he pushed his feet so hard against the floor that the chair moved backward.

"What is it?" Hesam sensed his panic.

Bahram looked around wildly to see if he was about to be attacked. "Asadi! He wants to kill me. Hesam, you need to do something."

"Who is he?"

"An idiot I went to school with." He recalled him perfectly now. "He has a grudge against me. He's never gonna let me go."

"What have you done to him?"

"It happened when we were in school."

"What did?"

Bahram slowly explained how he'd been the new kid at school. He described the brutal *falak* that led to the street fight with Asadi, who insulted him in front of everyone. How he'd turned the tables and beaten him up. How that afternoon marked a turning point in his life. How he tore up the 20-*toman* bill and threw it back in Asadi's face to earn the respect of his peers again. How he completely disgraced him in public by…

"Say what?" Hesam jumped out of his chair.

"I had to teach him a lesson," Bahram rationalized.

"What lesson?"

Bahram scowled at having to relive this episode. How could Hesam understand? He was a university student. He had never lost his honor, family and home just because he acted on his instincts. He didn't know the ordeals Bahram had to go through in a new city. "I had no other choice," Bahram justified. "Either that or I would've been the laughing stock of the whole neighborhood."

"Great!" Hesam said, louder than Bahram expected. "You…" He threw his hands up in the air, unable to convey his aggravation. "On my commander…" He started pacing. "And you want me to find a way of getting you out of here."

Suddenly it sank in. Bahram felt defeated. He had no way out of this prison. Now Asadi had complete power, and was guided by a vendetta that had begun years ago. Bahram and Hesam couldn't prevent Asadi from taking his revenge. "He's not gonna let me go."

"We have to think of a strategy."

"He ordered you to whip me?"

Hesam inhaled deeply and nodded.

"Then you'll just have to do it. But make sure you give me painkillers afterward."

"I'm not gonna go through with it, you silly." Hesam approached Bahram and squatted down. "We're going to think of something. But I'm not gonna hurt you. I love you, Bahram."

Bahram realized that the feeling was mutual. He no longer had to pretend. He was in love with Hesam. "That's why you have to do it," Bahram replied. "If you don't whip me, Asadi will come after you. And he's gonna have me flogged anyway. It's not a big deal. I can take it." He trembled.

"Bahram, you're a fighter." Hesam grabbed his knee. "You have to remain a fighter. I can't do it alone." Hesam looked again at the window, making sure nobody was watching. He didn't see anyone watching. "We need to think of a way out. But until then, we play their game." Hesam reached into his pants pocket and brought out a small container. "I'm gonna bandage your feet with old cloth and put some ketchup on it so it looks swollen and bloody."

"Ketchup? Are you kidding?"

"Let's make a pact. Unless you have a better plan, you don't get to mock my ideas. OK?"

Bahram didn't say anything.

Hesam stood up and explained the scenario. "It's time to put on a performance. And make it a good one. You have to lie on your stomach on the bed and scream each time I hit the ground with the cable. It should sound like you're suffering deeply." Hesam untied Bahram's hands and led him to the metal bed. "Lie on your stomach."

Bahram couldn't believe what was happening. He just obeyed.

Hesam loosely wrapped some rope around the detainee's wrists and the metal bedframe. He then did the same to his feet.

Bahram was facing the floor. The tile was gray and the cement between tiles had broken down into pieces. As he lay stretched on the bed, Bahram understood the extent of Hesam's affection. No other man had ever sacrificed so much for him. Not Daniar. Not Talib. Not even Majid. *We should be making love, instead of faking a flogging.*

"Remember to scream every time the cable hits the ground," Hesam reminded him.

Bahram heard the crack of the wire on the concrete

floor. The cable didn't even scratch the tiles but it would have cut through human flesh on contact. He couldn't make a sound.

"Scream," Hesam whispered.

The cable smacked the floor again.

"What's wrong with you? Scream!"

Another strike. More silence.

In frustration, Hesam supplied the screams himself. To Bahram, Hesam's screams sounded funny. Like a bad actor in a low-rated Iranian movie where the hero is shot a dozen times but is somehow still walking around to attack the enemy. Bahram tried to suppress his giggles, but the laughs finally burst out.

Hesam lunged forward and used his free hand to cover Bahram's mouth. "What are you doing? You need to sound like you're in pain."

Bahram shook his head as laughter shook his abdominal muscles.

Hesam lifted his hand from his mouth.

"It looks like a circus," Bahram explained. "You lashing the floor and screaming like a madman. Swish, ahh. Swish, ahh!" Bahram laughed harder and felt Hesam's hand pressing over his mouth again.

"This isn't a game. This is life and death—for both of us."

Bahram understood the gravity of the situation, but he could not stop laughing. His belly started to hurt.

Hesam looked at him with fascination.

"Or like a virgin boy who can't even do it right the first time. Ahh! Ahh!"

Soon they both laughed as quietly as they could.

Hesam checked the window yet again, then he kissed Bahram on the lips.

JULY 2, 1980

Karoun Prison, Ahwaz

As Hesam drove his Jeep into the prison gates, he passed by a protest sign on the side of the street: "This is neither Islamic, nor a republic." Hesam wondered why no one had removed the sign already. Since the executions last week, protests were happening spontaneously, appearing at the prison or city hall. As it turned out, one of the men executed had been a well-respected doctor from Jondi Shapour University Hospital. A university student had also been executed at the same time, a SOALS sympathizer. Healthcare professionals went on strike and held protests in several cities, including Tehran.

As Hesam came into the office, Gholam and Saeed were debating something. They didn't acknowledge his greeting.

"I'm pretty sure it's a myth. Plus, I've heard it can be harmful if ingested," Saeed explained.

"Well, we can run a test of our own."

"Testing what?" Hesam intervened.

"That camphor can reduce sensual temptation," replied Gholam.

"Sensual temptation?" Hesam wasn't sure what sort of a conversation he had walked into.

"You know these criminals in here. They're like animals. Unless we do something, they'd be sodomizing each other. We can't have that," he declared. "So we give them all camphor."

Hesam wanted to appear homophobic but didn't know where this was leading.

"But at the cost of getting them all sick?" Saeed objected. "We have no evidence that it works."

"Who cares if they get a bit of tummy ache?" Gholam asked. He looked at Hesam for affirmation.

"Who indeed?" Hesam was forced to agree.

"Why don't you go to the kitchen and ask if they're already adding camphor," Gholam instructed Hesam. "Maybe they're better cooks than we think."

"Better cooks than we think? Now I know you're delusional," Saeed mocked.

"Well, if you don't like the food, then get married and have your wife bring you home-cooked meals," Gholam told Saeed.

"Like Naser," Saeed mumbled.

Hesam didn't like how the conversation had turned. "All right, I'll go to the kitchen and ask."

"One more thing, Hesam," Gholam said. "Good job flogging that detainee, Karimi. I saw his feet have grown under the lash."

Hesam noted Saeed's questioning look.

"Commander, I've beaten him. Flogged him. Put him in solitary. No confession from this guy. I must say I'm starting to think he's really not guilty." Hesam was hoping Saeed would back him up, so that Gholam would end the vengeance.

"I know. You wanted me to free him, remember?" Gholam appeared unconvinced.

Hesam said nothing further. He knew why Gholam hated Bahram.

"I'll think of something to extract his confession."

Hesam stayed quiet so Gholam would reveal himself.

"We find out who his friends are. If they are politically involved in oppositional organizations."

"I've investigated him for a few weeks now," Hesam found himself saying. "I even went to Abadan. He is an orphan. He lives with an old widow, an illiterate woman. She doesn't know anything about politics."

"Well, then just beat him. Play soccer with him."

"I'm sorry?"

"Have the guards form a circle, put him in the middle, punch and kick him and pass him around. Like a soccer ball."

"Haj Agha doesn't allow that," Saeed interjected.

"Then just kill him," Gholam huffed. "He should have been executed instead of that doctor last week. If we kill Karimi, there'll be no family to organize protests."

"Execute him just because he's an orphan?" Saeed objected. "Commander, Brother Hesam may take your jokes seriously."

"I am serious." Gholam scowled.

"Commander, we're all here to serve our country, to protect our nation. I respectfully ask you to reconsider this case."

Hesam noted that Saeed had the courage to speak his mind, despite the risk of getting fired.

"Fine. Don't kill him. But don't release him either," Gholam ordered Hesam.

Mansoor rushed into the office. "Commander, protestors are gathering again outside the gates. They're chanting slogans."

"Oh, damn them," Gholam said, throwing up his hands. "Didn't the families sign a release to shut the hell up in exchange for getting back the bodies of the executed?"

"Yes, but these are not necessarily the families."

"I'll take care of this." Gholam stood up from his chair. "Fire some shots in the air and the dust will settle. These troublemakers are nothing more than dust."

Mansoor followed Gholam as he left the office. Hesam looked at Saeed. He felt ashamed that Saeed thought he was a ruthless guy, flogging Bahram. But he couldn't tell him the truth.

JULY 7, 1980

Karoun Prison, Ahwaz

Hesam looked at his watch. It was half past one. The call to prayer was ten minutes ago. With Ramadan approaching, the guards in the office agreed to pray together. Hesam thought quickly and volunteered to watch the office in case something urgent happened. That meant no one would notice when he went to see Bahram.

Hesam peeked into the washroom. His colleagues were performing ablution, washing their faces, hands, and feet before the prayer. Hesam again felt different.

He used to think religious practices were strange, something he looked down at. After all, he'd grown up in a family with socialist beliefs. But Saeed had changed his mind. He spoke up against injustice when Hesam didn't have the courage. And he used his beliefs to do good.

Saeed would lead the prayer. The leader was to be the most pious, the most righteous. For a second, Hesam wished he could participate. To be part of the group. To belong. But he couldn't pretend to believe something he didn't. That would be disrespectful to those who did. To Saeed.

He walked the hallways to the interrogation room. Bahram had just finished the sandwich Hesam had given him earlier. Bahram's feet were still wrapped in bandage rolls to simulate the injuries from flogging.

"They're praying. We have a little while to be alone."

Bahram nodded.

Hesam sat in the chair in front of Bahram's and held his hands. "Bahram, I need to ask you something."

"OK."

"Have you had any…stomach upset or…indigestion?"

"Ahh…no. Why?"

"Nothing at all?"

"What are you talking about?" Bahram tried to pull his hands away.

But Hesam didn't let go. He looked at the door to make sure no one was around before he leaned in to speak. "Gholam came up with a new scheme—camphor in prisoners' food."

"Yuck! Why?"

"He thinks it lowers sexual desires. Otherwise, the prisoners would be…" Hesam didn't even know how to talk about it.

"Climbing each other?" Bahram finished.

"I…I just wanted to make sure you're OK."

"Wait a second. You don't want me to eat their food because you're wondering if it's true. That I wouldn't have sex with you as a result of this?"

"Bahram…" Hesam leaned back in his chair.

"You can't keep me hungry because of your insecurities."

"It's not that. I just wanna make sure you don't get sick."

Bahram squeezed Hesam's hand. "Hesam. You're kind. Considerate…and I find you kinda cute."

Hesam blushed at the unsolicited compliments from Bahram. He wanted to believe there was no ulterior motive.

"The only reason I didn't wanna sleep with you is that…"

Hesam noticed that Bahram had used the past tense.

"I'd be using my body to get out of prison. I'd lose all self-respect if I did that."

Hesam pressed his lips together. "I wouldn't be *using* your body."

"If sex with you is the only way to get out of this hell, let's just do it."

"I'm not using this detention against you. I will ask Saeed to help me get you released. Everyone respects Saeed. If he asks, Gholam will allow it."

"He won't. He wants to punish me more," Bahram said, shifting his bandage-covered feet. "This isn't enough for him." Bahram shook his head.

"I will get you out of here. I promise. Once outside of here, if you still wanna be with me…"

Bahram placed his hand on Hesam's thigh.

When Gholam arrived at the prison, he went directly to the office. But he saw nobody there. He had told his team that one guard should remain on duty—even during the prayer. Gholam walked through the yard to check on the political ward. But then he heard something. He heard talk from the second interrogation room. He quietly cracked the door and saw Bahram.

"Well, let's see who we got here," he declared as he barged in. "Oh yeah, the little fatherless boy," Gholam said, taunting Bahram, whose eyes widened to see him. That pleased Gholam and he sneered, "See how fate has brought us back together?" He walked closer to Bahram and stepped on his feet with his boot.

Bahram screeched with pain.

Gholam smiled. "You scream like a girl. Not such a thug

anymore?" He looked at Hesam. "Good job, Brother. Next time, call me. I'll flog his back until I see bones." He lowered his head and looked at Bahram, "So happy to see you, butt-boy!"

Gholam touched the side of Bahram's face and the detainee jerked back. He laughed at the reaction. He headed for the door, but suddenly turned around. "Tell you what, Brother," Gholam said to Hesam. "Let's set him free. Hasn't he suffered enough?"

Hesam looked bewildered.

"We will free him. But only after he is of service. A pretty boy like that shouldn't go to waste." Gholam grabbed his crotch.

Bahram didn't flinch. But Gholam could feel that he was getting scared.

"You'll have him first. I'll do it after you," Gholam announced. "In fact, we will include more of the Brothers. As many as I can gather. We will take our turns with him. And once we're done, we'll let him go."

"Commander, I don't think—"

Gholam waved his hand to dismiss Hesam's objection. "Trust me. He will never be able to raise his head again."

Walking back to the main building, Gholam couldn't help but smile. He felt like a schoolboy again. It had taken three years, but he would finally have his long-awaited revenge for his degradation.

Bahram will be obliterated, Gholam thought. *He will never feel like a man again, torn apart by the guards. The pain and indignity will suit him well.*

Gholam looked into the prayer hall. The guards were sitting on their mats, and Saeed was leading the prayer.

Gholam wanted to have the punishment happen immediately. But how to bring up the topic with the guards casually, without offending them? Furthermore, he had to keep it quiet and not tell everyone. Saeed would never agree to such a thing.

Gholam watched the prayer continue. It wasn't prudent for all the guards to know about his plan. Maybe he needed some time to think it over. But an idea came to him and he knew how to proceed.

Then, Gholam returned to the second interrogation room. It was empty. He squinted. Was he mistaken? Were they in another interrogation room? He walked in.

Gholam heard a noise behind him and turned around. Bahram emerged from behind the door, holding a pistol with a silencer. The detainee's knuckles had turned white from the pressure of holding the gun tight. "Do not make a sound."

"How the hell did you—"

Hesam closed the door.

"How did he get your gun?" Gholam yelled hoarsely at Hesam. "You idiot!" He glared back at Bahram. "You filthy trash," he hissed, as he slowly reached for his gun.

"Drop your gun." Bahram's voice was deeper than Gholam remembered. "Slowly."

Gholam realized he was not bluffing. They had planned this together. Hesam was a traitor.

"Kick the gun over to Hesam," Bahram instructed.

Gholam looked at Hesam with fury and began yelling at him. "Why? What did he promise you? He has no money, nothing to give you." Gholam looked back at Bahram. How had he convinced Hesam this was a good idea?

"Kick the gun over," Hesam repeated.

Gholam had no option. Bahram seemed eager to shoot. Gholam kicked the gun over.

Hesam picked it up. Now, two barrels were aimed at his heart.

"Take off your clothes," Bahram said calmly.

The prayer will soon be over, Gholam thought. *The guards will come out and save me. I just need to stall.*

"Are you deaf? Take off your clothes," Hesam repeated.

"You ungrateful bastard," Gholam spat at the guard. "I knew I shouldn't trust someone who doesn't pray. You're an infiltrator. That's what you are. Well, your days are numbered. I will hunt you down and every member of your family. You will regret this."

"Hurry up," Bahram said. "And don't make me shoot you. You've seen what I'm capable of doing."

Ahwaz

Gholam was now stripped down and tied up in the solitary cell and Bahram was wearing the commander's uniform. The detainee's goal was to walk out of the prison, the cap low on his forehead to conceal his identity. Could he do it without attracting attention? His chest was already soaked with sweat and his face felt like a furnace. Anyone could easily observe something was wrong. His feet hurt in Gholam's shoes.

He wanted to run, but that would get him noticed. The prayer was over and the guards had returned to their posts. Bahram lowered his head and continued to walk through the office building, heading for the gate.

Suddenly, he slammed into another guard, full-body impact. The cap fell on the floor.

"The hell is wrong with you?"

"I'm sorry. I didn't see you." Bahram's heart was about to jump out of his chest.

"Who the hell are you? I haven't seen you before."

"Recent recruit. Night shift." Bahram wondered if the guard could tell that his voice trembled. He bent down to pick up his cap.

"Well, go get some sleep. You're walking like a zombie."

"I'm sorry." Bahram walked away as fast as he thought acceptable.

"And fix your uniform. This is the Revolutionary Guards Corps, not some local revolutionary committee in your village."

Bahram looked down on his chest. In his haste, he had missed a button hole so his uniform was longer on one side. He quickly tucked the uneven side into his pants.

A few steps down the hall, he ran into another guard with a cigarette between his lips. "Hey, do you have fire?"

"Sorry, Brother."

Bahram reached the front of the office building. The sun was shining, but he had no time to enjoy the light. Not now. He felt like it took him an eternity to find Hesam's yellow Jeep. Hesam wasn't there yet. Bahram leaned against the vehicle and kicked the gravel on the ground, hoping to look natural.

What if he got caught? Would Asadi get him a life imprisonment? Or make sure he was gang-raped? Would they do it in front of Hesam? Or would they flog Hesam in front of him? Would they both get executed tomorrow at dawn?

Hesam arrived and opened the car door. "Get in."

The Jeep was like a baking oven. They both opened the windows as Hesam switched on the engine.

"Hide this," Hesam said as he tossed him his folder. They drove toward the prison gate.

"Brother Hesam?" The guard at the gate greeted them.

"How are you, Ahmad *Agha*?"

"Praise God. I'm well. Who do you have?"

"This? Ah…a new recruit from the night shift."

Bahram gave a half-hearted military salute, making sure the cap partially covered his face. Ahmad had seen him as a detainee several times.

"We're doing an excellent job of recruiting the finest."

"Oh…he's on probation."

"Right. But before you know, he's gonna be our new commander."

"I'm going to drop him off," Hesam offered.

"Babysitting a recruit. I don't even know what to say."

Bahram lowered his head in supposed shame. Would this conversation ever end?

Finally, Ahmad opened the gate.

"Thanks. I'll see you in a half-hour or so."

"God bless."

Hesam pushed down the accelerator. The two of them remained silent, Hesam looking into the rearview mirror constantly in case someone was following them. He did not speak until turning right into the Ahwaz-Abadan road.

"I was afraid they'd find out and start shooting at any moment," Bahram confessed.

"Me too."

"I admire your composure. How much time do you think we got?"

"Not long. Someone will soon look for us both in the interrogation room. And someone will discover Gholam in solitary, tied up."

Bahram didn't respond.

"Bahram, I…I don't have a plan. What should we do now?"

"Well, I guess it's safe to say you don't have to return to duty." Bahram offered a joke to ease the tension.

"Funny," Hesam criticized.

"We should go to Abadan," Bahram suggested.

"You're kidding, right?"

"Where else do you wanna go?"

"Bahram," Hesam said slowly, "You're a fugitive, and I'm a traitor. I had a commander of the Revolutionary Guards Corps tied up. We're not common criminals. We're high-level political offenders now."

Bahram wasn't ready to let go of the idea to return to Abadan. "Majid will help us."

"If anyone in Abadan knows that Majid is working with SOALS, they'll be watching him. Helping us is enough to get him killed."

"I'm just a regular guy. I was arrested for no reason at all."

"That story has expired, Bahram. Now you're an enemy of the Revolution who escaped from prison with an infiltrator," Hesam said, his voice now cracking.

"Does anyone know you're a sympathizer of the Socialist Party?" Bahram asked. "I have friends who can help us cross the border into Iraq."

Hesam shook his head. "There's been unease at the borders. The guards are on edge. When Majid took me to the riverside, they started shooting at a raft."

"We can swim to the other side of the river." Bahram was grasping at straws, but he had to exhaust every last resort, before being forced to tell Hesam his secret.

"If Iranians think all Iraqis are enemies, why would Iraqis help us?"

"We can go to Kuwait. I know a guy there," Bahram imagined Talib would be willing to help.

"Is he gonna be waiting for us at the Iran-Iraq border?"

"Yeah, of course. I had my helicopter bring him in." Bahram was losing his patience at Hesam's ongoing disapproval.

"Don't get snappy with me."

"We have to go to Abadan," Bahram insisted. "Everyone I know is in Abadan. My contacts, my friends."

"Did you hit your head somewhere? That's the first place the Revolutionary Guards will be looking for you. For us."

Bahram was starting to sweat again. "So what do you suggest?" He was still contemplating telling Hesam the truth.

"My family is in Mashhad. What if we can hide somewhere in Khorasan?"

Khorasan is too far, Bahram thought. "We have to leave the country. Asadi is not one to wait around."

"What if we get across the border into Afghanistan?"

"And do what? Join the Red Army?" Bahram mocked.

"If the Afghan Mujahideen don't get us first," Hesam admitted.

"We're not going to Afghanistan. That's ludicrous."

"What about Turkey? Saeed is from Tabriz. I wish I had asked him before…"

Bahram had to tell him that Turkey was a solution. He knew people who could help. But he first had to explain to Hesam *how* he knew them. He noticed Hesam passing another car in the road. The wind slapped him in the face with the speed Hesam was going.

"Can you please slow down? This escape won't be worth much if we die in a car crash."

Hesam quickly pulled over. "Fine," he sounded irritated. "Let's make a plan. I need to know where to drive to."

They got out of the vehicle.

Hesam leaned against the Jeep and took out a pack of cigarettes. "There's only one left. We have to share." Hesam lit the last cigarette and inhaled.

Bahram sat on the ground. The sand was hot. "Hesam?" he whispered, still feeling unsure.

Hesam sat next to him and held out the cigarette. "If we go to Tehran and then to Tabriz…how do we cross the border into Turkey? They'll telegraph our names and pictures. We don't have passports." The ashes of the cigarette flew over the sand.

Bahram repeated, "Hesam?"

"What?" Hesam asked peevishly.

Bahram reached for the cigarette and took a deep inhale. "I have to tell you something."

"What?" he repeated, more softly this time.

Bahram had to buy some time. He kicked off one of Gholam's boots. "These stupid things are too small." He took off the other one as well.

"What do you have to say? Just tell me."

"Promise not to go berserk."

"What is it, baby?" Hesam said more gently and then took another puff.

Bahram put his hand on Hesam's knee. "I think we can go through Kurdistan."

"I think not," Hesam countered. "There's a civil war going on. We have no artillery. That's a great idea only if you wanna lose your head. Kurds behead the Revolutionary Guards."

"No," Bahram disagreed. "It's the army and the Revolutionary Guards who are killing the Kurds. They executed wounded men, even one on a stretcher. The picture was in the newspapers. We can go through Kurdistan," he insisted.

"Whatever the case, we are both wearing the Revolutionary Guards uniforms. How do we go there without getting involved in the war?" Hesam's voice escalated.

Bahram didn't know how to tell him. He removed his socks and began wiping the dried ketchup off his feet.

"I have contacts. I…"

"Bahram, are you Kurdish?"

Bahram took a handful of sand and continued scrubbing.

"Are you going to pretend you didn't hear my question?" Hesam put his boot mildly on Bahram's toes to stop the rubbing.

Bahram looked up and nodded.

"How do you even know that? If you don't have a family, who told you about your—"

"I'm not an orphan."

Hesam jumped up, fire in his eyes.

Bahram reached up to get him to sit down. He worried that everything was about to implode. If he couldn't calm Hesam down, he would lose him forever. "Don't walk away," Bahram begged. "You promised not to get angry."

"I promised you one thing only: to get you out of prison. I did that. You, on the other hand…you just lied to me. You're still lying. You…destroyed my career. Turned me into a fugitive. And still you tell me lies."

"I'm telling you the truth now."

"And what truth is that? That you're a Kurd? Who is Bibi? A liar like you? Or a fool like me?"

"I'm almost an orphan."

"Oh, you're full of it. Tell me—is Bahram even your real name?"

Bahram felt soreness in his nose and fought back his tears. How could he convince Hesam that he meant no harm?

Hesam began to walk away. "Even your name is a lie."

"Hesam! Hesam!" Bahram quickly walked after Hesam, his feet burning on the hot sand. "Please give me a chance to explain. I beg you."

"No more chances. You used up all of your chances."

"This may be the only way for us to get out of the country."

"Whatever. Let them take me. I don't care anymore." Hesam walked faster.

"My family threw me out," Bahram yelled. "When I was fourteen." His vision got blurry as tears welled up in his eyes. "For being gay."

Hesam stood still.

"My family found out and threw me out like garbage. They sent me away overnight." Bahram wiped the tears off his cheek. He told Hesam that his family had banished him to Tehran, but he ran away and ended up in Abadan. "I told everyone I was an orphan. And told them my name was Bahram."

Hesam stared at him. "So what's your real name?"

"Foad." Bahram broke into sobs.

"Foad?"

"I wanted to be someone else. Not a butt-boy thrown out like trash." Bahram wiped his face. "I wanted to be someone respectable. I wanted to be a man."

Hesam stepped forward. He wrapped his arm on Bahram's shoulder. "You are a man, Foad," he relented.

Foad took a short breath. He was relieved. He had finally told the truth and his lover was still by his side. But his jaw trembled as tears still flowed.

Hesam hugged him. "I don't know what you do to me to make me so weak that I can't resist, despite your lies."

"I was scared to tell you. I'm sorry, Hesam. I love you. I

never lied about that," Foad declared.

Hesam caressed his hair.

"I love you."

Hesam kissed his forehead. "Our names no longer rhyme." He gave a sad chuckle. "Never mind. It's stupid."

Bahram took Hesam's hand.

"So who is your contact who can help us cross the border?"

Bahram sniffled.

"Wait. If your family threw you out, how can you go back now? With a boyfriend of all things?"

"I don't know. I hope the war has scared them. They didn't kill me three years ago, even though that was the easier option for them. They just banished me. I think if they see my life is in danger, they'll help." Foad hoped this was true. "Plus, I think they'll be happy to find out I'm still alive."

"You haven't reached out to them in three years?" Hesam put two and two together. "Well, I think it's a bad idea. But the least bad idea you had." Hesam slightly pushed Foad toward the Jeep. "You can't get anywhere barefoot. Go, pick up Gholam's boots."

Foad looked at them on the sand in the distance. "Nah, those things hurt my feet." Foad opened the door and got in. His foot touched a piece of cloth on the floor. Foad pulled the *keffiyeh* from under his seat.

"I assume that belongs to Talib, your ex," Hesam said quietly as he turned the Jeep into the right lane.

"You keep the criminal evidence in your car?"

"I'd forgotten all about it."

"Have you ever worn one? I bet you look hot in it."

"Yeah, that's the only thing that's missing in this getaway. Me wearing a *keffiyeh* with the Revolutionary Guards uniform. Perfect, while driving toward Kurdistan with a male lover. Should we just write 'shoot me' on our foreheads?"

"I used to wear this. Talib liked it." Foad smelled it. Any trace of Talib's cologne was already gone. It smelled of dust.

"You loved Talib."

Foad opened the window. "Yes. I did." He threw the magazine and the *keffiyeh* out of the window. "But I found me a man I love even more." He put his hand on Hesam's thigh.

"It's ridiculous that I can't stay mad at you." Hesam smiled. "You're such a charmer. It makes me angry."

Hesam took Foad's hand, brought it up to his lips, and kissed it.

Foad raised their clasped hands and kissed Hesam's.

"Enough romance for now. Remember, we're on the run."

"I hope we survive today," Foad replied.

JULY 8, 1980
Sanandaj

Foad sat silently as Hesam drove north. Hesam had warned him that the next time Foad lied to him would be the last time he'd ever see him. Foad didn't want to test the threat.

They were stopped at various checkpoints by the Revolutionary Guards, but they were allowed to pass when Hesam explained they were returning from a mission. Just outside Sanandaj, there was another checkpoint, this time a Kurdish post. Foad spoke Kurdish with the guard. He told him the truth. He even told him his real name. Once the soldier heard he was a member of the Karimi tribe, he let them pass. Foad had translated the conversation for Hesam, keeping his promise that he'd tell Hesam the truth.

They reached Sanandaj after midnight. The streets were dim and deserted. A city in war. They passed by piles of ruins, probably the aftermath of rocket-propelled grenades. Foad saw bullet holes in the walls here and there. He found it difficult to navigate the streets now. The war had changed their look.

"Make a left here."

Hesam followed Foad's directions. "Where are we going again?"

"Daniar—a guy I grew up with. He and his wife, Atefeh. They probably have a couple of kids by now."

"And this is better than visiting your parents?"

"Daniar would know the contacts who can get us to Turkey."

"You don't wanna see your parents?"

"They're the ones who don't wanna see me," Foad said coldly.

"I assume Daniar is…" Hesam didn't finish his sentence.

"A guy I had slept with."

"And therefore the reason you were sent away."

"Mhmm."

"And you wanna go to his house? Even though his blabbing cost you everything?"

"He's not…vicious. He probably just boasted to someone that he had the matriarch's son. And things got out of hand." Foad offered his best guess.

"Wait, your mother is the matriarch of the tribe?"

"That's her. Banoo Karimi."

"So you don't wanna see her to punish her for sending you away?"

"They wanted me to disappear. So I did. They probably think I'm dead anyway."

"That must be hurtful."

"Stop here." Foad detected a familiar sight. "I'm pretty sure he lives here."

Hesam parked the car. "Are you sure it's OK to go there wearing this?" Hesam pointed to his uniform.

"Better than being naked."

Hesam didn't laugh.

Foad got out of the car barefoot. He knocked. No answer. "I wonder if they left after the war began." Foad knocked harder.

Hesam kept looking around, afraid of getting caught.

Foad was poised to knock a third time when the door opened. Banoo was standing in front of him. Foad felt like a dried piece of *hamour* fish, salted and stiff.

Banoo just stared at him as if seeing a ghost. Foad was a ghost. Even to himself. He had been Bahram for over three years.

"Who is it?" He heard Atefeh's voice. She rushed to the door and her eyes widened. "Foad?" Atefeh exclaimed. "Foad! Foad! Oh my God. You're alive." She repeated it in Kurdish. "Daniar, come here. Foad is back!"

Foad stared at Banoo. She looked ten years older. Her hair had grayed. Wrinkles had taken shape around her eyes. Her mouth sagged at the ends. Foad noticed a trail of tears twinkling in the dim light. She stepped forward and hugged him.

He knew he should say something, but what?

Daniar came limping toward him, cane in hand. "Foad! It's really you."

"My son has come back to me," Banoo said to Daniar.

Daniar hugged Foad and kissed him on the cheeks.

"We thought you had died on the road," Daniar said.

"I'm here." Despite the circumstances, Foad enjoyed surprising Daniar. "This is Hesam." He put his hand on Hesam's shoulder and slightly pushed him forward. "Speak Persian so he can understand."

"Welcome, Hesam," Daniar said. Hesam paused and timidly extended his hand. Daniar ignored the hand and pulled him to his chest. "Don't act like a stranger." Daniar kissed him on the cheeks also. "You brought Foad back to us. You're family."

Foad wanted to clarify that *he* had decided to return home. That detail could wait until later.

"Oh my God, I can't believe it. Come in, come in," Atefeh said hysterically.

"Come in," Daniar repeated. "Do you have any luggage?" He noticed Foad's bare feet. "I'm sure you have a lot to say."

"We need a change of clothes. I hate to be wearing this," Foad replied.

"Why are you wearing these in the first place?" Daniar inquired, eager to hear the story.

"Hesam helped me escape from prison. This was the only way to get out. We haven't stopped since."

"You were in prison?" Daniar asked.

"Are you injured?" Atefeh interrupted.

"No, thanks to Hesam. I'll explain in a minute."

They entered the living room, lit by a low-wattage lamp. Everyone sat.

"Where…have you been?" Banoo struggled to finish her question.

"I stayed away. I thought you didn't wanna hear from me." Foad attacked.

"We love you, Foad." Banoo sounded deflated.

"You must be hungry," Atefeh interjected. "I'm gonna bring something to eat."

"Make some tea also," Daniar asked her. "Thank you."

"I mourned your loss for years, son." Banoo whimpered. "Where were you all this time?"

"Abadan." Foad didn't elaborate. "And later, in prison in Ahwaz."

"He was in the wrong place at the wrong time," Hesam clarified. "Ended up a political prisoner."

Foad was happy that Hesam noted right away that he wasn't in prison for a sexual offense.

"Are you affiliated with the Democratic Party?" Daniar asked.

The Kurdish Socialist Democratic Party, Foad wanted to explain to Hesam. "No," he answered out loud. "But I have a few friends from SOALS."

"SOALS. Their sympathizers come here to fight with us against the army."

"Is that how you got wounded?"

"Your father," Banoo cut in, "has gone to Tehran to rent a place so we *all* can leave." She perhaps hoped Foad and Hesam would be joining them. Her face was not hard or cold. Rather, it was sad.

"At least he's not here to be disgraced by his own son." Foad felt anger rising in his throat, as he indirectly reproached her.

"You're not a disgrace. In my house, you're a guest of honor." Daniar wrapped his arms around him.

Banoo glanced at Daniar, visibly needing him to mediate.

Foad noticed that his host spoke of his house. *His* house. While Banoo used to be the matriarch of the tribe, Daniar was now the man of the house. And he had changed the rules. He made sure nobody made a mistake, the way they had three years ago.

"We never had a guest more welcome than you, Foad *jan*," Atefeh said as she emerged from the kitchen.

Foad looked around him and couldn't believe it. His family had banished him just a few years before for an indiscretion. Today, they welcomed his boyfriend into their house. As Foad stared at Hesam, he realized he had never seen him without the Revolutionary Guards uniform.

Sensing the tension in the room, Hesam asked Daniar, "Can you give me something to wear?"

Daniar nodded and led the two guests to a bedroom. "That uniform…I can't wait for you to take it off."

Foad burst into laughter. "You haven't changed." That was the same thing Daniar had told him that eventful afternoon, a few years ago.

Daniar giggled. "Not in that way."

"I'd love to wear anything else," Hesam said, apparently worried that his uniform was upsetting the family.

Atefeh yelled out from the kitchen that she'd turned on the water heater.

Daniar opened the closet door and offered them to take anything they wanted, plus T-shirts and underwear from his drawer. "I'll bring you fresh towels for your bath."

"Thanks, Daniar," Foad said, finally confident he was home and welcome.

"I'm so happy you're back."

Foad asked the condition of Daniar's wound and suggested he sit on the bed. He sat next to him.

"Foad, I'm so sorry I…"

Hesam was listening, but pretended to be busy selecting a shirt.

Daniar continued, "I should have been a lot more careful and insist on what I wanted."

"I don't blame you," Foad said, "anymore." He paused for a second, then added, "You weren't the one who exiled me."

"Not in a million years…" Daniar stared at Foad guiltily. "I never meant my…curiosity to cause you any harm."

"It's not your fault." Foad didn't know what else to say.

"I wish I could take it back. I'm sorry."

"It's OK," he smiled. "I had a crush on you, but you're straight. I get it." Foad felt lighter acknowledging what they'd never before said aloud. "You had to figure it out. And so did I."

"I missed you, man." Daniar rubbed Foad's shoulder. "Atefeh apologized a thousand times."

"Atefeh?" So it was she who'd told him, Foad concluded.

Daniar lowered his head. "I'm sorry."

Foad thought about how strange destiny was. He was sent away, which hurt a lot. But if Foad had stayed in Sanandaj, he might have been killed in the war, or wounded like Daniar.

"Atefeh was young and…your mother acted out of fear. She didn't know any better. You have to forgive her." Daniar pulled Foad close. "Foad *jan*, I don't know what you've been through. But don't be too harsh on your mother. That is exactly the way *she* treated you."

Foad looked at Hesam, who nodded in agreement.

"Trust me, she's suffered enough. She's mourned your loss. Didn't you notice how much she aged? I mean…" Daniar paused. "Just know that she has changed. She's opened her heart to you. Please consider doing the same."

Foad looked at Daniar's bandaged leg. "OK, I'll think about it."

"*Ghorbounet beram*. But don't think for too long. Time is limited."

Hesam gave a smile and added, "I think my mother would have reacted even worse if she found out."

Foad considered the advice.

"How rude of me," Daniar used Foad's shoulder as support to get up. "I'll let the two of you have a moment. The hot water for your shower should be ready in an hour or so."

"Thank you for everything," Foad told Daniar as he was walking out the room. "But I have one more favor to ask of you. And it's a big one. You have to help send us to Turkey."

A grave expression settled on Daniar's face. "So you're not staying," he hesitated. "OK, of course. I'll ask around."

"Quickly! We have to leave tomorrow."

"No way," Daniar said. "You just came back."

"I know, but we can't stay. The more we wait, the more time they have to hunt us down. We don't want to endanger you too."

"So you were a political prisoner?"

"Yes. Luckily, Hesam hid the evidence. But an old enemy caught up with me in prison. We had to run without a plan or anything."

"You're the man I wasn't courageous enough to be," Daniar addressed Hesam.

Foad grabbed Hesam's arm as he blushed at the accolade.

"Sorry if I talk too openly too fast. That's what war did to me. I learned to say everything quickly and honestly— because otherwise, I may not get a chance to say it at all. Don't mind me. Change and let's go eat." Daniar limped out of the room.

Foad looked at Hesam as he started changing his clothes. "Turn around," he asked Hesam softly.

Hesam did as told, smiling.

"You've seen me topless. Now it's my turn." Foad put his hand on Hesam's chest. It was firm and hairy. "I think I like you," he teased.

"Your mom is in the next room."

"You heard Daniar. In *his* house, I'm the guest of honor," Foad laughed.

"He's smart. I agree with him. You should forgive your mom. Actually, all of them. Look how nice they've been since we arrived. They even welcomed me with open arms."

"They'd better be nice to you. You're my man." Foad kissed Hesam on the lips. "And tonight, we finally share a bed."

JULY 8, 1980

Orumiyeh

After a short discussion, Foad had convinced everyone that Daniar shouldn't take them to the border. Three young men traveling out of the conflict area would look suspicious. Especially with one of them already wounded. They devised a plan: It would be a lot more believable if they pretended Hesam and Atefeh were a married couple and Foad was the wife's brother. At least he and Atefeh both spoke Kurdish, in case they had to convince a skeptical guard at a checkpoint. To add urgency to their plot, Atefeh would be pregnant. She had tied a small cushion to her belly. They also switched the yellow Jeep for Daniar's aged Paykan. That would look more plausible for people fleeing the war.

Atefeh had invented the rest of their backstory: They were running away from the war so she could deliver the baby in the city where her parents lived. They reached Orumiyeh late in the afternoon without incident. Foad and Hesam said goodbye to Atefeh as they dropped her near the bus terminal. She was going back to Sanandaj, this time not pregnant. Meanwhile, the two young men placed themselves two blocks from the bus station and waited for their smuggler.

With nothing to do other than wait, Hesam confessed to Foad that he'd left Italy to escape his relationship with Umberto, using the excuse of serving the revolution. But now, he was running away from revolutionary Iran, hoping to perhaps make it back to Italy.

Foad felt guilty for turning Hesam into a fugitive, but happy he'd quit the Revolutionary Guards Corps in the meanwhile.

The Revolutionary Guards definitely had a picture of Hesam. It was the picture he'd provided when he joined. Finding a picture of Foad would be more difficult. After all, Hesam had taken Foad's prison folder with him when they left. Daniar had set it on fire earlier that morning. Still, all Asadi had to do was to raid Bibi's house, and then: mission accomplished. Picture obtained.

It had been more than twenty-four hours since they'd fled. So it could be a matter of minutes before the pictures were telegraphed to all posts of the Revolutionary Guards throughout the country.

Hesam popped the hood of the Paykan open.

"What are you doing?" Foad wondered.

"Making up an excuse for having parked on the side of the road for a whole hour," Hesam said and got out of the vehicle.

How long before their contact showed up? The smuggler was an acquaintance, but they took no chances. They hid their cash, just in case he decided to jack up his price. Foad felt ashamed for accepting Daniar's money. At least they gave him Hesam's Jeep in exchange.

Daniar was the first man Foad fell in love with. And now, three years later, Daniar had made amends. He found an escape route for Foad and his new boyfriend. Banoo had quietly watched the plan take form with wet eyes. And Atefeh, the reason Foad's secret was disclosed in the first place, insisted that *her* cover story was more believable and *she* should accompany them to Orumiyeh. Everybody had offered an act of kindness to fix the previous wrongs, to offer apologies.

Before leaving Daniar's house, Foad had taken a small picture of them as a keepsake.

As they waited, Foad noticed a Benz approaching. The driver was wearing a Revolutionary Guards Corps uniform. The car slowed down and stopped. Foad lowered his head and sank into his car seat.

"Good evening." The guard approached Hesam.

Foad wondered if he should try to imitate the Azeri dialect, should the guard ask him any questions. No. What if the guard started speaking Azeri?

"Hello." Hesam walked over to the guard.

"Can this even drive?" He looked at the Paykan.

"Yeah. It still has some life in it."

"Well, at least clean it then. What happened to your car tags?"

Daniar had insisted they be removed to make it harder to track down.

"Fell off in an accident," Hesam shrugged. "I didn't notice it until later."

The guard looked at the empty spot where the tags once had been. "You're not from here." The guard had picked up on Hesam's accent.

"No, I'm a guest. From…"

Pick a place without a recognizable accent, Foad told himself as he opened the car door. "From Karaj," he intervened.

"That's a long way."

"Yeah, I guess that's why the car started to act up."

"How long did the trip take you?"

Foad had to quickly estimate the proper time. "About twelve hours."

"Twelve hours?" The guard frowned, suggesting that was too long. "What brings you here?"

"Came to visit my uncle."

The guard looked at Hesam. "And you?"

"He's my cousin," Foad answered too fast. "We came to visit the family."

The guard surveyed them as if searching for proof they were related. "Yeah? Where at?"

"We called and asked them to come here and tow the car. I mean, if this thing doesn't start by the time my uncle arrives." Foad wanted to give an opportunity to Hesam to speak.

"My car is good. It's just overheated." Hesam got the clue. "Once it cools down a bit, it'll drive again."

"Well, don't leave it here."

"My uncle should be here any minute," Foad said. "He can tow us."

"I told you, it's just overheated," Hesam countered. "Don't worry, Brother," he turned to the guard. "We won't leave the car here. I'm gonna drive it home."

The guard looked at Foad.

"I don't know why you even drive in this shabby cart." Foad faked a dispute with his supposed cousin. "It could have broken down anywhere on the road."

"Then why didn't you drive us in your own Cadillac, cousin?" Hesam mocked.

The guard laughed. "Your cousin is right," he told Foad. "Don't be ungrateful." He then turned to Hesam with newfound respect. "Some people are always ready to criticize," he told Hesam, loudly enough for Foad to hear. "If you get hungry, there's a teahouse down the street," he said to Hesam as if the teahouse would refuse to serve Foad.

"Thank you, Brother. May God give you strength."

Foad hung his head low, but furtively watched the guard slowly walk back to his Benz and drive away. Only then did he resume breathing.

Hesam walked over to Foad and leaned against the car. "Turns out I'm quite likeable."

"That was too close. I'm scared." Foad put his hand on the window, his fingertips against Hesam's hand. He wanted Hesam to reassure him that the smuggler would soon arrive and save them.

"How much longer do we have to wait?" Hesam murmured.

Foad felt responsible. If not for him, Hesam would be in Ahwaz, reigning over his detainees. Was Bibi also in danger? Would Asadi presume she knew something? What about Majid?

Foad felt that everywhere he went, he created a path of destruction. Exile. Escape. New identity. Fight with Asadi. Loss of Talib. Arrest. Putting Bibi's and Majid's lives in danger. Now, his love for Hesam made him a fugitive.

He shook the thoughts from his head. There was too much to think about. Foad had obliterated everything and everyone in his path. Maybe he deserved to get caught, so he wouldn't destroy another life.

"I'm so sorry, Hesam," Foad muttered. He felt as if Asadi was tightening a noose around his neck. He gasped for air. Would he be hanged or shot by a firing squad? And what would happen to Hesam?

He had to run away. Leave Hesam alone so his lover had a better chance to survive. But Asadi would find them both.

Foad had an idea to save his man. He asked Hesam to join him back in the car.

Hesam sat in the driver seat and looked at Foad curiously. "OK, what is it?"

"What time is it?" Foad grasped for the last trace of hope.

Hesam looked at his watch. "Past seven."

Foad couldn't reasonably expect that that the smuggler would still show up. "The guy should have been here more than two hours ago. He's not coming."

Hesam exhaled loudly. "Can you think of someone else who can help? Should we call Daniar?"

Foad couldn't believe Hesam was still hopeful. "There's nothing we can do anymore. We have to cut our losses short."

"What does that mean?"

"We can't leave the country, Hesam. Our pictures are probably at every border checkpoint already."

"You don't know that for sure."

"Yeah, I do."

"So what do you suggest?"

"Hesam, you have to turn me in," Foad pleaded.

"You've lost your mind," Hesam patronized him. "Too much stress."

"If we get caught, we both get killed. You have to save yourself."

"Yeah, sure." He reached over to touch Foad's forehead for a fever.

"Tell them I took your gun or something. You have to turn me in."

"I won't do that," he dismissed the idea.

"God damn it, Hesam." Foad banged his hand on the glove compartment.

"We have a whole life ahead of us," Hesam insisted. "There are tons of places I wanna show you in Rome."

"We won't make it there. There's no time. Come on. Turn me in. If they catch you with me like this, they'll kill you too."

"You know what Asadi wants to do to you. I can't give you up to him."

Foad punched Hesam in the arm. "You have to." He hit him again. "We don't have another option." He beat Hesam some more.

Hesam grabbed Foad's arms harshly. "Stop it. Get a grip. This is not the time to lose your cool."

Foad's eyes were burning. He tried to free his hands. Hesam let go.

"You don't understand," Foad said. "I destroy everyone's life. Save yourself while you can."

"You're under a lot of pressure, Foad. I get it. But you have to pull yourself together."

"Take me to the Revolutionary Guards Corps."

"The only place I am taking you is Turkey. We'll be safe there, until the UN refugee agency can send us over to Italy."

Foad felt tears streaming down his face. "You have to go."

"We'll go together. That's the only way."

As Foad wiped his face, Hesam leaned back in the driver seat. "I will call Saeed. He's from Tabriz. He might know someone in Orumiyeh also."

"You can't call him. I don't wanna risk his life, too. His phone may be tapped. After all, his former roommate was an infiltrator."

"I'll change my voice."

"Too risky. Plus, how would he know it's you?"

"Come." Hesam stepped out of the car. He walked over and pulled Foad out of the car and held him as he cried.

A passerby glanced at them. "So sorry for your loss," he offered, assuming Foad was mourning.

Foad waited for the stranger to walk away. "We can't escape the country. We're done," Foad whispered as he wiped his eyes.

Hesam pushed a bottle of water into Foad's hands and insisted he drink.

After his tears ran out, Hesam described his plan for Foad and took him to a phone booth. Hesam dialed a number and gave the receiver to Foad. "Sound natural," he instructed.

Foad reluctantly took the phone. "Hello? Saeed *jan*?" His voice was different after sobbing. "Is it you? Did you recognize my voice, man? It's Mohsen."

Hesam nodded in approval.

Foad continued. "Thanks so much for the gifts." Foad took a breath. "Especially the green plastic cup." He paused for Saeed to say something, indicating he knew what Foad was talking about.

Finally Saeed spoke, going along with the story. Obviously, he still remembered the green plastic cup he had left for the prisoner in the shower, about ten days ago.

"Good. He's good. Yeah, yeah. We're in Orumiyeh visiting uncle Rahman. But I lost the address." Foad offered the cover story as an excuse for asking for a possible safe house in the city, just in case the phone was being monitored. He hoped Saeed would take the hint.

"Here it is," said Hesam as he parked.

Foad looked at the tall green minaret and the faded blue of the façade of the mosque. "Is this a good idea?"

Hesam switched off the engine. "Saeed is a trustworthy guy. He constantly criticized me when he thought I was beating you or flogging you."

"He might have changed his mind. Maybe he *wants* us to get caught," Foad objected.

"I lived with Saeed. He's a good guy. He was nice to you in prison."

Foad had doubts. "I'm still afraid."

"Remember you're a fighter, Foad. Courageous. I saw that in prison. Reach in and find that in yourself. Just like you did in the desert near Ahwaz."

At the moment, Foad didn't feel strong. He was tired.

"You went to Abadan with nothing and you managed to build a life. You can do that again. This is not the time to give up." Hesam looked at the mosque and swallowed. "I can't do this alone. Find your strength. Do it for me."

Foad slowly nodded. He had to follow Hesam's directions.

"Come, let's go."

As they reached the mosque, a middle-aged man with a thick black beard and religious cloak welcomed them. Hesam explained that they were friends of Saeed Towfiq and asked if they could stay over for the night. The name must have meant something, since the cleric invited them in. They took off their shoes as they entered.

"Religion should be kept sacred," the cleric explained unprompted as if he had suspicions about the circumstances of their arrival. "Separate from politics. You see, politics will make some happy and some upset. It will push some to the right or left. But if politics are kept separate from religion, all people will keep true to their faith, regardless of politics of the day." He showed them a room.

"Thank you," Hesam said.

"Have you had dinner yet?"

Hesam shook his head. "Not hungry. Thank you so much."

"I'll check on you in a while."

Foad entered the room. A red rug stretched over the floor and there were calligraphy verses of the Quran, framed, hanging on the walls. The room smelled of rosewater. Foad sat cross-legged on a small thick rug and leaned against a cushion. Hesam sat next to him.

"What next?" Foad asked.

"I'll figure it out. You rest. You look awful."

Foad didn't have the energy to argue. He wished he could stretch out his legs, but not in a mosque. He closed his eyes.

JULY 9, 1980

Orumiyeh

Foad opened his eyes. Hesam was shaking his shoulder. "Get up. Come on," he said. "We have to go."

"Ha?" Foad rubbed his eyes.

"We have to go. *Now.*"

"What's going on?" Foad looked around and saw the cleric.

"My son, we heard some news. It may not be true. But it's best to be cautious."

"What news?" Foad sat up.

"Rumors that…there might be a coup," Hesam said, helping Foad get up.

"You better go in a hurry," the cleric stressed, then left the room.

"We have to go. It's not a joke." Hesam ordered.

The cleric led the way through the hall quickly.

"I don't understand," Foad objected.

"We have to cross the border immediately," Hesam said, grabbing Foad roughly by the shoulders to stop his delay. "It's now or never."

"If there truly is a coup, the borders will surely be shut down," the cleric explained.

"What if they recognize us at the border?"

"It's a chance we have to take." Hesam thanked the cleric.

"God is the savior. I'm just a servant."

Hesam turned on the engine and they sped away. He had obviously asked for directions in advance. The Turkish border was only thirty miles away.

Foad couldn't see much of the landscape. The headlights just illuminated the road ahead and the cracks on the asphalt. They approached a guard's post.

Hesam stopped the car. "Foad," he whispered. "Look normal and say nothing."

A guard in uniform appeared at Hesam's window. "Passports."

"Good evening, Brother. How are you doing?"

The guard looked at Foad. "Passports," he repeated coldly.

"We had a long journey. I just became a father, you see."

Foad pressed his hands into his thighs so they would not shake. He noticed Hesam was clutching the steering wheel.

"Get your passports and open the trunk."

In front of them, Foad saw the fence, framed in barbwire. Just beyond the fence, Turkey lay with extended arms. Only about a hundred-fifty yards away. But it looked so distant. At the Iranian border police post, two guards were standing by the gate. One of them was saying something into his wireless device. He then signaled to the other guard to close the gate.

"Are you deaf? Show me your passports before I shoot your brains out," said the guard at Hesam's window.

The guard with the wireless yelled out, "Hojjat, come over here."

"Wait here," the guard named Hojjat told Hesam as he walked to the gate.

"They're closing the border," Foad warned.

Hesam whispered something but Foad couldn't hear. The air filled with the sound of screeching tires. The force pushed Foad back against the seat. One guard was blowing a whistle. Another raised a paddle, signaling them to stop. Hesam picked up speed.

"Stop! Stop!" Hojjat yelled. The guards scurried out of the way. The old Paykan slammed into the barbwire across the closed gate. Foad watched the barbwire scratch the car hood and windshield. It sounded as if it could shatter the glass. But the barbwire broke and allowed them through.

Foad heard bullets. Then a different loud pop. The car twitched as it sped over the dirt road. One of the tires had just been punctured by a bullet. There was a second gate and barbwire fence. Two guards stood in front, aiming their guns at the car. One yelled something in a foreign language.

Foad noticed the guards take aim. Suddenly Hesam slammmed on the brakes. Dust blurred their vision. Hesam held up his hands. Foad did the same.

"Don't shoot," Hesam said in English.

The Turkish guards would turn them back to the Iranians, Foad thought. This was the moment of surrender. Foad had already experienced so much. Loved so much. This was the time for him to admit defeat.

Foad saw the two guards come closer, to both sides of the car. They each pointed a gun at the two passengers.

"We are refugees," Hesam said in Persian. "We refugee," he repeated in broken English.

The guards ordered them out of the car, as they both kept their hands up. But instead of forcing them to walk back toward the border, they guided them to a cabin. One of them yelled something in Turkish at the Iranian guards.

"Traitors," Hojjat yelled out.

Foad turned around and saw Hojjat walk back, farther into the Iranian territory. Foad was shivering, too shocked to react.

Hesam peered at Foad, hands still in the air. He grinned but remained wide-eyed, still in disbelief. "We made it."

With misty eyes, Foad nodded and smiled back.

Author's Note

Dear readers,
Thank you for picking up this book and reading it all the way to the end.

I started writing this more than a decade ago, without even realizing that I'd begun a manuscript. Hesam's character is fictitious, but I was inspired by the true story of a young Iranian socialist who returned from university abroad to serve his country. Despite supporting the government, he was suspected of espionage and arrested. He died under torture. I found myself thinking of him, imagining his life if it hadn't been brutally cut short. I felt compelled to bring dignity and humanity to his memory, for having been subjected to degrading treatment and having paid the ultimate price for his political beliefs.

I spent years researching the historical details to bring this story to life, but I also had to study the book publishing industry. After much thought, I chose to publish independently of large publishing houses to maintain artistic control over the project, specifically to keep the historical details as accurate as possible.

Reader reviews are the lifeline of independent authors. Without reviews, books get little visibility. I'd be very grateful if you would write an honest review on the platform where you purchased this book. You can text or call me so I'm able to thank you personally: +1 301 660 6165.

With sincere appreciation,
Hamour

Discussion Questions

1. After reading the book, have you changed your mind about anything related to Iran? Do you feel differently about anything?
2. What is the one most vivid image that came to your mind as you read?
3. Considering that the title of book, in what situations was it most tangible to you that the character was conflicted about being on the right side?
4. Which character did you find most relatable? Why?
5. If you were to make a soundtrack for this book, which songs would you choose?
6. If you could meet any of the characters, who would you pick?
7. Can you pick a passage that you found particularly interesting or profound?
8. Hesam has joined the Revolutionary Guards Corps to serve his country. What prevents him from assimilating into the group? Why does he stand out?

9. With the exception of his ex, Bahram has been lying to everyone about who he is. Did it influence your impression of him?
10. What role did Umberto play in the story?

For more book club resources, please visit www.HamourBaika.com.

If you'd like me to join your meeting on Skype, please contact me: hamourbaika@gmail.com.

Acknowledgements

Anand, you made it possible for me to work on this project. Thank you for making space for me, for taking over more house chores so I could write, and for tolerating my "going dark" when wearing headphones and listening to podcasts so I could learn more about writing and publishing. I love you to the moon and back.

Maman, thank you for encouraging to me and even sending one of my novellas to a publisher so many years ago. I continue to write because of the support I received as a child.

Jay Blotcher, thank you for boosting my self-confidence and encouraging me, but also correcting me when needed. Thank you for helping me identify what to shorten and what to expand. And also, thanks for your ACT-UP work. We in the LGBT community owe our freedom and rights to those who came before us and paved the way in a very different social landscape.

My sincere thanks go to Jules Hucke for proofreading. I could feel your kindness from behind the computer screen. We chuckled as I jokingly blamed *All That She Wants* for too many "that's" in my writing. But honestly, I learned English partly through studying song lyrics by Ace of Base, Savage Garden, Michael Jackson, and Madonna. I write thanks to them.

I am indebted to Roya and Ladan Boroumand. Thank you for reinforcing in me your unwavering quest for truth and uncompromising ethics to tell it, even when inconvenient.

My heartfelt thanks to Monireh Baradaran for reading the manuscript and pointing out areas for improvement and a couple of historical details I had to revisit.

I'd like to express my gratitude to Nasim Khaksar for talking to me about Karoun Prison and life conditions in it. I'm sorry I reminded you of such unpleasant facts. I found inspiration in *Little Intellectual*. Thank you for your writings.

Research for this book was daunting but it was possible because of the courage of those who told their stories. Thanks to writers of prison memoirs. Special thanks to Iran Archive (iran-archive.com) and the Library of Congress for making resources available to the public free of charge.

Tina Ehsanipour, thank you for reading the manuscript and helping me improve it. You've made me semi-allergic to exclamation marks. So much so, that Jules had to put back several of them that I'd previously removed. Reliable testing has shown me that I'm allergic to hyphens too. I removed as many as I could, hopefully without messing up Miraj's design!

Joanna Penn, you're a well of knowledge. I'm so grateful for *the Creative Penn podcast* and for all the wisdom you share with the world.

Jessica Bell, I delayed the publication date just so I could fit myself into your schedule. I never regretted that decision. You beautifully covered my ideas for this book, better than I could've envisaged.

Mirajul Kayal, I spent hours on various software programs just to conclude that my visual aspirations needed a true designer. Thank you so much for carrying out my vision. You're so kind and considerate, like a brother I've never met.

Patrick, I'm so grateful for your help in proofing. Rica, thank you so very much for your design suggestions. Thank you from the bottom of my heart to Ashley, Bota, Cheyenne, Goli, Jackie, John, and Kourosh for helping with my questions and requests, and for your kind and reassuring words. I'm so lucky to be friends with you.

Appreciation is also due to the *Wells Street Journal* for publishing me when I doubted I could write.

I'm so grateful. This would not have been possible without each and every one of you.

Printed in Great Britain
by Amazon